No worries if not!

HarperNorth
Windmill Green
24 Mount Street
Manchester M2 3NX

A division of
HarperCollins*Publishers*
1 London Bridge Street
London SE1 9GF

www.harpercollins.co.uk

HarperCollinsPublishers
Macken House
39/40 Mayor Street Upper
Dublin 1
D01 C9W8

First published by HarperNorth in 2023

1 3 5 7 9 10 8 6 4 2

A catalogue record for this book
is available from the British Library

ISBN: 978-0-00-855870-3

Printed and bound in Great Britain by
CPI Group (UK) Ltd, Croydon

MIX
Paper | Supporting
responsible forestry
FSC™ C007454

No worries if not!

LUCY NICHOL

Harper
North

For all the difficult women who unapologetically light up the world and make it a better place.

Prologue

17th January 2011

I'm not a psychopath or anything. I mean, if I'm watching a thriller or something and there's a scene early on where one of the good characters fills up a cat food bowl and calls for Mr Whiskers or whoever then I turn it off straight away because – come on – we all know how that's going to end. Ditto a dog food bowl. Or a rabbit hutch. I know I won't be able to cope with what's coming because deep down I'm a softy. And I can live with that.

But this? I didn't feel sad about this. I felt angry. I mean, how could I be sad about someone who turned out not to be the person I thought they were? No, I was fuming. Although, if I'm being honest, I was also really embarrassed by all the rumours at school. All I wanted to do was hide away in my room. But of course Mam took that to mean I was missing him. Which couldn't be further from the truth.

She always thought the sun shone out Liam's arse. Our family had known his family for years and, to be fair, he'd always been a decent boyfriend – up until the point when we had sex. When I told her Liam had dumped me she didn't look shocked. I mean, why bother asking when he was coming for his tea when she clearly already knew we'd broken up?

Liam's auntie must've told her. They went to Zumba together every Tuesday and they were right gobshites when they got together – always gossiping. But of course she won't have heard the full story – about the rumours he'd been spreading. He probably told his mam, who probably told his auntie, who probably told my mam, that it was some kind of tragic and devastating break up . . .

Anyway, I put Mam straight. I told her I didn't want him back and that we only broke up because it turns out he was a knob. I wasn't about to go into detail about what he had been saying about me because that would have confirmed that we had slept together and on top of everything else I wasn't prepared for the Spanish Inquisition.

Mam said my language wasn't very 'ladylike'. I told her to piss off and she said, 'You're just hiding your hurt with anger, Charlotte. Apologise please, for using those words under my roof.'

She said that I should call him, say sorry for whatever it is that's happened and work it out. I was like 'No, Mam, I've done nothing wrong, Liam's a prick, end of.'

She took the huff at that and left me to fizz away with rage in my room, listening to Pink and Gwen Stefani because they'd understand.

I think Mam had an inkling that we might be having sex. I'm seventeen after all. We've had 'the talk' and she's banged on about me taking the pill, being sensible and all that. Saying that, she never explicitly said the word 'sex'. The same way she always mouthed the word 'vagina'. There was a reason we'd always called it my fairy. If we had to call it anything at all, that is.

Anyway, Mam had just got back in from the big shop and she came straight upstairs and pushed a copy of Cosmopolitan *under my bedroom door. I thought it was quite sweet, a nice treat, until I saw that she'd stuck a Post-it Note on one of the pages with the words 'This should help xx' in scribbly blue Biro.*

It was stuck to a double page feature on 'How to Get Your Man Back'. But there were two key problems with this gesture.

Firstly, I don't want him back.

Secondly, I DON'T WANT HIM BACK!!

I went downstairs and had it out with her while she was putting the shopping away. I told her that I didn't need crappy advice on getting a man back – especially one that I didn't even want in the first place. She stood by the open fridge, pointing at me with a piece of broccoli, still convinced that I wanted him back. 'Cutting your nose off to spite your face,' came out more than once, followed by 'Sorry shouldn't be the hardest word' – which made me feel sick with cringe cos I knew she'd stolen it from that stupid song. There wasn't even a hint of irony either.

Anyway, I said to her, again (because it didn't seem to be sinking in) that I had nothing whatsoever to apologise for. I'd done nothing wrong. And she said it doesn't matter, sometimes we just need to keep the peace and an apology, whether we mean it or not, is the easiest way to do that. And as much as I protested, she said, 'Unfortunately, Charlotte, for us women to get what we want, we sometimes need to say sorry first . . .

'Nobody likes a difficult woman,' she said.

1

A gigantic clip art of a tug-of-war came hurtling towards us on the screen, typography popping out in bright purple capitals. One. After. The. Other.

T.E.A.M

B.U.I.L.D.I.N.G

T.A.S.K F.O.R.C.E

After last night's tequila, Jamie's needlessly animated presentation was threatening to have the same effect on me as the Nemesis at Alton Towers back in 2004. 'Chris Rea could write a Christmas hit about getting stuck in a queue like that. We'll come back when it's quieter,' Dad had said, before dragging us off for a double cheeseburger.

It all came flooding back. My stomach lurched.

'So, I've come up with some thoughts on activities and I'd like to get everyone's take.' Jamie was in his element. Project management 101.

We were to start the year with a planned activity to 'diffuse our differences and spark dynamic output.' Oh, and the activity will be 'co-created by a specially curated team in the spirit of its ultimate ambition.' Specially curated team being his unlucky team, aka us lot.

As far as bosses go, he was a right fucking prick.

'So, option number one on the team-building away day menu, paintballing followed by Italian tapas.'

My carefully curated colleagues shifted uncomfortably in their seats as capital letters and a massive 3D paintball gun overwhelmed the screen.

'Thoughts?' He pressed on, eyeing us all one by one while standing proudly by the shiny smart board. He was a few years older than me and most of the team, early forties maybe. But his additional years of supposed 'professional' experience were hidden beneath a glossy veneer and a bad suit. He wanted to portray himself as the party animal, the one who could work and play harder than the rest of us. Which was fine, if only he actually worked hard instead of strutting around the office till all hours *pretending* he was.

It felt to me as though the office was simply his pre-drinks, and the main event happened when he and his awful mate Danny hit the pub at 6 p.m.

I glanced to my left. Maya, our planner, was slouched backwards in her chair, her knees jutting off the base of the seat and her eyes concentrating on her bright orange New Balance trainers, which clashed with the bright yellow carpet. Her feet were impatiently and repetitively tapping against the floor under vast swathes of worn-away baggy jeans. If feet could talk, they'd be walking her straight out of here at any moment.

David, our insights executive, was sitting stiffly in his chair, hands clasped tightly on his lap, staring straight ahead. He seemed to be studying the smart board intensely, as if deep in thought as to the pros and cons of the option presented to us. I knew what he was *really* thinking. *I'm a number cruncher, get me out of here.*

Nobody wants to be running around dodging Jamie's bullets – we already had to do that on a daily basis.

Pete, who only joined us about six months ago after Tina mysteriously left without any notice, took his usual approach. Focusing his stare on the desk in front of him like he was the only sober audience member in the front row of a comedy gig. Unfortunately for him, his stare was about as subtle as a paper bag over his head. I could never understand why he endured this job, his LinkedIn profile was proof that he'd left a much more senior role before coming to this hellhole.

'Thoughts, Pete?' Jamie demanded.

'Um. I . . . sure. Great idea. Really . . . great.'

All eyes bore into Pete, his mottled red cheeks screaming his discomfort. He was a people pleaser, but he was struggling to hide his disdain for this team-building activity.

'Option two.' Jamie pushed on, an audible sigh providing the soundtrack to the click of his clicker. The paintball graphics retreated into the background while the words 'AXE THROWING' lurched forward.

More silence shrouded the room, Maya's trainers shuffling more loudly as she continued her relentless fidgeting. It was having the same effect on my brain as nails down a blackboard.

'You can't seriously tell me there isn't a strong contender here already?' Jamie snapped, eyeballing each of us individually.

The silence was getting awkward. We obviously all felt it as we let out a combination of 'yeah' and 'sure' in quiet, understated faux-enthusiasm.

'OK.' He pushed on. 'Option three . . . '

I suppressed a sigh, telling myself that, as far as forced fun goes, we were probably over the worst.

But I was wrong.

As Axe Throwing fractured into a million tiny pixels and disappeared off screen, images of mud, barbed wire and . . . oh my God . . . people holding hands . . . appeared in its place.

'I was saving this beauty till last.' Jamie had a glint of something in his eye. Evil, perhaps . . . he clapped his palms together loudly, 'So then, who's got enough grit to take on the Warrior Mud Challeeeeenggggggge?!'

You could've heard a feather drop on the garish carpet tiles. We all felt as awkward as Jamie looked as he stood there waiting for something, anything. Just someone to affirm his belief that he really *was* the king of office entertainment.

'I—I mean, we.' I cleared my throat and looked pleadingly at my colleagues as I spoke. I needed them to rally. I couldn't be the only one to shatter Jamie's dreams. 'We'd be happy just, you know, having a lunchtime picnic in the office or something. Fish 'n' chips maybe. A few tunes . . . '

Jamie fixed his eyes on me. If you could 'see' thunder, then this is what it looked like. A rumble in the distance, threatening, ready to explode. Like his eyes could shoot blood in a split second.

'An office party,' he spat. 'What is this? 1991?'

We were one of *those* offices. You know, where the culture and atmosphere are dire, but the décor screams loudly over the top of it. Like some kind of screwy pinball machine on acid. Table football, bright orange and green comfy chairs, quirkily named glass meeting 'pods' and 'bring your dog to work' days. We were only one step away from installing Wendy houses in HR.

'We just. I mean, it's about spending time together isn't it. No pressure and all that. Maybe, a few words from, you – *obviously.*' I added the obviously to purposefully pander to his seniority. 'And, you know, a bring your own buffet?'

'If you didn't want to do anything you should have just said,' he huffed. 'I wouldn't have wasted my time . . . '

And they say women are over-sensitive and emotional. Jeez . . .

Maya piped up, her voice soulless and unapologetic. 'What she's trying to say, *boss*, is that nobody wants forced fun.' I shot her a glare so sharp it could've laser corrected her bad eyesight.

'Forced fun?' he snapped, looking directly at me, as if *I* was the one who dared to utter those damning words. I felt compelled to apologise.

'Sorry.' I started, 'it's just that, well, I think what we'd really like is an informal kind of . . . office thing. You know. Just really relaxed. A few well-dones for last year, a re-cap of our goals for this year, a bit of music, a few pizzas, maybe a quiz . . . ' I made sure to chuck the work element in, although given it was Jamie, it probably didn't matter that much. He played the game, sure, but because of who promoted him, he didn't have to try *too* hard.

'So an office "do",' he spat, bending his knees slightly and using his fingers as quotation marks. 'So everybody thinks we can't afford to do things properly.' He let out a highly audible harrumph and momentarily stared out of the window – clearly looking for comeback inspiration. 'You do realise floor eight had an all-expenses-paid trip to Torremolinos for their team-building event last year, don't you? It might not have been our best year, but it hasn't been . . . '

Maya looked up at him, 'But floor eight are . . . '

'I know,' I said, abruptly stopping Maya in her tracks before the words we were all thinking fell out of her mouth. Floor eight *are* flashy wankers. It's true. But in that moment in time, I was just desperate to save us all from Jamie's bubbling wrath. The wrath that we knew from experience was always worse when he felt belittled or unappreciated. 'I'm not saying we can't afford it.' I continued. 'It's just, we asked around when we knew we had this meeting, to prep, like, and that was the consensus. Low key. But we could always go out, you know, drinks down the Quayside or something. I mean, if that's . . . well, no worries either way. We'd be happy with anything, really.'

We wouldn't be happy with anything, but his face was beginning to contort like a clubber on a bad pill.

'Right then.' He put his pointer on the table, gave us all one last look each, then randomly left the room without another word.

'Well, that's that then.' Maya said standing up out of her chair, her gigantic puddle jeans owning the room.

'*You* didn't help,' I said, stopping her in her tracks before she reached the door. She turned round.

'Too much pussyfooting around, Char,' she said with a smirk.

'But he's our boss, Maya. And now he clearly thinks that what you said was what I was thinking.'

'It *was* what you were thinking.'

'Aye, but *he* doesn't need to know that.'

'Look, what would you rather? A mini tantrum from the boss or a day rolling around in mud with him?'

We all looked back up at the images on the screen. Swamps of people swimming around together, up to their necks in mud. Supporting each other by holding hands while balancing on some kind of triangular walkway. Clambering up over wooden walls while being dragged in front by one person and unashamedly pushed up by the arse by another . . .

Maya spoke without taking her eyes off the pictures. 'Nobody, and I mean *nobody*, is getting me to take part in a wet T-shirt competition disguised as a team-building exercise.'

'Ah, Maya. Come on, it's not . . . '

'For fuck's sake, Charlotte. It's *Jamie*,' she said.

I had no riposte. I just spluttered a couple of 'buts' and 'ifs' and before I could articulate anything of any meaning she was gone, leaving me sitting speechless in my chair while Pete and David quietly lugged themselves up out of their seats as if they were wading through peanut butter.

'And thanks for your support,' I said sarcastically, as they too retreated back to their desks, leaving me with nothing more than a shrug of their shoulders.

I took a detour to the kitchen, in need of a strong builder's brew while I tried to figure out how to redeem myself to the boss, who was clearly upset. A prize prick, but the boss nonetheless.

Jamie headed up the partnerships and research team for Platform – the media buying agency we all worked for. He was all external facing and preoccupied with how we *looked* to people. It was likely to be less a team-building day and more a parade. He'd probably even book a photographer to capture 'informal' documentary style pics for our Instagram account.

Unfortunately for me, he was also my line manager. He was Maya's too, but, I don't think Jamie knew how to handle her. She usually said very little but what she did say always had punch. Maya said what we *all* wanted to say. I envied her for that.

On the other hand, maybe I tried too hard to placate him. He was a tricky customer, all gloss and fun on the outside, but impatient and moody close up. He'd got worse since his divorce. On both counts. So I was always trying to walk a fine line. Without being too attentive, of course. There was something unnerving about the way he looked at you some-times . . .

Jamie was jealous of the creative marketing agencies on the floor below – Harpers and Troy and Storycraft. We worked with them sometimes, collaborated on client campaigns, and they were all about vision and art. Meanwhile we negotiated the media deals. We were all about numbers – costs, viewing figures, spots, slots. I think Jamie thought he was some kind of frustrated artist who'd been left to rot. To be honest, *I* was always on the lookout for any jobs that might be going with Storycraft. They did some really cool stuff, and I was desperate to make a move in that direction. Plus, they didn't need to carpet their offices in loud primary colours to stand out. They just . . . did. They stood out for the right reasons.

The daily roar from the recruitment firm on floor eight above didn't help Jamie's style of management, either. 10 a.m. on the dot, it was like some kind of warm up for the day ahead. It began with a 'woooo' and ended with a 'oooooaaaaaaarrrrrr' and about twenty pairs of feet stamping hard on our ceiling, shaking the contents of my wooden elephant desk tidy. It always made me laugh how they sounded as though they were gearing up for a rugby game – or perhaps a Warrior Mud Challenge – when, in fact, they were just about to get on the phone to the HR officer of some call centre to see if they needed any more temps that week.

The problem was Jamie was bezzie mates with their sales director, Danny, and the competitive nature of their friendship was continuously affecting every single one of us.

I set my cup of tea down on my desk and started thinking about how to diffuse the Jamie situation without pissing him off. We had our appraisals coming up and I needed him on side. His report could be the difference between a decent increment or a measly cost of living pay rise. Not just for me, but for everyone. Mediating didn't especially make me popular with either Jamie *or* the rest of the team, but if nobody else was going to do it . . .

I opened an email and typed the subject header 'Team away day' but got distracted as my phone pinged. A TikTok DM from my housemate Mush. I decided that could wait. He'd gotten into the habit of sending me funny cat clips and there was no way I could properly enjoy watching someone's cute kitty making a comedy appearance on a Zoom meeting until I got this bloody email out the way.

Hi Jamie,

Sorry to bother you. I just wanted to quickly follow up on the meeting.
We really appreciate the thought, and would normally really love to take part in the Warrior Mud Challenge – it's a great idea! However, as already mentioned . . .

I reflected on those last three words. Hmm . . . perhaps they could be seen as passive aggressive . . . I quickly deleted them . . .

. . . However, we did a quick straw poll and most colleagues said they'd prefer to do something low key in the office over lunch. I think everyone's just got so much on this month. Although, I'm sure we're not wedded to the idea, so it's no biggie either way.

I decided that I'd also need to acknowledge his seniority and autonomy . . . he liked that. Plus, it was a softener. And he might have pity on us then. As our leader. As someone who could make our lives easier. He had the power. I think that was his favourite part of the job. It certainly wasn't balancing departmental budgets. He always kicked that chore over to me, describing it as 'admin'.

Even if we didn't get the low-key office picnic, at least we could negotiate from that point. Perhaps we could wangle axe throwing as a compromise.

Psychology, innit.

I continued typing . . .

. . . Of course, I'll leave it to you. Let me know if you need me to sort anything if we're doing the office picnic. Food, drinks, etc. Or the Italian tapas – that sounds like a great idea. No worries if not, though, as I say, we're pretty chilled either way. And we really do appreciate your ideas and the investment senior management are clearly willing to make in an away day.

Charlotte

I pressed send and took a slurp of my hot tea, picking my phone back up to see what feline funnies Mush had sent this time.

You gotta check this guy out.

Oh? I clicked on the profile he'd sent me, watched a few seconds and typed back.

```
So what. It's a guy reviewing chocolate
bars.
Yeah. But look at him.
Cute. So
Works in my office. He's single.
```

Oh!

I took a closer look, picking my cuppa back up to settle into stalking some random confectionary obsessive on TikTok. He looked about my age, ish. Maybe slightly younger. Maybe mid-twenties? And he was definitely cute. Top marks on that smile . . . which was kind of hard to miss given his whiter than white teeth . . . and nice, slate grey eyes, topped off with blonde hair styled in a definitely-not-styled way – messy, carefree, long . . . he had surfy vibes about him. Mush knew my weak spots – and I knew when he was trying to tempt me out of my dating rut.

I chucked my AirPods in so I could have a listen.

He was reviewing chocolate bars like he was pairing fine wine, teaming them up for those special moments in our lives. Telling people what it meant if a Mars bar was your emergency newsagent purchase of choice (solid, no nonsense, gets the job done). I scrolled up . . .

Next up a Twix . . . to embrace your individuality (no two people eat a Twix bar the same way) . . . and then a stern warning as to why you should never eat a Ripple on a first date.

I found myself chuckling at his Ripple disaster story. So what, he said, if melted chocolate is meant to be all sexy and romantic when it comes to dipping strawberries and the like. It's less seductive when you've got suspicious brown marks melting into your white shirt. There was no denying it. He was funny.

And fit.

```
Good call Mushtaq!
```

I typed back. His recent suggestions for dates had been way off the mark. It had been easier to swipe left to those and focus on work. But perhaps, this time, there was genuine potential.

```
I'll engineer a meet-up. We were in a meeting
the other day and he let slip he was single.
```

He replied and I felt momentarily satisfied . . .

Then I noticed an email pop up on my screen. It was from Jamie.

Thanks Charlotte.

Seeing as your email didn't seem too concerned either way, I've booked the Warrior Mud Challenge.

Jamie

Fuck.

2

'Heads you call, tails I call.'

Mush tossed the coin that would seal my fate for the next . . . probably like three hours or something. It rotated in the air a few times before Mush caught it in his palm and flipped it onto the back of his hand.

'Tails. Sorry, Char.'

Fuck. I lifted my chin and shook my head in disappointment.

'Well, what're you waiting for?' Mush lunged backwards into the slouchy blue sofa letting out a satisfied exhale.

'You're such a twat sometimes,' I snapped, grabbing my phone.

'Good luck.' He grinned, leaning forward to pick *his* phone up then chucking his legs horizontally in front of him onto the coffee table. I huffily pulled at the paper broadband bill that was caught beneath his feet and began punching the customer service number violently into my iPhone screen.

I wasn't going to sit down. Pacing the living room while angrily voicing the stupid numbers to the stupid automated menu thingy would reinforce just how pissed off I was.

14

'On hold. Wrong department apparently.' I put the phone on speaker and placed it on the coffee table. It soon started loudly exclaiming *'We're sorry for your wait, one of our team will be with you as soon as possible,'* before returning to some wanky music that randomly got louder when you were least expecting it. Every time one track ended, I thought it was a human finally picking up – but then another burst of muzak started up.

'You do realise I'm gonna be on this call for the next twenty hours don't you? You better make me a cuppa.'

Mush half-heartedly jumped up and sloped off to the kitchen, leaving a human-sized crater in the soft fabric of our prehistoric settee – one of the many soft furnishings his mam donated when we first decided to flat-share after uni. Almost seven years ago. Shit. Where did that go?

We hadn't *consistently* flat-shared over the seven years. And it was more Mush's flat really. He was the one who found it in the first place, plus he'd been here since day dot, while I had lived here sporadically – moving out for a while to my cousin's funky warehouse flat near the Ouseburn Valley a couple of years back. It was when I noticed his last serious girlfriend had all but moved in – and I wasn't very good at playing gooseberry. It made me feel . . . like a bit of a failure to be honest. Not having got my shit together when Mush was clearly embracing the whole 'adulting' thing. Steady job, steady accommodation, steady girlfriend . . .

They were a great couple, Mush and Rachel. Everyone thought he was set for life. Loved up, having loads of fun, both doing great at work. That was where they'd met, in the law offices on the Quayside. But then I got a drunken and desperate voice message one night.

I rushed round to find him in a giant snotty mess on the sofa, cuddling one of the squishy cushions and wringing his feet so hard one of his Baby Yoda socks was hanging off his toes.

'What's Thailand got that I haven't?' he'd wailed, as I comforted him with tissues and Nutella mug cake.

After that, I never went back to my cousin's place. I just moved my stuff back in, bit by bit, until gradually I was paying my rent to Mush again. And now here we were, back in domesticated housemate bliss in the middle of Studentville, with fairy lights and tinsel still shining from Christmas-just-past.

Well, bliss aside from the fact that our broadband provider was being a greedy bastard.

We'd been putting this call off for days, but after seeing the direct debit shoot up by almost double we were livid. Why is it that the things that go the most badly wrong are the things that always involve navigating some stupid bloody automated menu system and then sitting on hold for the equivalent of, I don't know, the entire *Lord of the Rings* trilogy, only to speak to someone who's been trained *never* to say yes.

It's like those games, when you can't say yes or no. Except in the call centre game, you actually get extra bonus points for saying no. You get commission for saying no. You get a goddamn standing ovation for saying no. At least that's how it feels when you're on the receiving end of a relentless string of *no, no, definitely not, no.*

Mush wandered back through with the cuppas. 'Extra strong He-Man tea to keep your stamina up.'

'I'm not sure extra caffeine's what I need right now . . . ' I murmured, my jaw already firmly clenched with the prospect of dealing with *'computer says no'*.

'Just trying to be nice.'

'I know. Soz.'

The hold music stopped – again – and the automated far-too-jolly voice piped up – '*We're sorry for your wait . . .* '

Mush picked his phone back up, clearly flicking through TikTok or Facebook reels. 'Running up that Hill' by Kate Bush blasted out, alongside a computerised American voice saying *'When your treadmill fails you.'* He immediately turned the volume down and pulled his AirPods from his pocket to placate me.

'*We're sorry for your wait, one of our team will be with you as soon as possible.*'

'Sorry for the wait, my arse.' I whinged. 'If they were actually sorry for my wait, they'd employ enough people to answer the phones.'

'You always said it was good manners,' he said.

'What?'

'Apologising.'

I shrugged. 'Yeah but it's a human thing. A computerised voice can't feel sorry so what's the point in it saying it.'

'To keep the peace?'

'You can't have a row with a computerised voice.'

'*You* seem to be doing a pretty good job of it.'

'*You are now number four in the queue. Someone will be with you shortly.*'

'I. Hate. Queuing.' I moaned, just as Mush was attempting to block out the hellish hold music I was subject to. He could at least endure that part of this ordeal.

He lowered his AirPods back down. 'It's such a British thing.'

'What is?'

'Queuing. Apparently we're just really good at it.'

'What, waiting in line? What's the alternative?'

Mush shrugged. 'Getting your elbows out and charging ahead regardless?'

'I guess. Plenty of that after a few pints mind.'

'Aye,' he said, attempting to place his AirPods in his ears again before being jolted back into the room by a memory and stopping. 'Remember when we queued for *ages* in the rain to get into Groovy that night.' Mush was clearly trying to improve my prickly mood with nostalgic tales. I think it was his attempt at keeping me calm.

I smiled, joining in with his reminisce. 'Why were we even . . . ?'

'Dunno. Someone's birthday I think.'

'Must've been someone we liked. A lot. You normally couldn't pay to get me in that place.'

'Queueing. For fucking Groovy. I mean . . . '

'Ugh.' I shuddered just thinking about it. Terrible seventies megamixes, sticky floors and the almost-human dregs of the night hollering at the bar or attempting semi-comatose Bee Gees moves on the dance floor. We had tons of decent bars in town. No idea why we always seemed to end up in the cheesiest of places at the end of a big night. 'You did all right though,' I said, remembering the attention he was getting.

'Aye. At first.' Mush took a slurp of his tea and appeared lost in thought. He was clearly daydreaming about the two girls who were chatting him up in line that night. He always gets heaps of attention. He's a good looking lad. Beautiful brown skin, dark eyes, neat black stubble and the glossiest black hair that flops lazily across his face.

Thankfully for our friendship, we got any notion of sexual awkwardness out the way as soon as we met, back in our first year of uni.

Back then, we were sharing with a bunch of others in student halls on the edge of town, just over the River Tyne. You could see our modern, purpose-built student high rise as you drove over the Tyne Bridge towards Gateshead. It was like a student oasis that seemed to light up the night sky. We had everything we needed on site – a cafe, shop, launderette, we barely needed to leave. Until we remembered the small matter of actually studying. But it was just a hop and a skip across the iconic green bridge to reach our lecture halls on the main campus . . . and all the bars.

We'd been living together a couple of months when we ventured beyond the 'just friends' boundary. We both got totally mortal, completely steaming, on a student night in town, and staggered back home over the bridge, holding hands and giggling. Almost as soon as we put the keycard in the door we were snogging. We ended up falling into my room – mine being the closest to the flat door – and carried on snogging on my teeny tiny little student bed. I think we thought that, because we got on so well and, well, because he's fit and he reckons I am too (he's always dead nice about me), that we'd totally hit it off in the bedroom. But it couldn't have been further from the truth. We had too much in common. You know, like a brother and sister. Well, not like me and Ben. We grew up hating everything about each other – our taste in clothes, music, movies. No, with Mush and me, we loved all the same things. But so much so that we couldn't get past that 'mates' thing. On paper, great, in bed . . .

The moment I felt his hand on my arse the giggles engulfed me. For a split second he looked hurt. I mean you would, wouldn't you. But then he knew it too. And any hint of embarrassment melted into extreme relief. We were far more suited to watching *Star Wars* together with microwaved mug cakes than tearing each other's clothes off.

We never went back there again. Never even had the urge. Regardless of how dry a spell we'd been in.

I was glad we got it out the way, though. Especially now we live together properly – no en-suite bathrooms in this place. We share the lot. And with my long hair jamming up the plug, coated with scuzzy soap and old toothpaste, and his habit of leaving his Primarni boxer shorts and Simpsons socks on the bathroom floor, there wasn't anything even remotely romantic about our relationship.

'*We're sorry for your wait, one of our team will be with you as soon as possible.*'

'Fuck's sake.' I grumbled.

'They *were* fit though.'

20

'Who?'

'Those two lasses.'

'Oh, yeah. Shame you puked on your shoes when the one in the ridiculously high heels was chatting you up.'

'Aye. She was wearing open-toed sandals. Could've been at least third date potential there if I'd been able to hold my drink. She was well lush. *And* she laughed at my jokes,' he sighed, the possibility of true love dancing briefly in his eyes as his thoughts wandered away from our front room and to an altogether more romantic place . . .

'I'll tell you what's definitely *not* lush . . . ' I said.

'Go on . . . '

I filled Mush in on the excruciating team-building task force meeting and the looming Warrior Mud Challenge as hold 'music' continued to infect our house with cheesy monotony.

'I don't get it though,' he said. 'Why would you tell him you didn't mind if you did?'

'Good manners isn't it.'

'Is it?'

'Well yeah, but everybody knows that we don't *really* mean it when we say no worries either way. Who the hell takes these things literally?'

'Your boss.'

'Aye.' I sighed. 'But it's like when you bump into someone from school and you get all enthusiastic going we *must* catch up it's been *ages* and everyone knows that it's just a way to get the hell away from the conversation without being rude.'

'Is that a thing?' Mush looked genuinely perplexed.

'Of course it is,' I said. But then I remembered how ridiculously popular Mush was. Anyone asking him for a catch up would have been genuine.

'You say it a lot, mind,' he said, nodding towards me.

'Say what?'

'No worries if not.'

'Do I?'

'Yeah, at one point I wondered if it was part of your email signature, because it was a constant sign off.'

'Was it?'

'Yeah. Like, even with me. You ask me something nice, like, if I want to go to the pub after work, or if I want a steak bake picking up from Greggs, and you add "no worries if not".'

'I do not,' I snapped defensively, while internally contemplating the idea that he might be onto something . . .

'You do, it's like you're begging people to say no to you. Even when you're actually doing something *for them*.'

'It's not begging people to say no. It's just . . . giving them a get-out clause.'

'But why give them a get-out clause?'

'It's polite. And well, I guess it makes me feel ready for rejection if they say no.'

Mush rolled his eyes before changing the subject. 'Jamie's a right doylem,' he said. 'But worse than just being a doylem,' he continued, 'he's actually a sleaze. Even I can see that and I'm a bloke. I don't know how you and Maya put up with him.'

'I know. Although, to be honest, I think I get the tough end of the bargain.'

'Well, he must know he stands no chance with Maya.'

'Er, I'll have you know he stands no chance with me either!'

'I know that, I just mean, he's hardly Maya's type.'

'I don't think Jamie's anyone's type. I think that's why we get the attention.'

I pondered on it. Since Jamie and his ex had split up, he was always banging on about some girl or other – although we never knew if they were real or made up. But he also paid me a little too much attention. At least that's how it felt sometimes. I was never sure if he truly valued my ideas or just wanted to reinforce his position as manager over me. He was definitely power hungry and I think he saw his position in the office as his most attractive feature.

'*We're sorry for your wait, one of our team will be with you as soon as possible.*'

Mush picked his phone back up and I finished the dregs of my tea, while an urgency down below began to develop.

'So, Char. TimTok . . . '

'Eh?'

'Tim. On TikTok.'

'Oh! Yes! No definitely. Do it.'

'I'll message him now . . . '

At least I had something nice to think about while hanging on for some customer service operative to pick the phone up. I looked back at my phone, the minutes clocking up. How much longer was this gonna take?

'Listen, Mush, you're gonna need to watch the call. I need a piss.'

'Fuck no. You'll be up there ages. Not doing it.'

'I'm only going for a wee.'

'Take it with you then.'

'Jesus Mush.'

'You lost, remember.'

I reluctantly grabbed my phone off the coffee table and stomped out the room. I'd been on hold for . . . forty-eight minutes so far, so there was no way I was dropping the call now.

'We're sorry for your wait, one of our team will be with you as soon as possible.'

I headed into the bathroom and shoved my phone on the floor where it was just within reach but not too close to the loo to be considered gross. But I needed it within reach just in case, by way of a miracle, a human being might actually pick up. I'm all for hygiene but when you've been on hold for over three quarters of an hour something's got to give . . .

I put the toilet seat down, pulled my jeans in the same direction and started to let out the now-urgent stream.

Ahh . . . that's better . . .

'Hello? Hello can I help you?'

I froze stock still on the loo, holding in my urgent stream with all my muscular might.

'Hello? Is there anyone there?'

I was supposed to put the bloody thing on mute. Why didn't I put it on mute?

'Yes, um, sorry.' I could barely breathe for the strength it was taking to hold back the deluge. It was one of those loaded ones after too many cups of tea. You know, like an early morning one. Where it's been waiting patiently for its freedom but was now poised to let loose. I just knew it wasn't going to drip away quietly.

'What can I help you with today?'

'Yes, it's our, um, it's our bill,' I said, still desperately concentrating on my pelvic floor muscles. I cursed myself for never practising my Kegel exercises regularly like Mam always said.

'Yes, I can see that it's jumped up quite a bit lately.'

'Well yes,' I said, trying to sound authoritative, wiggling my bum around on the seat, as if squeezing my thighs together would act as some kind of barrier. All the confidence I had tried to muster had dripped away while my pee was waiting impatiently, banging at the urethra door, desperate to be let out.

Why as the customer do we always try to overcompensate. Why couldn't I ask her to please hold the line, I will be with you in one minute, as soon as I've pissed like a racehorse and zipped my bloody pants back up . . . I could've stuck the phone on hold for just three seconds and that would be it.

At least now I know how to get someone to pick up the phone. Have a bloody piss while you're on hold.

'It has jumped up,' I continued. 'But we haven't changed anything, so we don't understand . . . '

'No. I think that's the problem.'

'What?'

'You didn't switch. You're still on our old package which we stopped rolling out some time ago . . . '

'Right?' I was struggling to concentrate. I was never good at multi-tasking.

'You've been on it for two years now . . . '

'OK . . . ?'

'You should've moved to our new package around nine months ago.' Her patronising tone angered me.

'I'm sorry . . . what are you telling me? That we're paying double because you cancelled our package – or rather, didn't cancel it officially because we're still on it. But because you put it up . . . ' I felt my pelvic muscles flutter so squeezed again hard with all my strength, holding my breath as if that was the stopper.

By this point I could hear Mush hovering outside the door. This was beginning to feel like the most public pee I'd ever had.

As I squirmed awkwardly on the loo seat, I knew that if I let out even a teeny dribble more, that would be it. Seal well and truly broken. Floodgates wide open. I took another risky deep breath, as if my pelvic floor muscles were like some kind of puppet on a string, controlled by my breathing.

'Yes. You will have received an email explaining that your old package was going up in price and for you to switch to a new one . . . '

'OK, it's just that we receive lots of emails . . . many go to junk . . . ' I couldn't even form full sentences anymore. It was starting to hurt . . .

'Ah, so you do need to ensure that all your providers are saved as contacts . . . ' How was she telling me off right now? I thought the customer was always right?

'But, I don't recall . . . '

'So what you need to do now is upgrade your package to the new one . . . '

'Upgrade? But how is it an upgrade if it's cheaper?'

'You get faster broadband speed.'

'But . . . sorry, we get faster broadband speed for less?' It was beginning to leak out now. Like an interim splish-splash-splash. I tensed my muscles again intermittently stopping the flow. I was now hovering high above the toilet, thighs tightly clenched, teeth gritted. I caught sight of my face in the mirror. Red as gammon. 'OK, look, can you just do that for me now I need to get . . . '

'No, I'm afraid that's something the customer needs to do. The package you're on isn't one we offer anymore.'

See, there's that 'no'.

This was no good. I couldn't argue. I hadn't the strength and neither had my bladder. I'd been waiting fifty minutes and three seconds for this piss now. Why didn't I go before. 'OK. And how do I upgrade then?' I asked, sounding clearly breathless due to my plank-level Kegel efforts.

She blathered on about something or other that I needed to do with our online account which, to my knowledge, neither of us had ever accessed before, but I was in no position now to go into further detail. I'd just have to suss it out.

'Right then . . . ' I was seeping . . . and sweating . . .

'It will take ninety days to take effect. Your current contract doesn't expire until April.'

'Ninety days?! What the?!' The shock shook my bladder and unwittingly released all my muscles. It all came gushing out − the swooshing, the splashing. It was LOUD.

'Is everything OK?' she asked.

'Yeah, um, sorry, my . . . friend's a bit sick. He's being sick.' Charlotte, really? Is that even better? Is it even believable?

'Oh. Right. OK.' I could tell she didn't believe me, there was a muffled sound, like she was trying to stifle laughter. Was this a regular thing? Did they often catch customers having a piss – or worse – because they kept them on hold for ever and ever?

She carried on, strange little intakes of breath as she spoke. 'Well, really you need to keep an eye on your account . . . and . . . make sure you're switching to the best deals . . . '

How was this woman making me feel so small. And why couldn't she just get off the phone now.

'OK, sorry,' I said, immediately hating myself.

'Is there anything else I can help you with today?'

'No, no that's all. Thanks.'

'Thanks for your call.'

Oh my God just hang up already!

'Thanks. Bye.' I hung up.

And at that moment every last drop contained within my now Olympic-medal worthy bladder came flooding out with immense relief. Then the door flung open.

'You well and truly fucked that up, Char,' Mush said, giggling like mad.

'Do you mind?' I snapped, kicking out towards the door, my foot unable to reach it.

'Should've gone before you made the call.'

I half stood up and pushed the door on Mush before grabbing too many sheets of loo roll in anger, blotting away frantically at my nether regions. I could still hear him laughing and snorting away behind the door.

I was livid. Not with Mush – with the bloody stupid broadband provider. This was corporate gaslighting. Thieving corporate wankers!

'Right that's it,' I said, zipping my trousers back up and opening the door. 'If we can't suss this online thingy out, you're making the next call. Tails or no tails.'

'All right, chill yer boots. Fancy another cuppa?'

'Go on then.'

He made his way to the door before pausing and putting on a silly voice. 'My friend's being sick. Good one. She so knew what was really going on.'

I shook my head and couldn't help but laugh. 'Well, you've got to learn to multitask when dealing with these people.'

'Yeah, and you've got to learn that they're the ones who should be apologising,' he said more seriously. 'He-Man brew coming up.'

'Ta,' I said.

'Oh, and TimTok's on for a date! I'll send you his number . . . But I think he's gonna follow you too?'

'On TikTok? Shit. I can't remember what's on there . . . ?' I grabbed my phone and started to review my cheesy content.

'Lighten up. There's nothing he won't see when you're two pints in. Call it "managing expectations". '

'It's mainly videos of me mam's cat so . . . '

'Cool. Oh but I've also just tagged you in that one of you trying to hold in your wee while on hold to the broadband company . . . '

'Mush you . . . !' I desperately refreshed my notifications.
'As if,' he laughed.
'Well, TimTok better not keep me waiting . . . ' I said.
'If he does, do not apologise.'
Easier said than done, I thought. Given my track record.

3

17th August 2002

People I like today:
Me
Dad

People I don't like today:
Ben
Mam
The lady in the shop

We went shopping today. Ben didn't go cos Mam said he didn't have to and that, anyway, I could choose my own T-shirt.
Ben always gets out of shopping.
I wanted to play out on Brickfield cos Kelly and Laura were going now we're allowed to the park ourselves but Mam said I had to go with her to the shops. And I reckon that Ben was going to the park and I know Laura fancies him.
I feel sick that they were all playing out together while I wasn't there.

31

To make matters worse, when we went to choose a T-shirt, Mam wouldn't let me pick anyway!!!!!!

She's such a liar. She said I couldn't have a T-shirt from the boys' section – but it didn't even say it was for boys.

We went to the boys' bit first and Mam picked up a T-shirt that said 'adventurer' which I thought was stupid cos Ben's not an adventurer, he's boring. With a capital 'B'. All Ben does is hang around the park trying to look cool. Then she picked out another one that said 'icon' and that one was really nice. It was green, short-sleeved and it had big letters saying ICON and inside the letters it looked like New York or something. All big buildings and things. And I love New York because it was in Home Alone 2 *and I really want to go for Christmas and Mam KNOWS that.*

So I asked for that one but Mam said no!! And I told her that she said *I could pick one and she said that I could, but I had to pick one from the girls' section and when I asked why she just said it was because I was a girl.*

So we went into the girls' section and the T-shirts were BORING! They all said things like 'be happy' or 'positive vibes' and I told Mam I wasn't a hippy and I didn't want a stupid girls' T-shirt I wanted the icon one and she said no, I couldn't have it, Ben was having that one and I had to pick another.

I hate her. I hate the stupid shop and I hate the stupid lady in the stupid shop who laughed at me for wanting the boys' T-shirt. It's not like it's even got a boy on it. And so I said why didn't they make nice ones for girls as well then and Mam told me off for being rude and made me apologise.

And when I did she said, 'apologise like you mean it.' So then I had to say it again which is just shan.

So I never got a new T-shirt. And I heard Dad saying why couldn't she just have got me it anyway and Mam was mean to him too.

We're having pizza tonight.

4

Jamie emerged from his office earlier than usual. 'Pub drinks?' he said, as breezily as he could, to our two banks of desks. We were only two weeks into the New Year and he was already looking for any excuse for an early flyer.

'Sure.'

'Aye, grand.'

'Why not?'

He walked back into his office and we all watched like nervous hawks as he picked up his mobile phone, his fingers frantically texting. We knew what that meant. And the deflated office mumbles confirmed that *nobody* was happy:

'FFS.'

'I was gonna make soup tonight.'

'As if that Warrior shite wasn't enough . . . '

You see, you didn't say no to Jamie, however breezy his invitations seemed. He was the boss. And he was clearly texting Danny from floor eight to agree to meet up by the Quayside. Danny would parade his sycophantic team of highly enthusiastic, sales-driven recruitment consultants in shiny shoes and slick hair, and Jamie would want to keep up. So he'd drag us lot along. After all, we knew the drill: make Jamie feel good in front of his mate and we'd get bonus points for 'living the values' in our next appraisal.

I finished typing up an email to one of our clients and couldn't help but notice all eyes on me, peering unkindly over the desk dividers.

I glanced up. 'What?'

'Why can't you just say no?' Pete complained.

'Me? You lot weren't exactly in opposition. Besides, I didn't even say anything.'

'Exactly.' Maya sighed. '*You're* the most senior. *You're* meant to have influence. Now we've got after work drinks with floor eight *and* that fucking mud bath from hell to look forward to.'

'I'm not *really* senior,' I shrugged. In reality, it was in title only. Assistant director. My pay grade didn't really reflect any level of seniority, and I couldn't really see any change in my responsibilities other than being given a new job spec that had an extra line added to it saying '*assist the partnerships director with strategic vision and creative implementation thereof*'. What the fuck did that even mean?

Still, the change in title was enough to see me move from 'current teammate' to 'potential team traitor'. I never asked for it either. I think Jamie just wanted to say he had an assistant director – like it was some kind of indicator of success. And he tended to treat me more like a PA since my promotion, which was ironic. If I had a pound for every latte and bacon sarnie I've had to pick up for him over the last three months, I'd have enough money to not even worry about the sky-high broadband package.

I tried to ignore the comments and finished typing up my email. I was trying to delicately explain to one of our long-standing clients that taking out an ad in a range of new publications probably *was* a good way to attract more diverse applicants to jobs. *However,* the content needed careful consideration . . . because promoting a 'reggae-themed' recruitment event and using questionable pictorial tropes was . . . well, it was . . .

How could I explain it to them without calling them a little bit racist . . .

Hmm . . .

'I'd urge you to reconsider the content for this ad . . . ' I typed. *'It's not especially inclusive. It might just be best to perhaps . . . '*

I took a moment to think through my next few words carefully . . .

Oh God. Whatever I said, however I said it, it was going to be awkward . . .

' . . . review the demographics of the readership and provide content that is inclusive rather than . . . '

Umm . . .

' . . . tokenistic.'

Maybe not.

' . . . niche.'

There. Niche. That was a safe bet. I finished the rest of the email, adding, *'Apologies if you feel I'm over-stepping the mark but I just thought it was worth mentioning. No pressure, of course.'* Then I pressed send.

'Ready to rock 'n' roll folks.' Jamie had re-emerged from his office, clearly excited about the team-off he was about to have down the pub, using us poor souls as the pawns. He had his tan coloured woollen overcoat on over his petrol blue suit. You couldn't miss him. He stood in front of us and loosened his tie – a sign that he was ready for business. His favourite kind of business. Then he turned his coat collar up and made towards the door, a sign for us to follow.

As everyone unsmilingly closed down their laptops and multi screens and grabbed their coats I had a last minute email ping through.

Charlotte.

I find your email ironic, as by excluding reggae and recognisable and relatable imagery, it seems that it is in fact you who isn't being inclusive in this matter.
Please place the ad with our original content as requested.

FFS. Should I just spell it out? Don't. Be. Racist.

However, the ongoing work we got from Stanton House-builders was significant, so I had to play it carefully. But I always thought of myself as an ally – and didn't allies speak up?

I had asked early on in the campaign briefing stage about what evidence they had to back up their problems with diversity. I mean, was it really a problem with the diversity of applications received? Or was it more to do with the short-listing and interview process. I had a sneaky suspicion it was the latter but it wasn't really my place to say. After all, even commenting on the ad content seemed to go down like a ton of bricks.

I shut the laptop down regardless. We had over a week until the deadline for the mag closed. And besides, bolshy client was on leave for the next few days. I'd think of a good way to respond to her next week.

'Charlotte!' Jamie yelled. 'You're making us all wait. I feel as if my throat's been cut over here!'

'Coming.' I hollered, making sure the laptop was properly switched off before turning both screens off too and grabbing my coat from the back of my chair.

I scanned the rest of the office, it was still fairly quiet, with most people sitting, staring at their screens with their heads down in concentration. Jamie had clearly got us up to leave much earlier than we were meant to. Again. I glanced up at the funky wall clock. One of those huge contemporary types with no numbers. It was basically just two arms moving around on some funky paint-splashed plastic background. Very on-brand. It was so early though even the lack of numbers didn't hide the fact we were leaving *way* sooner than we should be.

I secretly hoped the rest of management knew that, as far as we were concerned, this was boss's orders. We were simply doing our jobs. I had a feeling he would spin it as 'networking' anyway.

As we all sloped off down the many flights of stairs and out into the cold evening air we could see some of floor eight in the distance making their way towards the pub, its on-trend rusty looking shipping container structures surrounded by a shimmering glow of fairy lights and laughter. The air between us and the pub was thick with the clink clank of high heels and the smarting tones of too much aftershave and deodorant floating back towards us from the floor eight gang like a less appealing Bisto gravy.

Meanwhile, Jamie's partnerships and research team, aka us lot, were reluctantly following our leader, making very little noise compared to our forerunners, thanks to our stifled chit chat and rubber-soled footwear. I had a feeling everyone was probably trying to come up with a reasonable excuse to abandon ship in half an hour. But our lack of enthusiasm became even more apparent as a party boat with some kind of birthday celebration or something came chugging past us on the Tyne – squeals of delight and laughter replacing our empty silences.

As we walked into the pub Jamie made a point of shouting that the first round was on him. 'I'll get you all your usual,' he said, not knowing what our usual really was, just what he had become accustomed to buying for us.

'I guess I'm not getting a pint then.' Maya whispered angrily in my ear.

'At least it's a free bevvy,' I offered, trying to see the bright side, even though it irked me that he never asked what we wanted. It's like when you've worked with someone for ages and never asked their name, then too much time has passed to do so without insulting them. Still, I think he preferred to see me and Maya with Prosecco over pints.

Jamie ushered us towards the table where some of floor eight were sitting, as if he were swatting us away like flies. The excitable group had commandeered one of the huge chunky industrial-looking tables, and the one right next to them was, unfortunately for us, vacant bar a couple of dirty plates and empty pint glasses.

It was one of those places where rust was celebrated and hues of brown and orange made the big container spaces feel almost homely. This place was part of the Quayside's newer additions, with a bar, restaurant and backyard bike shop and cafe. They even hosted outdoor street food markets and micro-brewery stalls in the summer, often with a live DJ and a nice, laidback buzz. The Hawker Market it was called. And it was all nestled on the Gateshead side of the river, looking across to Newcastle's grand old buildings and warehouses.

We loved it down here – when the company was right.

The conversation at the busy table was already in full flow with Prosecco chilling in ice buckets and pints of IPA refreshing mouths that worked even harder in the pub than they did on the phones.

'Hi,' I said, trying to sound cheery, plonking myself in a seat on the next table. Maya nodded sternly in their direction and sat on the other side of me, forcing me to budge up so as not to appear to be keeping my distance from our floor eight peers.

We never really knew the name of their company. It was Fletcher and something. But we knew them as floor eight because they were above us and we whole-heartedly resented the sound of their stamping feet, hollering and daily sales brags in the busy lifts.

'What did you lot do for your Christmas do then?' Jessica piped up, her pinky-red glossy lipstick still looking freshly painted on, despite it being the end of the working day. She was one of the more popular consultants from floor eight. She looked after call centre temps and sales staff, and her patter was almost as competitive in nature as Danny's was. We knew all about Jessica because we were often advised to '*Be more Jessica*'.

We hated Jessica.

'Team trip to Fiji.' Maya piped up, nudging her funky, heavy rimmed glasses back up her nose and concentrating on Jessica's reaction.

'How lush!' Jessica gushed with delight. 'That in the Bigg Market or on the Quayside?'

Maya looked disappointed that her sarcasm had spectacularly backfired. Jessica might look and sound like a soft, pretty-in-pink angel, but she was as equally sharp and cutting as Maya.

Jamie returned with a couple of pints in his hands, David in tow, struggling to carry the ice bucket and Prosecco glasses. 'Here we go J-Team!'

Yes. That's what he called us. And no – no irony intended.

He gestured frantically at David to pass me and Maya a glass and plonk the fizz down in front of us. 'Thanks,' I said. We would've killed for a nice cold pint of Italian lager. At least he got the region right.

'Budge up then.' Jamie shimmied in between me and Maya, plonking his own nice cold pint right in front of our hop-thirsty eyes. Maya immediately stood up. 'Off for a ciggie', she said, making a detour to the bar.

Jamie watched her leave then turned to me, his voice becoming lower. 'I'm glad we got this opportunity to chat,' he said, smiling at me. I smiled back, wondering where this was going to go . . . I hated it when he went all serious. It either meant he was going to get mardy about something or that, well, he was going to get personal. 'I've got something to run by you,' he said.

'Ooh interesting.' I replied, pouring myself a glass of fizz and hoping that this was going to be professional. There was no point pouring Maya one.

I hated pretending to be nice, and I'm sure Jamie had a nice side to his personality hidden somewhere. But we were just so fed up with playing along. We wanted substance — mentoring, sound advice when our clients were being tricky, briefings and a heads-up re news from the senior management team that he sat on. Instead we were mostly left in the dark, fending for ourselves without a clue as to what was happening in the business. Perhaps he didn't even know — maybe he just didn't understand it? He had been promoted to his current position by the previous MD who was a friend of his uncle's or something. He was still involved — from a distance. Which I think was the main reason Jamie got to float along doing sweet FA and being a pain in the backside. And even though we did well as a team, we usually met our targets and clients seemed to like us (most of them anyway), we felt aggrieved. Like, we were putting in the leg work while Jamie was prancing about going to dinners and networking business breakfasts with Danny.

'OK, so bit of a heads-up,' Jamie continued, as I caught his eyes flick down my shirt and back up again. I pulled at the back of my top to nudge the front of it up a little higher. It wasn't even low. He just set me on edge. 'There's likely going to be a development. A scale-up and rebrand. This is strictly confidential of course.' He held his pint steadily in front of me, signalling for me to acknowledge his words. I nodded. 'Of course' I said. He took a slurp and let out a thirst-quenched *hahhhh*. Was he trying to build up the suspense like some terrible game show host?

'So,' he continued. 'We might be looking at bringing some creative work into the fold. A new department so to speak.'

'That's exciting,' I said, feeling genuinely interested and uplifted. I'd always wanted to get more involved in content. It felt more me. I always enjoyed seeing the clever lines of copy or wondering how I might improve campaign imagery or metaphors. I might not be hugely proactive on my own social media accounts, more often preferring to observe rather than put myself out there. But I knew if I could work on a social media strategy for a brand I'd be bursting with ideas.

So, for once, perhaps Jamie's words were worth hearing.

'The thing is,' he continued. 'And this is strictly between you and me, the thing is I'll likely be moving into a new role, heading up both teams. Which means that we'll need somebody to step up and be more hands on with the J-Team. Someone to be the new me – I know you love the detail and the numbers – you'll keep any new creative types in check,' he said. I had to bite my tongue.

'OK, of course, sounds interesting,' I said, wishing that there was no 'between you and me' about this conversation because it somehow felt a bit wrong . . .

'So I'm thinking, if you were up for applying for an assistant director role . . . '

'I thought I *was* an assistant director . . . '

'Well, no, not really. You're assistant *to* the director aren't you . . . ?'

'Erm . . . ' I hesitated — figuring not agreeing was nearly as good as actively disagreeing.

'So I'm thinking you should apply. I'll support your application, give you a glowing review. What do you think?'

'I'll definitely have a think about it,' I said, smiling on the outside, even though inside I felt deflated. Just those fleeting seconds of creative opportunity really got me feeling positive. I guess I'd have to look elsewhere to do something like that. But surely this would be an actual step-up, one with a pay rise and proper responsibility . . .

Jamie looked hurt at my lack of commitment. 'I mean, it sounds fantastic, but I'll have to read the job spec, check I feel ready for it.'

'Are you doubting my talent spotting ability? You remind me of how I was at your age — if you play your cards right, you could be sitting here in a few years,' he said, putting on a stupid voice like some kind of local radio voiceover guy. I didn't want to break it to him that a) I was sitting there already and b) I didn't want to be him. But bursting his bubble that he was some kind of great business guru wouldn't help things.

'No, no,' I said, picking up my glass and downing some of the fizz.

'Good. Cos I think you'll be great,' he said, one elbow on the back of my seat, as though he were putting his torso on show, his almost untied tie dangling lazily down his shirt. Then he leaned in, slowly, his knee touching my leg — and I had to concentrate hard to stop myself from visibly flinching. He put his hand on my shoulder. For what felt like an age. And he was talking to me almost over my shoulder. I could feel his boozy breath fluttering my hair into my face. Ugh. What the fuck?

Then it got worse.

'I think *you're* great, Charlotte.' He spoke the words softly, slowly, letting them hit my consciousness from behind. It was proper creepy. He was only on his first pint. Not that booze was an excuse or anything. But surely he knew this was overstepping the mark.

I immediately felt the back of my neck shiver cold. Jamie didn't do sincerity, and this felt . . . horribly sincere. I looked down, feeling unprepared, not sure what else to do, and I smiled. 'Thanks,' I said. Thanks?! Jesus. What was I thankful for? For being infected with my boss's smarm? His hand stayed there . . . lingering on my shoulder . . .

Was I imagining things? He wasn't usually what you would call tactile. Thankfully. For all the sleazy comments and looks nothing ever went further. But right now, he was positively handsy. It wasn't even firm, like, you know, in a matey sort of way. It was . . . soft. Affectionate.

I looked back at him, trying to figure out what I needed to say to get him to move it.

Maybe he was just trying to let me know that I was great at my job? I mean, just because I'm female and he's male doesn't mean . . .

No. We're a true mismatch professionally, personally, platon-ically, romantically . . . we only worked together because we had to. I'd never given him any vibes had I? I'd never encouraged him? And we'd worked together for almost two years with nothing this icky happening before.

Was I imagining it?

Maya came striding back, half-drunk pint in hand, and Jamie immediately snatched his hand away from my arm.

She put her drink down and gave me a concerned look to let me know she'd seen the offending move. I glanced away, desperate not to let Jamie know his move had been noticed, yet at the same time feeling furious that he felt it was OK to invade my space like that. To practically whisper in my ear. Like I was some kind of dog on heat that he had every right to corner.

But it wasn't just about his proximity. I mean, we sometimes all have to squash up in a pub on a night out. It doesn't matter mostly. Because it's just what you do. If your knees touch because you're all bunched up round a table so be it. It doesn't feel intentional.

This, however, felt very considered, very intentional. There was plenty of space, why'd he have to get so close? And I know, sometimes it's hard to hear, but it wasn't even 6 p.m., the pub was fairly quiet. It wasn't that. This was loaded. With something I didn't want to think about.

I tried to change the subject, to keep things formal, work-related.

I took a sip of my drink trying to think of what to say next, to set a boundary. I cleared my throat. 'While we're on the subject of work,' I said, desperately hoping that his last comment really *was* on the subject of work. 'I'm having a few issues with Stanton Housebuilders.'

'How so?' Jamie asked, backing off a bit, picking his pint back up to exhibit a sense of nonchalance.

'The new marketing director wants to place an ad in a media title that promotes the voices of people of colour. They're trying to be more inclusive in their recruitment practices . . .'

'Which is a good thing, am I right?' he said, looking simultaneously perplexed and disinterested.

'Well, yes. But they want to run this ad that's, well, it's kind of . . . racist.'

'We're on a night out, Charlotte,' he interrupted. 'Relax why don't you?' He barked it as though it was an order. Then within seconds he was up out of his chair facing the two tables, gesturing wildly as if giving an enthusiastic TED Talk. 'Who's man enough for a shot!'

Maya rolled her eyes and raised her hand while supping the last of her pint. She elbowed me in the side. 'Might as well make it bearable,' she whispered forcibly. I nodded and raised my hand. Jamie began reversing his way to the bar, both arms out in front of him, tipping the occasional thumbs up and nod of the head as more and more people agreed that they were 'man enough' to down a shot. I'm not sure this pleased him . . .

'Oi, chief' Jamie hollered in Danny's direction. 'Business bad? You mucking in for these drinks or what?'

Danny flicked him the V but then stood up and joined him anyway, his team giving out an appreciative roar as he, in similar style to Jamie, reversed his way to the bar, this time treating us all to a dramatic bow or three en route, before tripping up over a couple of girls that were unlucky enough to be walking past. He managed to steady himself and turned away instantly, while Jamie pretended to pummel him in the ribs.

'What do you think they see in each other?' I asked Maya.

'Themselves,' she said, glancing over at them both with scorn. 'And, deep down, they don't really like themselves, so they don't really like each other. Which is why it's all bullshit banter and competition.'

'Get you Freud!'

'Come on, they're textbook,' she said, her eyes still fixated on the two swaggering blokes at the bar, who were by now jeering each other on as they eyed up the poor lasses Danny almost toppled a moment ago. 'What was he doing touching you up anyway?'

'He wasn't touching me up,' I spat, feeling weirdly guilty, as if I had been the one to step beyond the professional dynamic. 'It was more a motivational grip. I think . . . '

'I saw your face. It wasn't a happy one. Not with that smarmy hand on your shoulder. What the fuck?'

'Just Jamie being Jamie,' I shrugged.

'Well if Jamie gets any more Jamie he'll need a slap sharpish.'

'Yep,' I agreed, replaying the moment in my head to see if it was me just making too big a deal of it.

Jamie soon returned to the table carrying a tray loaded with tequila. Not again. God, it was bad enough having tequila before my first day back after the Christmas break. It was only a Tuesday night.

'Right, need the loo,' I said, excusing myself from the increasingly loud bravado of our two tables.

The bar was beginning to get busy now so I had to wait for a gap in the traffic before making my way towards the loos – which were outside in another container unit. I'd just made a move for it when I felt a thud from my right almost knocking me sideways.

I regained my balance feeling a bit confused. 'Sorry,' I said to the girl who stumbled over me, before realising that her drink was, in fact, soaking through my white shirt. I glanced down at the dark chocolate coloured stain. Damn the popularity of espresso martinis. I looked up at the girl, expecting a gushing apology to end all gushing apologies. Her eyes were well oiled and barely focusing.

'What'chit!' It would've been aggressively sharp if it wasn't slightly slurred.

''Scuse me?' I said, gesturing to my top. She rolled her eyes and walked by.

'Oi,' Maya stood up, thunder clouds raging through her face.

'Don't bother, Maya. It'll just make things worse.'

'I wasn't shouting at *her*. I was shouting at *you*. What the fuck did you apologise to her for? The daft cow fell into *you*.'

'I didn't know she'd poured her bloody drink down my top at that point.'

'Aye, but as soon as you apologise, she's got one up on you.'

'How so?' I asked, barely interested but continuing the chat anyway as I tried to wipe the dark stain from my shirt with the aid of a serviette left on the table next to us.

'Because you've let her know you're a walkover.'

'I am *not* a walkover.'

'*Sorry*,' she repeated in a high pitched whiny voice. 'Honestly Charlotte. Man up will you?'

'Man up?'

'I was being ironic.'

'Sarcastic, you mean.'

'Whatever.'

'Come on girls,' Jamie tried to intervene, for once looking unsure of himself, 'No harm done, eh?'

'Girls?' Maya repeated, clearly irked. Jamie shrugged.

I hadn't the energy for this. 'Maya, just give it a rest will you?'

'Fine. But you'd have far less bother if you didn't assume blame all the time.'

'Whatever,' I shrugged, getting in the last word like a livid teenager.

But I *was* livid. Livid because I knew she was right. And livid because, even though I *knew* she was right, I couldn't shake the feeling that I'd done something wrong just now.

5

Tim and I had spent a few days exchanging DMs on TikTok since Mush had first introduced us . . . but they were mostly just links to other TikToks. Showing off our best finds to demonstrate our social media prowess and quirky personality without really having to reveal anything personal: it was like a TikTok mating dance.

Still, it's what you do isn't it? Sharing videos to avoid sharing anything more personal. And, anyway, I was meeting him tonight for actual IRL drinks – so the TikTok shield would be well and truly down. And I'd get to find out who TimTok *really* is . . .

I still had a final hour of work to get through before the date and I was feeling impatiently excited, procrastinating over work and instead re-watching TimTok's cute videos and enjoying his surfy vibes. I loved the confidence he had. I had a good feeling about this. And it had been a good few months since I'd been on a date or even enjoyed any semblance of romance other than time to myself when Mush was out.

An email from Jamie momentarily jolted me away from date anticipation. He'd carried on since hand-on-shoulder-gate as though nothing had happened. But something definitely had. Something as unwanted as a bout of gonorrhoea. I opened the email. Subject header 'Movin' on up', complete with winking emoji.

He had sent me some details about the role he was on about the other night. Well, the details weren't exactly detailed, it wasn't a job spec, as such, more a kind of . . . vision. He suggested that I put forward an 'expression of interest' for 'leading the J-Team' – which seemed strange given that it was his job and they hadn't announced anything about the new department yet. And besides, I really wanted the chance to get onto the new content team – to flex my creative muscle and all that. Even if I took a sideways step, I'd be happy learning the ropes in a new area where I could step away from data, spreadsheets and reports, and into something more fluid and imaginative.

Like TikTok chocolate bar reviews maybe . . . or TikTok date reviews . . . ?

But Jamie's weird comment, unwanted (and lingering) squeeze of the shoulder and his stomach-churning whisper were still playing on my mind. I couldn't shake it. I couldn't decide what would make it worse – if it was a genuine overstepping the mark or a pissed up overstepping the mark. I didn't want either, frankly. But knowing that he did it sober made me feel that he could talk to me like that any time. Perhaps even in the safety of the office. I shuddered at the thought of our next one-to-one. It's rare anyone looks forward to an appraisal, but at least it meant we had formalities to work through at our next meeting together. It'd keep things on track.

Anyway, now there was a job opportunity tied up in this new cringey dynamic that he'd created. He said in the email that Harriet, the director above him, would be looking at whether anyone in the organisation could step up. But, he said, she had form to always think 'new is best'. So he'd help me overcome that adding – wait for it – *'I'll help you shine.'*

For actual fuck's sake.

If I had to work more closely with him before I even got the job was it really worth it? He'd still be line managing me anyway. But perhaps it would make things a bit better? If the team was bigger it might make things less . . . intense.

My phone pinged. It was Mush.

```
Ready for the big night? X
Yeah, looking forward to it. X
So's he. He's been asking about you.
What have you said?
All good stuff.
```

I turned back to my emails and tapped in a reply to Jamie, asking him if it would *really* be OK to put myself forward for a job that hadn't even been announced yet. I mean, wouldn't it be a bit . . . arrogant? I suggested it might be best if I waited until Harriet announced things formally. But he was adamant in his reply. He said it was 'showing initiative and ambition' and that they're great leadership qualities. He said that I should just let Harriet know that, should there be an opportunity to move upwards in the organisation, I'd be very interested in working my way up and supporting Jamie in leading the partnerships and research team.

He even mentioned adding something about how I enjoyed his coaching. Which I felt I'd have to type through gritted fingers.

No. I wasn't going to go that far.

It all smelled a bit . . . off. But seeing as opportunities for promotion come along as often as good dates, and seeing as Jamie was practically ordering me to make a noise about it, I thought I should probably say *something* to the big boss. Perhaps just *not exactly* the thing Jamie was suggesting.

Besides, coming up with my own ideas was surely part of that initiative and ambition he was talking about . . .

So I typed out an email . . .

Dear Harriet,

Hmm . . . Harriet wasn't really known for being a dear . . .

Harriet,

I've heard through the grapevine that there may be some opportunities coming up and a new agency focus on content. I'm sorry if this is being a little too presumptuous, but I just wanted to throw my hat into the ring early.

I'm really keen to flex creatively, and content has long been an area I'm passionate about. If there's ever an opportunity to chat further do let me know. Of course, no worries if not, I appreciate this is possibly a bit premature.

Best wishes,
Charlotte

Best wishes?

Regards,
Charlotte

Hmm . . . perhaps I need a light touch of nice in my sign off . . . she'd appreciate a *little* nicety . . . show a flash of personality . . .

Kind regards,
Charlotte xxx

SEND

Suddenly, a fuzzy band of anxiety washed down my face and into my fingertips which I realised had just committed a heinous crime on my behalf.

FUCK! FUCK! FUCK! Where's the fucking recall button. Kisses. Three flamin' kisses. That's that out the window then. Why did my fingers do that to me? Why?

Too late. It was gone. Harriet, the world's least fluffy person, was about to receive a load of kisses from me, someone she didn't work too closely with, someone who was asking about a promotion.

It was like the world's biggest suck up. And it was not cool.

I sat staring at my screen, my hand hovering over the mouse, stifled by indecision – or frozen by shame. I wasn't sure. I craned my neck over the desk divider to see if Harriet was in her little glass office in the corner at the bottom of the room. It looked like she was having a meeting in the chairs by her desk. She wouldn't have seen the offending sloppy kiss yet, but there was nothing I could do about it. It was inevitable.

You don't suck up to Harriet. You just don't.

Harriet was officially the executive director of business growth, but she was more like the CEO. Her counterpart was John, executive director of finance and operations. But John seemed to just keep his head hidden in spreadsheets.

I liked Harriet in that I respected her and she seemed fair and reasonable for the most part. But I couldn't pretend that I wasn't a bit fearful of her. She wasn't one for chit chat, and she'd cut you off mid-sentence if you went off on a tangent. But she was efficient. Unlike Jamie. And she could actually be a right laugh when she was off duty. She was often the last one standing on a work's night out, but there was something about her demeanour in the office the next day that reminded you not to mix fun Harriet up with boss Harriet during daylight hours.

I wasn't sure what to do. Leave it and hope she wouldn't notice, or make very clear it wasn't intended for her. I checked the time, there was no time to think about it. I needed to head out for my date with a TikTok star.

I made a quick detour to the loos to add some red lippy – it was my way of distinguishing between work-Charlotte and off-duty Charlotte. Application neat and successful, I was perfecting my pout in the mirror as Maya strolled in, grabbed a cubicle, locked the door and started having a piss.

'Spill!' She hollered from behind the door.

'Eh?'

'The lipstick.'

'Ah. Got a date.'

'Better not be with Jamie.' I could hear her angrily pulling out sheets of loo roll one by one from the dispenser.

The automatic air freshener released a timely scented cloud reminding me to grab my perfume from my bag for a quick spritz . . . I certainly didn't want to rock up to my date stinking of pine-fresh disinfectant.

'I told you, that was just . . . Jamie being Jamie,' I said, dabbing my skin with Miss Dior and just remembering to stop myself before I rubbed my wrists together and diluted the scent. 'Anyway, I'll put him in his place next time, promise.'

'You better.' She jangled about a bit, flushed, and was standing next to me in an instant, washing her hands and checking her teeth in the mirror while I touched up my liquid liner.

She looked me up and down on her way to the drier. 'Looking good,' she said. 'So who is he?'

The blast came on and I had to shout. 'Some guy off TikTok. Works with Mush.'

'Eh?'

I raised my voice as loudly as I could. 'Some guy off . . . ' the drier suddenly cut out and I was left hollering the words, 'Tik Tok!'

'Oh. I'll check him out, what's his name?' She pulled her iPhone from her pocket and opened the app.

'TimTo—I mean. Tim. His account's called Sweet Like Chocolate, I think.'

'Don't pretend you don't know,' she winked.

I giggled.

'Ooh cute,' she said. 'If you like that kind of thing.'

I shook my head giggling to myself.

'OK well have fun. Text me if you need a get out.'

'Will do.'

Maya headed out the door and I gave myself a final mirror check. My long brown hair was tied up in a messy bun, and my face was bare other than my red lipstick and eyeliner flicks, enhanced by black mascara that magically lengthened my lashes by about three inches. This was my *comfy* version of wearing heels in the pursuit of femininity. Whatever that is. Besides, even though I hated them as a kid, I had started to really love my freckles. The pursuit of alabaster skin wasn't worth sacrificing the freckles for.

I hadn't dressed up – I didn't want to look like I'd tried too hard. So I was about to head down there in my baggy black trousers, docs and long-sleeved fitted black polo. Classy, yet understated.

Tim had let me choose the venue, so I'd decided to go for something where the focus wouldn't be on our conversation. You know, to ease us in to getting to know each other.

I picked a stand-up comedy night. At the Stand Comedy Club that was tucked away down a little cobbled street. You could grab a drink before the acts came on, it was pretty chilled and it was bound to be a good laugh. And TimTok was clearly a good laugh and definitely into comedy judging by his content . . . Plus, if we didn't get on, it wouldn't be a complete waste of our time.

I was a few minutes early but, as I pushed on the door, I could see Tim already in situ. He'd bagged us a booth by the upstairs bar, which was at street level (the comedy took place in the basement), and he already had a pint in front of him. He didn't see me so I wandered across to let him know I'd arrived, taking my coat and scarf off as I went.

Tim was sitting playing on his iPhone.

'Hi,' I said, making myself known by standing at the side of the table, my hands hugging my coat in front of me. 'Charlotte.'

'Hi,' he said, standing up and smiling. 'Tim.' He sat back down. God he was so dreamy. I mentally told myself off. Dreamy? I hadn't even thought of calling anyone dreamy since my teenage diaries. But, as I glanced at him again, I realised the word wasn't far off. His beachy hair fell in straggly waves just above his shoulders, and his eyes were more piercing than his videos gave them credit. But he seemed somehow . . . less in your face. More reserved, perhaps. Although I'm not sure what I was expecting. Just because he was a TikTok star it didn't mean he was going to greet me with a slightly disjointed digital accent saying something like '*5 ways of greeting someone on a first date. No 1. Hi Charlotte . . .* '

I realised I was looking a bit too deeply into his eyes as my brain was whirring. 'I'll just dump my coat and grab a drink. Need another?'

'No, I'm good.'

I placed my coat on the seat opposite and stood in line.

Was I blushing? Or was it just too warm in here? If the former, that was a good sign! If the latter . . .

I tried to discreetly waft my top from my chest and get some air circulating. Maybe the polo neck was a bad idea.

I ordered a nice cold pint, then took it back to our booth, sitting down opposite him. He had obviously come straight from work too. He was wearing a dark charcoal suit, but with a black T-shirt underneath the jacket instead of a shirt.

'How's your day been?' he asked, smiling up at me. Damn, those teeth were even more white and perfect in real life.

'Good. January's almost over so I'm nearly over my Christmas lament.'

'You too? I'm terrible for that every January.'

'I know. It's the darkness,' I said. 'Makes you feel as though there's nothing else in your day other than work and sleep. Nothing that a little comedy won't fix though eh?' I put my glass to my mouth and downed a good glug of beer. I loved a first date but they were always slightly nerve-wracking. How do you break the ice? What do you talk about? What would you think of him?

What would *he* think of *you*?

'What about you anyway?' I asked. 'How was your day?'

'Not bad,' he sighed, and I noticed he had his iPhone glued to his hand as he flipped it over to check whatever must've just pinged through. Maybe it was work?

I sat awkwardly in silence for a moment as he finished looking at whatever he was looking at, his thumb swiping upwards which made me think it probably wasn't a work email after all.

'So,' I said. 'Have you seen any of the acts on tonight?'

'Hm?' He finally put his phone down and looked back up. 'Oh, um. I haven't looked actually. Who's on again?'

'All local comics,' I said confidently. 'Gav Webster's compering, he's great fun. Proper Geordie comedy. Then there's Lauren Pattison, she's real funny too. And, oh, I can't remember the others. Haven't seen them before.'

'Cool.'

Was it me or was his demeanour cool too, to the point of frosty? I mean, he didn't have to come on this date.

Then he suddenly grabbed his bag. Was he leaving already? 'Oh. I er . . . haha. I got you something.'

'Oh, thanks,' I said, wondering what on earth he could have brought me. He rummaged around in his bag and then pulled out a Galaxy Ripple. Of course. Chocolate. That's what he was all about after all.

'Lush!' I said. 'Thanks. You'll have to tell me though. What does the giving of a Ripple symbolise then?' I decided it was only fair to indulge him.

'Well, you're a classy lady right?' He seemed to perk up a bit more now we were talking about chocolate. He seemed a bit more like his TikTok persona. 'And the Ripple beats the Flake hands down because of the bonus chocolate layer.'

I giggled, taking the chocolate bar from him. 'Bonus chocolate. I guess it does have that doesn't it. Have you reviewed this one on your channel?'

He picked his phone back up. 'I think I did. Two ticks.'

He sat there concentrating hard, his thumbs swiping up and down on the screen. Meanwhile, I sat in another awkward silence as he tried to find the video.

'It's OK,' I said. 'Maybe I'll send you a review of it.'

'Would you?'

I smiled, but inside I was so confused. My fluttery stomach was no longer fluttering. I mean, here was this gorgeous guy, sitting right in front of me, with the most piercing slate grey eyes and beaming white smile. But there was just . . . something missing. I couldn't put my finger on it. Was it me? Was he used to dating better looking women? Funnier women? Wasn't I sparking enough of a vibe for him? I wasn't sure, but the craic really wasn't what I'd signed up for, and the chemistry was as poor as my respective GCSE result.

By this point, I was already wondering about whether or not I might text Maya, you know, to accidentally join us or something. Relieve the awkwardness. But my brain was full of conflict. The guy was objectively so, *so*, cute. He was definitely funny, even though I hadn't seen any evidence in real life yet. Maybe he was just a bit nervous too?

'So,' I said, attempting to move on from the flatlined conversation. 'I hope Mush hasn't been giving all my secrets away?'

'No, don't worry.' He smiled, picking his half-drunk pint back up and glancing around the bar.

God this wasn't getting any easier.

'So, do you and Mush work closely together?' I asked, our conversation flowing as freely as a blocked toilet.

'We're on the same floor, but different departments,' he said. 'We both do digital stuff but he's based in marcomms and I'm in the IT team. So . . . yeah, I guess. A bit anyway.'

'OK.' I realised I'd been hoping for a conversation that felt less like an HR chat. 'Ooh I know. Shall we do a favourites ice breaker? Go on. Fave movie?' I wiggled around in my seat settling in for a bit of easy chat.

'Um . . . let me think . . . I love a bit of fantasy or sci-fi.' He was responding to me as though I was interviewing him for a job. As though we were both drinking water across a boardroom table rather than beer in a comedy club. I guess in some ways all dates are like interviews really – interviewing each other to see if you're good enough for date number two. I wasn't very good at job interviews – maybe that also explained my dodgy record when it came to first dates.

'Big *Star Wars* fan over here,' I said trying to feel a bit more enthused. 'Me and Mush did the entire back catalogue in one weekend a few years ago.'

'Ah. Yes. Popular if a bit over-done. I'll just go grab another beer,' he said. 'Want one?'

'I'm good,' I said, nodding towards my half-full pint. 'Thanks though.'

I watched him stand up and walk over to the bar tentatively, and I felt thoroughly disappointed. There was a big queue by now, so I knew he'd be a few minutes. I got my phone out and texted Mush.

```
OK, Mush, he's GORGEOUS. But he either
hates me or he's seriously awkward.
Oh. Bad chemistry?
Just no chemistry, really. Gotta go.
```

I typed as I noticed Tim paying for his pint.
Mush text back.

```
Aw. Sorry mate. X
```

I shoved my phone back in my bag as I saw TimTok walking back towards me with a half-smile.

'I think we need to go downstairs and grab our seats,' he said, looking as excited as if we were about to file into some kind of funeral wake.

Thank fuck for the comedy. 'Great.' I said. 'I'll just find the tickets.'

As I fannied around trying to find the right email, the rest of the bar seemed to be making their way downstairs ahead of us. 'Found them!' I proclaimed, and we followed suit at the tail end of the crowd, making our way down the stairs, the dark red walls plastered with hundreds of posters of acts that were soon to be gracing the stage.

When we got to the ground floor, we must've hovered at the door looking like two lost puppies, barely a word between us, when somebody in a Stand T-shirt came over to us. 'There's a couple of cabaret seats up front.' he pointed towards the stage.

We glanced over to the only vacant table in the room, a wave of fear enveloping us.

If there's one thing I know about places like this, it's that you never, under any circumstances (unless you've got a masochistic streak) sit in the front row of a comedy gig. Maybe this wasn't a good idea after all.

We took our seats and placed our drinks on the table, and our coats on the back of our seats. 'This could be a bit of a rollercoaster,' I whispered to him, still trying to crack the ice. But he looked like a frightened rabbit in the headlights.

I began to realise that maybe he wasn't arrogant after all. Maybe he was just shy? Maybe all that TikTok stuff was just a persona. You know like Beyoncé has one. Sasha Fierce or whatever. Maybe TimTok was his social media personality, and real Tim was a lot less comfortable without his phone as his comfort blanket.

We took our seats as our host, Gavin Webster, was announced. I was starting to wish I'd got another pint in now.

After a few minutes, we realised we'd been spared the *what's your name and where do you come from?*' routine. Perhaps we screamed awkwardness? As a couple of others got the joy of being singled out I hoped that perhaps the light was hiding our faces from the acts or something. Finally I felt my shoulders unclench. We were in the dark, with no pressure to talk to each other, just watch the stage. Simple.

We roared with laughter at jokes about posh people from Jesmond and pandas and I started to loosen up. Then Gavin introduced the next act; Lauren was just my age and was doing brilliant things on the comedy circuit. She went to the same uni me and Mush had but while we were studying marketing in the business school, and bar prices at the union, she was clearly honing her comedy genius across campus.

Next up was a young bloke called Darryl Thompson who appeared on stage in a bright yellow T-shirt, jeans and Converse.

Darryl made his way to the mic stand. 'Hello Newcastle!' he roared. 'Now then, who've we got in tonight.' He leaned forward, his hand above his eyes scanning the room. Then he stopped, flinched a little and pretended he couldn't see. 'Steady on. Anyone got a pair of sunglasses? There's a canny pair of *Love Island* style Turkey teeth blinding me from the front row.'

I realised he was looking at us. At Tim to be precise. I thought his teeth had looked extra white upstairs. In here, maybe they were positively glowing. Like UV at a crime scene.

I painted a big grin on my face to show willing, even if I knew my gnashers wouldn't have the same unearthly glow as Tim's, and looked over at him, who, all of a sudden, picked his phone up and started playing with it! He was doing that thing Pete does at work, trying to make it look like he hadn't heard, as if he didn't realise someone was talking to – and about – him. But I knew this was a gigantic red flag. Visibly getting your phone out at a comedy gig when it was in full flow was a big no-no. Jesus fucking Christ. We were gonna get roasted.

Then Darryl starts making these jokes about how the radiation clearly emanating from Tim's teeth won't mix well with the radiation emanating from his mobile phone and that if he doesn't put it down we might all be obliterated, and that Tim'll be the only one who they'll be able to identify because of his nuclear strength teeth.

By this point, grin still firmly painted on my face, I was sinking lower into my seat in the hope that I might disappear, but it was too late. Darryl the comedian stuck the mic in front of me, put on a fifties style radio voice and says, '*Tell me young lady, what was it that you first noticed about your partner.*' I laughed, probably way harder than I should have. I mean, it *was* funny.

The mic was still waving around in front of me, Darryl's eyes boring into me. I had to say something, no matter how lame . . .

'All girls love good dental hygiene,' I joked, looking across at Tim and giving him a wink, trying to show him that it was OK, it was harmless. His skin was now turning a kind of grey. It was like every last drop of blood had drained from him. Like this evil vampire comedian was draining him dry of every ounce of self-respect.

He wasn't smiling. Not even grimacing. There was no grit your teeth and bear it. I could feel his unease and the urge to go on the defensive. And then he said those words . . . the ones that will *always* get you into more trouble because, even if it's fair, it's too much of an open target for anyone to resist. Tim opened his mouth and, in his finest TikTok voice (which I hadn't yet heard this evening), but with an accompanying quiver, said, 'Come on, leave us alone, we're just out trying to have a nice time.'

Darryl raised his eyebrows. 'So you're not having a nice time? Hokay. Shall we try and make this a bit more fun ladies and gents?' Then he leaned back towards us. 'OK, OK, I'm just joshing with you. What're your names?'

I look over at Tim but he looked as though rigor mortis had set in. His lips were firmly shut and he was just kind of staring.

So I jumped in. 'Charlotte and TimTok'. And then I realised what I'd said, and of course TimTok doesn't know I've been calling him TimTok so he shoots me a glare.

Darryl raised his eyebrows. 'Sorry, what? TimTok?

Fuck.

'Oh haha. Um. Yeah. He's a TikTok star,' I said proudly. 'You might recognise him.'

By this point Tim's looking at me, clearly trying to tell me something with his eyes. I think he was torn between wanting to kill me and begging for mercy. But I didn't know what else to say. I was put on the spot. And I mean, he's got over a quarter of a million followers so, it's not like I'm exaggerating. In TikTok land he's way better known than this dude.

'TimTok from TikTok, eh?' Darryl said, shoving the mic in front of Tim now.

'Well, no. That's not my actual name,' he delivered it with a definite tone of resentment.

Then Darryl addressed the audience. 'Want to hear from a genuine TikTok star ladies and gents?'

The crowd started whooping and cheering, and I had a terrible feeling about what was coming next.

Then the tech guy shouted something from the side of the stage, and Darryl gave him a thumbs up . . . and all of a sudden I was back at the school disco as Gwen Stefani played through the speakers . . . it was that song . . . *tik tok tik tok tik tok* . . .

Tim remained seated. It was getting really, *really* awkward by now. Like some kind of stand-off between a TikTok star, who was seemingly nowhere near as outgoing in real life as his alter ego, and a stand-up comedian.

The stand-up comedian was clearly winning on all counts. And he wasn't giving up . . .

Gwen Stefani's voice was blasting through the speakers . . . *'What you wait what you wait what you waiting for . . . '*

I gave Tim a little nudge and he eventually stood up and made his way onto the stage.

I'd only had one pint. He'd only had two. And I was dying inside but all I could think was *at least I'm not where TimTok is standing right now.*

He stood there stock still, like some kind of human statue you see at the seaside. And Darryl the comedian's doing all these clockwork style dance moves around Tim. Then the music stops after its brief blast. And there's been this huge build up for our very own TikTok star.

But rather than ride with it . . . it dropped like a twenty ton rock.

Darryl stopped dancing, and jumped forward towards Tim with the mic, his endless enthusiasm desperately trying to energise this frozen social media star. 'So tell us then, what made you a TikTok sensation?'

Tim stood there. Silent. His mouth began to open in slow motion, as though he were about to say something, but then it just hung there. Gaping. Like he was in shock. Like a struggling bee that needed reviving with sugar water.

The audience laughed along but you could feel the unease growing in the room. Tonight's social anxiety had become one highly contagious beast. Even Darryl seemed unsure as to what to do next.

'Off you pop then. Ordeal over,' Darryl said, tapping Tim softly on his shoulder with an undeniable sense of pity. Both stand-up comic and TikTok star were equally freaked out now. TimTok had to live down a very public social downfall. And

Darryl now had the mammoth task of bringing the audience back to its former hysterical glory.

Darryl moved onto a kind of observational skit about modern day communication and short-form attention spans. I wasn't really taking it in, but the crowd seemed to perk back up at this point. He'd pulled them back. All was well on stage.

Tim, meanwhile, grabbed his coat.

6

I walked in the front door and could see the blue and grey colours of the TV lighting up the front room in random flashing patterns. Through the crack of the lounge door I could see that Mush's socks were sticking out off the end of the sofa, surrounded by baggy denim. There was something homely about coming back to my best mate's feet up on the sofa. And it was a sign I could properly relax. Well, usually, anyway . . .

'So?' he shouted.

'So what?' I hollered back, hanging my heavy vintage sheepskin coat up on the increasingly wobbly hooks in the hallway. It had started snowing on my short walk home from the Metro station. Those cute little flakes that land like feathers before melting into one great big damp patch on your coat. I tried to brush them off but it just seemed to make the coat more wet. And probably more heavy. Snow at Christmas always makes you feel like you're in some kind of festive romcom. Snow after Christmas? More of a disaster movie.

'*So* what kind of chocolate bar perfectly describes him?' Mush asked as I walked through to the lounge, his neck twisting backwards from the sofa, desperate to see if his matchmaking skills had paid off. 'Is he smooth and rich? Or sweet and melting?'

I rolled my eyes and chucked myself back on the armchair. 'Ah Mush, not now.'

'What? We always debrief. And besides, I set you up . . . '

'Yeah, thanks for that.'

'Come on, it can't have been all bad. You fancied him didn't you?'

'I *did*, yes.'

'Then spill. I've been bored shitless all night,' he said, motioning towards the TV. It looked like he'd been watching some kind of serial killer documentary or something. The kind where they zoom in on some serious-looking bloke with a gruff voice sitting at a bar drinking whiskey.

'Well, where to start?' I sighed.

'Like I asked. Start with confectionary. Was he top tier chocolate? Are we talking artisanal unique flavours or the past-its-sell-by-date stuff on the newsagent's counter?'

'Hmm . . . ' I paused to gather my thoughts for our traditional post-date debrief – which was often way more forensic than any of those old whiskey-soaked detectives off the telly. But I didn't want to relive what had just happened. I couldn't. I still felt bad for him. Should I have defended him?

'I don't really know,' I said, jumping back up to hijack the throw from behind him on the sofa. I retreated back to the armchair tucking my feet into it and completely cocooning myself in blanket. 'Maybe like . . . I don't know. Like the chocolate in one of those cheap advent calendars me mam always got us.'

'Eh?'

'Well they're always the same aren't they. There's this huge presence on the outside. Big brand, big personality. You know, like some Marvel character or SpongeBob SquarePants or something. But it's never Cadbury or Mars that's filling the spaces behind the little doors.'

'You don't half sound bitter.'

'*Precisely*. It often is. Bitter, I mean.' I screwed my face up. 'Ah Mush. There was just no spark.'

Mush sighed. 'Ah well. Hope he's not too disappointed.'

'He won't be,' I said hiding my chin in the blanket and twirling the tassels that hung off the end of it between my agitated fingers. 'I've agreed to see him again . . . ' I mumbled.

'But . . . '

'I know. I *know*! As soon as I said I would, I felt like a fake. I felt like a . . . '

'Teaser bar?'

'Eh?'

'Maltesers. Teasers bar . . . you know, cos you're a . . . '

'Fuck off Mush. I just felt bad for him, that's all.'

'But why? It's just a date? Since when have you felt obliged to go on a second date just because you felt sorry for . . . oh, hang on, it's *you* we're talking about . . . '

'Yeah, well.' I snapped. 'I always think first dates are like, well, they're not exactly natural. Nobody's being themselves. It's like at a job interview. Where you're all artificial and on your best behaviour and sometimes that comes across well and sometimes it doesn't. So you kind of have to forgive the awkwardness. Because it's not real.' As the words left my mouth I realised that it wasn't just Mush I was trying to convince.

Mush started sniggering. 'Bet you wish you didn't forgive the awkwardness the time that tosser . . . ' he couldn't finish the sentence for laughing. 'That tosser in that restaurant . . . ' He was hitting the side of the sofa and holding his stomach while gasping for breath.

I held my hand up in front of him. 'Let's not got there shall we?'

Mush was referring to the Thai restaurant incident. The date in question seemed nice when we first met. I was on a pub crawl with some uni mates down the Ouseburn Valley – the artsy part of town full of converted warehouses and upcycling shops, tiny art galleries and pubs that served a vast array of pale ales and proper pub chips against a backdrop of live music. We were all sitting in the sunshine on the grassy bank outside the Cluny pub, plastic pints in hand and sunnies on our heads, when I clocked him. He seemed a bit over-dressed for the Ouseburn, shirt and proper shoes and all that, but I think he was on some kind of stag do or something and he seemed dead canny. We talked non-stop, and, at the end of the night we kissed. He was a good kisser, I'll give him that. So I agreed to meet up with him, and we swapped numbers and arranged to go for dinner in the week. But then, on that first date, rather than having me shake with visceral pleasure in the bedroom, he had me cringing in the middle of a Thai restaurant. I still don't know what possessed him to take his shirt clean off during the second course. OK, sure, it was August, but they had air con. And it was the evening so it wasn't even that hot . . .

God, he even did that weird flex thing where he made his pecs move independently of each other. I think I was meant to be impressed. Instead, I had to stop myself from hiding underneath the table. It was mortifying.

So, how did I deal with it? Yep, you guessed it. I signed up for round two. Why? The kiss, maybe? Or was it just because I felt bad. Or perhaps I figured it couldn't get any worse . . .

I was wrong.

He brought one of his mates along on date number two, rang the doorbell and held the door as I stepped into the car that was waiting outside. But I was confused as to why my date wasn't getting in . . .

Turned out he was gearing up to car-surf on the bonnet wearing a Union Jack flag, while his mate drove us up and down our street blasting that fucking terrible 'Sexy and I Know It' song. Mortified didn't cover it this time.

There I was, sitting in the back seat of his mate's Subaru Impreza, all dressed up for a night on the town and a few nice cocktails, while they dossed about trying to get all the wrong sort of attention. I could see Corinne's curtains twitching next door but one.

On reflection, *maybe* that was *his* way of getting out of a second date without having to say 'no thanks'.

Fair play if that was his plan. He nailed it.

So Mush had a point. And that wasn't the only time I'd gone along for the ride just to avoid having to reject someone romantically. The number of second dates I'd gone on just to try to *make* myself like them was probably close to double figures. I'm not saying that I had loads of choice or anything. I mean, sometimes *I* would be rejected and I'd just have to lump it. You just have to get over it don't you?

So I'm not sure why I couldn't enforce the 'just getting over it' principle to my below-tepid dates. If *I* had to 'just get on with it', why shouldn't they?

But tonight, well, turning him down after everything that happened would have been like the final nail in his self-esteem coffin.

'So remind me, *why* are you doing it again?'

'Oh just leave it Mush.'

'No come on.' He sat up more alert on the sofa, actively waiting for my response. 'Why on earth would you go on a second date if it was so awful?'

'Precisely because it *was* so awful. I felt sorry for him.'

Mush picked his phone up, checking the time. 'Considering it was so awful you managed to make a decent night of it. Did you . . . '

'No, God no. No not at all. We didn't even kiss.'

'Right Charlotte Thomas. What aren't you telling me?'

I pulled the throw higher up over my face, desperately wishing tonight had been a bad dream. In fact, it did remind me of one of those anxiety dreams. You know, like when you're naked in a shopping centre or your teeth are all falling out . . .

'Well.' I started. 'We went to the Stand. And . . . '

'Nice one. Who was on?'

'Lauren Pattison, Gav Webster, some other guy . . . '

'Did Gav Webster do his pandas routine.'

'Aye.'

'Love it!'

'Yeah, well, if only we ended our date there things might have turned out OK. It was this other act, the third act, that killed the night. Or rather, crucified TimTok.'

'Deets please.'

I took Mush through it. Step by excruciating step.

'Eeh stop it now, I'm literally dying here.' Mush sounded like Mutley. He was absolutely beside himself. 'I can't wait to see him at work tomorrow.'

'No. Mush, please. He looked so broken.'

'I'm not surprised. A so-called TikTok star. Stood like wood on stage.' By this point Mush was breathing into a cushion, his entire body exploding with laughs. How come blokes can do that? How come they can take the piss out of each other like that? I'd never dream of doing that to Kel. Or Maya. Or anyone for that matter. But with blokes, it was like, any humiliation was fair game.

'Mush. Can you stop laughing now? It was bloody horrific. You can see how there was no way I could turn him down for a second date after that. In fact, I didn't even have to say yes to him. *I* asked *him*. I apologised for the disaster of the night, said he can choose what we do next time and that it was on me.'

'So not only are you going on a second date with him, you're actually paying for it too?'

I nodded.

'Fuck me.'

'D'you know what?' I said. 'If that had worked out it might have saved me a load of hassle.'

Mush chucked the cushion at me, hitting me in the face. I grabbed it and clutched it tight, as though hiding beneath soft furnishings might make the memories of the evening spontaneously vanish. 'I just want to forget about it now,' I wailed.

We sat chatting on the sofa till gone midnight, playing Spotify playlists on a loop and eating biscuits while I bemoaned the state of my life.

Why was I always trying to make it up to people? Precisely *what* was I trying to make up for?

Where had this responsibility to make everything OK come from? I was life's scapegoat for every eventuality. A mediator, an appeaser, a soother . . . I mean, for God's sake . . . my mam even got me to eat all my veg as a kid by telling me the broccoli would be lonely without the spuds and Yorkshire puddings for company.

I literally grew up feeling responsible for broccoli. I empathised with fruit and veg. Funny how they never encouraged empathising with whatever unidentified meat was on my plate . . .

But while tonight's offer of a second date brought the ridiculousness of my behaviour to the fore, dealing with that really wasn't the priority. I could deal with date number two. It might even be fun.

Dealing with Jamie, however, needed immediate and careful consideration. I needed to seriously overhaul my approach.

'Honestly', I said, as Mush was busy searching for the next song to play. 'I need to kick myself up the arse. I've got to stop being sorry for everything. Taking the blame for everything.'

Mush continued scrolling through the app, without so much as a glance up at me.

'Are you listening? Mush!'

'What? Oh um, just picking a song.'

'I was saying. I've got to stop . . . '

'Love a bit of Elton John . . . '

'What?'

He slumped back into the sofa smirking, as slow melancholic piano notes began to emanate from the wireless speaker . . .

'What is this music? Anyway, I was saying, I've got to stop being so bloody apologetic all the time. I've got to stop absorbing Jamie's guilt. Maybe he doesn't even have any. Maybe he behaves like he does, and touches whoever's shoulders he wants, and talks like however he wants . . . and he doesn't even feel . . . '

I stopped mid-sentence as Mush became all animated, gesturing towards me as the song in the background built up . . . 'Sorry seems to be the hardest word . . . '

'Haha! You're an arse Mushtaq, you know that?'

'You could teach Elton a thing or two about how to make the word sorry roll off his tongue a little easier.'

'Yeah, yeah, I get it all right. Very funny.'

'On the other hand,' he said, clearly rifling through his Spotify app for another appropriate pop hit. 'Madonna doesn't want to hear it at all.'

'Doesn't want to hear what?'

'Sorry,' Mush said, tapping on his iPhone screen and rudely interrupting Elton's ballad with some late Madonna synth-pop. 'Madonna doesn't want to hear it, Charlotte. She's written an entire song about it. It's even called "Sorry".'

'So?'

'So . . . Be. More. Madonna!'

7

I tapped on his office door. He did that thing he does, when he doesn't look up but waves you in. Then you go in, start speaking and he instantly holds his hand up to shut you up.

I stifled a sigh and sat down on the chair by his desk as he continued typing something. His office was typically Jamie. A red and black desktop punch ball sat between us menacingly alongside a white, mostly empty ceramic pencil pot donning the words 'OFFICE CRAP'. And he had one of those light up letter boards sitting on the top of the cupboard behind him. Its phrase of the day was 'big cheese'.

He changed it every day. The letter board. It was important to him. He never explicitly said this, or indeed explained why it was so important to him to remember to do it every single day. But we noticed he did it and yet we all refused to outwardly acknowledge it.

I made sure to not let him catch me looking at it.

He finished typing his email or whatever it was by clicking his mouse with a big, animated gesture. He turned to me.

'Charlotte. Thanks for coming in.'

'No worries,' I said.

'Hokay. So . . . the thing is . . . you've sent an email to Harriet.'

Oh. My. God. She's been laughing at me hasn't she? Those kisses . . .

'Yeah,' I said, feeling massively embarrassed. 'I, um, made a bit of a mistake at the end of it.'

'You made a bit of a mistake in all of it,' he said, setting his pen down with a loud tap.

I felt my body preparing for some kind of confrontation. He looked directly in my eyes and I forced myself to hold his gaze. But then he looked away, smiled with an almost-laugh and said, 'I think you could do with a bit of prep work. Fancy some help?'

I felt confused. 'Sure,' I said, somehow managing to make a one syllable word inflect like a question.

'Yes,' he said, still fannying around with the pad in front of him. 'I believe you could do with some mentoring, you're not quite leadership material yet but I'm confident I could mould you.'

I felt nauseous. I didn't want anyone to mould me, let alone Jamie. 'Thanks,' I said, wishing I hadn't because he was making me feel massively patronised and a little bit unclean.

'Great,' he said, tapping his pen loudly on the pad three times. 'How about drinks, tomorrow?'

'I . . . sorry?'

'I'll take you out for a bottle of vino.'

Who the fuck says vino. And why does he want to take me for one?

'Err . . . thanks . . . I . . .'

'Just don't tell anyone. We don't want them thinking I've got a favourite now do we?' He winked at me.

He. Just. Winked. At. Me.

I mean, OK, I'd *agreed* to a second date with Tim Tok when I didn't really want one but that was different. We both knew the purpose of the date was to suss each other out, you know, romantically. *This* was different. This was . . . frowned upon. This wasn't two people on an equal footing.

There was no way . . . I couldn't . . . ugh.

He looked at me expectantly.

'I, I'm sorry. I can't. I'm . . . ' I thought hard and fast. 'I promised Mush a movie marathon.' I spluttered. To be fair, I also had my smear test to look forward to tomorrow, and one uncomfortable situation is more than enough for one day. But I certainly wasn't going to tell Jamie about that.

'Oh,' he said, nodding slowly and biting his bottom lip. 'I thought the job opportunity might take priority?'

'Oh God yes. And I'm so grateful for your help, really. It's just. He's just been dumped and . . . '

It was a lie of course. But how would Jamie know.

'OK, let's take a rain check. Maybe Thursday?'

I felt exhausted batting him off. 'I better just play it by ear, see how Mush is.'

Jamie's face sort of contorted, 'Right then.'

'He's pretty devastated.' I'd already told the lie, I might as well embellish it . . .

'OK,' he said impatiently, 'I'll check in with you Thursday morning. I'll make sure Harriet doesn't diarise anything with you before then.'

'Thanks,' I said, walking out the door wondering what on earth I was thankful for.

I sent Maya a Slack.

Lunch?

She half stood at her desk, twisting her body round to see me.

'You OK?' she mouthed silently. She'd obviously seen me emerging from Jamie's office. I shook my head. She grabbed her coat which I took to mean yes to lunch.

We wandered across the Millennium Bridge in haste towards a cafe by the river. We did the usual thing of not discussing the core topic of conversation until we had sat and ordered. It's the unwritten rule isn't it?

When we got seated Maya dived straight in with a complicated order of vegan cheese this and oat milk that and a request of dressing on the side.

I ordered cheese on toast and a regular cappuccino.

'Right then,' she said. 'What's happening girl?'

'He's on about some job I should apply for, but he's not given me any details of the job, just told me to email Harriet, with specific instructions as to what I should say. Which all felt a bit weird, if I'm honest. So I emailed her generally, like, just to show interest in case there *is* something happening, and he's caught wind of the fact that I wasn't approaching her *exactly* to his brief and so he's asked me out for a vino and I don't—'

'Woah . . . take a breath.' She stopped me in my blustered tracks. 'And anyway. A vino? Who goes out for a vino?'

'Jamie does! Oh my God, what if this was all a ploy. What if there's no job. What if he just wanted . . . ?'

'Probably.'

'Thanks for the reassurance,' I said, just as a mega protein oat milk latte arrived for Maya, and a plain little cappuccino was plonked next to me. I eyed her drink enviously while we both smiled impatiently at the poor waiter who was serving us, desperate to get back into the conversation.

'He's a sleaze, Char.'

The poor waiter turned around. Maya did nothing to reassure him we weren't talking about him.

'Yeah, I know. But if there's a promotion going, I could really do with the money and, you know, if it's content . . . I mean, not that I'd, you know . . . '

'Of course. Goes without saying. But you shouldn't have to do anything that makes you feel uncomfortable in order to be in with a chance of getting your promotion.'

'I know, but we've got appraisals coming up too and . . . I'll get out of it. I guess I'm just wondering *how* to get out of it without damaging his ego or whatever.'

'I wouldn't worry. That ego's so well-practised you'd need to drop a flamin' anvil on it from the top of the Tyne Bridge to even chip it. But yeah, there's definitely something happening restructure wise. The rumour mill's rife with content.'

'See I *so* want to work in that area. I want to *create* stuff, not just place it.'

'Yeah, and you've emailed Harriet so . . . '

'But I need Jamie's reference.'

'Bullshit, Char. Jamie's got no sway over Harriet. She can't stand him.'

'You think?'

'I *know*. I overheard her telling Chrissie that Jamie was so soulless his ultimate ambition was to own one of those Twitter accounts with tens of thousands of followers that follows nobody else . . . '

'Why would. . . ?'

'Cos he only likes the sound of his own voice.'

The food arrived. Maya immediately picked up a knife and fork to tuck into her delicious looking lunch. Meanwhile . . .

We both stared down at the toast on my plate that was piled high . . . with grated cheese.

'Well,' she said, finishing her mouthful. 'It's certainly cheese on toast. But I doubt it'd make Gordon Ramsey proud.'

'Maybe it's the new way of doing it. You know, like when they started putting drinks in jam jars. Someone on Twitter got their dinner in a fish bowl recently . . . '

'I doubt it. Everyone knows melted cheese can't be beaten. This is just bad food.'

I picked up my knife and fork and Maya immediately dropped hers and put her hand up in front of me. 'Woah . . . what're you doing?'

'Eating it.'

'But it's not what you ordered.'

'I guess it is. Literally.'

She stuck her hand up, ''Scuse me!' she yelled.

'Honestly, Maya, it's no bother. I'm not in the mood for
. . .'

'Course it flamin' is. Everyone knows the point of cheese
on toast is the dangerous delight of mouth-burning cheese.'

The waiter came over. Maya gestured towards me to speak.

'Yeah. I ordered cheese on toast.' He looked at me confused.
I pressed on. 'And this, well, it's not melted.'

'That's how we do it here,' he said, seemingly disinterested.
My hackles flared.

'Well, OK, but it's not what most people expect to see
when they order cheese on toast.'

He sighed. 'Want me to get the chef to re-make it?'

'Yes she does!' Maya interjected. He stared at Maya then
back at me.

'Yeah, please. If that's all right that'd be great. Sorry.'

Maya shook her head and sighed, then went back to tucking
into her meal. As the waiter walked off she made a point of
muttering the word 'sleaze' again so this time he really did
think we were talking about him.

Perhaps that's why I got shit cheese on toast.

Maya lifted her eyebrows at me accusingly, while continuing
to tuck into her colourful lunch bowl.

'What now?' I thundered.

'Charlotte, you've got to get a grip, girl. Why do you
apologise for everything?'

'I don't. I didn't.'

'You did. You were all like,' she put on a whiny voice. '*Yeah,
please if that's all right, sorry.*'

'It's just a turn of phrase. It's just polite.'

'It's fucking not. I told you before, sets you up for disadvantage. The other person will find it easier to say no to you if you're so apologetic about everything.'

'Where'd you get your psychology degree from?!'

'Scoff all you like. It's not right. You've got to assert yourself. You don't think Harriet got to where she is today by being apologetic?'

She was right. Harriet was a force of nature. She always seemed 100 per cent convinced in everything she was telling us. She could make me redundant and I'd somehow be the one apologising.

Harriet was in her early forties maybe – possibly around the same age as Jamie. But she always made him look like a little kid in comparison. Don't get me wrong, she wasn't dull. Not at all. She was a good laugh and her volume in the office didn't go unnoticed . . . but she towed the professional line far more strictly than Jamie.

He was like some kind of excitable toddler in an oversized suit with a massive ego.

That afternoon dragged at work. Every time Harriet left her office to make a cuppa I looked up smiling, hopefully, pleadingly. Hopeful that she hadn't been offended by my sloppy email kiss. And no doubt sycophantic in equal measure.

But, other than smiling back with a slightly puzzled look on her face, nothing was said.

It was also date night number two with TimTok and I was wishing I'd called it off. But it was a bit late in the day now. I'd arranged to meet him straight from work again, literally two days after our last date. I felt so bad. In some ways I was surprised he said yes.

Anyway, there was always a chance it could be good. Great, even. If I just gave him a chance . . .

I was relieved he hadn't picked our regular office haunt. I didn't want my potentially awkward date to be gatecrashed by the floor eight mob. Or maybe I did?

No, that could never be a good thing. Even if I ended up on a blind date with Jacob Rees-Mogg I don't think I'd want to be rescued by that lot. And I'd put the poor lad through enough already.

As I walked over the bridge towards the small bar he'd chosen I felt so lucky to live here. Even in the bleakest of January days, the Quayside sparkled with a laid back energy. The lights on the Millennium Bridge were morphing between violets and oranges and blues, brightening the dark smoky sky. There were little coffee stalls and cyclists making the riverside feel full of life even on a winter's night.

I was proud to be a Geordie. Growing up in my part of the city, to the east just bordering North Tyneside. It was quiet, and kind of unremarkable in many ways, but it was my home and I loved it. You rarely meet a Geordie who isn't proud of their hometown.

As I approached the bar I felt relieved that it didn't appear to be overly empty. Lack of buzz would've been excruciating on a difficult second date that I wasn't sure I should even be on. I could see fairy lights twinkling in the windows and steam clinging to the glass as people warmed up inside away from the January frost.

I ordered a drink at the bar and, realising that I'd beaten my date to it this time, I grabbed a seat away from the main area, shaking my coat onto the back of the chair and dismantling my hat and scarf combo. I sat down and cleared some of the steam from the window with the cuff of my jumper.

As I sat losing myself in civic pride, I was jolted back to the reality of my date as TimTok stood staring through my clear little gap of window waving at me like some kind of pixie. He had a beanie hat on his head and his straggly waves hung close to his face below it.

Seeing I had a drink already, he ordered himself a pint at the bar before wandering over to my table, smiling. He gave me an awkward kiss on the cheek and I was sad to feel absolutely nothing. Not a flutter, nor a pang of excitement. Nothing.

I just couldn't understand it. On paper he was everything. In looks he was gorgeous. Was I just not in the right frame of mind for a man right now? And dying on stage, I mean, God, even actors do that sometimes, don't they?

He held his pint up and we clinked glasses. 'I'm sorry about the awkward comedy thing,' I said. 'They can be pretty ruthless, can't they?'

'That's OK,' he said. 'It's a bit different being onstage than it is sitting in your kitchen with only your iPhone for company.'

'I imagine!' I said. 'To be honest, I'd struggle with either.'

We both laughed. Little, forced, nervous giggles, and we tried to chat about life and hobbies and careers and uni . . . but as the minutes ticked on slowly, I realised that, as lovely as he turned out to be, there was never going to be that spark between us. Comedian or no comedian. And even the fairy lights and overbearing laughter from the other tables couldn't cut through the silences.

By 8.15 p.m. I felt it was only right to put our excruciating date out of its misery and make my excuses.

'Right. So. I better . . . '

'Of course . . . '

'It's been lovely,' I said, picking up my coat from my seat.

He stood up to say goodbye and his eyes fixated on mine . . . for a moment too long.

Ah no. No, no, no. Surely there were no signs encouraging this. But nothing deterred him. He was going in for the kill . . . and I was less than prepared for it.

We locked eyes and he smiled that smile. That smile that I first saw beaming from this handsome TikTok star. It wasn't glaringly white. It was just . . . sexy. And, for a moment, a brief second, I wondered . . . could this be . . . good? I was completely and utterly conflicted in that second.

Then he leaned towards me, put his hand on my arm, firmly, confidently. I *really* wasn't expecting that. And, as his lips brushed against mine, there was a pang of something . . . a little jolt. A flurry . . .

. . . of saliva.

No, not a flurry, a deluge.

Was he . . . trying to eat me?

All I could think about as he gobbed away at my increasingly wet face, and as he squeezed my arm tighter with enthusiasm, was the cheese on toast. The abomination of that cheese on toast I was presented with earlier.

When you want something gloriously gooey you get bone dry grated cheese on stale bread. When you just want to disappear you get . . . gunged with saliva.

I pulled away. 'I'm so sorry,' I said, kicking myself as the words fell out of my mouth.

He looked at me with puppy dog eyes, lines spreading across his forehead. And my heart ached. He was a really nice guy, in the end, and I'd just made him feel awkward. Twice. But it wasn't my job to make all nice guys feel good about themselves was it? I had to tell him it wasn't working. To tell him I just wasn't that into him. But I couldn't.

The people on the next table were all eyes on this seemingly awkward first date. But it wasn't. It was never going to be a hit. It was the difficult second album. It was . . . the 'too polite to say no' date.

The only way I could make this more bearable – for both of us – was to take the blame. I tried, I really tried, to bite my tongue, but I heard myself carrying on regardless . . .

'It's not you it's me.'

8

11th March 2005

Today has been the worst day of my entire life. Ever.

It's like God was waiting for the perfect day to get back at me for chucking Ben's stupid Good Charlotte CD out his stupid bedroom window. I swear he only says he likes that band cos of their stupid name. I hate that band. I hate Ben*

*Me and Kel were going to totally **own** the dance floor. We know our Gwen Stefani 'Hollaback Girl' routine off. By. ❤. It's **PERFECT**. We've practiced for weeks now and it looked so cool when I did it in front of the mirror in my low jeans with the top folded down to make them even lower like what Gwen does.*

***He** was definitely going. I knew cos Kel had asked Jason at lunchtime (they're actually going out proper now – she's kissed him with her tongue **and** he asked if he could finger her but she said no because she didn't think he would even know how to do it anyway. **And** it sounds gross actually so me and Kel said neither of us would ever do **that** until we were like sixteen or something. Cos you have to then).*

*Anyway, Kel asked Jason who he was going with and he said he was going with Ryan so he was definitely going to be there. I decided tonight was going to be **the night**. I had it all planned. Me and Kel would do our **perfect** routine and I would glance over to him during the part where Gwen sings the bit about **ooh ooh this my shit** over and over and that would be it. I would be snogging the face off Year Nine's fittest lad EVER. And Caroline Taylor would be sooooo jealous and I'm allowed to be glad about that cos she snogged Jason **after** Kel was already going out with him which is like breaking a golden rule. The cow.*

*But then **it** happened. In Geography class. It was some lesson about tectonic plates or something.*

Me and Kel were sitting at the back in our usual spot, learning about fault lines and stuff and something felt weird down below. Like a fault line was erupting in my pants.

*My top lip was getting all sticky I could tell and my heart was all jittery because **how on earth** was I going to get up and go to the loo in front of class when I might have period blood on the back of my skirt. I know it's black (my skirt) but my white shirt was hanging over it and everyone knew that when Abigail Brammar started hers in class everyone saw and it's like a school legend or something. A bad one. People call her **Carrie**. I still don't know why, but I pretend I do.*

I couldn't tell if I was imagining it or not but I knew if I sat there for too long it might all soak through and that would be sooooo embarrassing. There was hot lava gushing on the telly screen and hot lava gushing out my knickers. Oh my God it was the worst feeling EVER. So I had to make a decision. I stuck my hand up.

Even if I changed my mind, at that point I knew I couldn't turn back.

'Yes, Charlotte?'

'I need the loo.'

'Quickly, then.'

I stood up out of my chair and tried to check the back of my skirt with my hand without anyone seeing what I was doing and then I tried to check that there was no red puddle on my seat but it felt like they were all staring at me. I must have raced out of that classroom at like fifty miles an hour or something.

Sometimes sitting at the back isn't good after all.

As soon as I closed the classroom door behind me I ran to the loos and luckily it was empty so I went into a cubicle and pulled down my pants and it had happened. **I'd started**. There was blood. Like dark brown blood. Is that even normal? Is it even blood?

I remember in junior school they sent the boys out to do some extra science lessons or something and made the girls watch programmes about periods – to prepare us they said – but they NEVER show you what it actually **looks** like. Was it even blood? What if it was something else? It was nearly black.

I couldn't stop looking at it. That had come out of my actual fairy.

I didn't have any of those panty liners Mam always told me to carry because there was **no way** I was letting the boys in class see them. Ben found them in my room once and spent the next hour singing some stupid song about period blood. Which was pure shan cos his mate Andy was round and he looks like Cillian Murphy in 28 Days Later so I was proper livid.

But even if I did have my panty liners, I didn't have my bag with me in the loos because if there's one thing that tells the entire class that you're having your period it's a girl walking out to go to the loo with her bag on her shoulder. There's those Lil-Lets tampons that are meant to fit in your hand so nobody can see them but then Mam said not to start on those cos you have to push them up inside of you and you need to practice first.

Anyway, I had to stuff loads of that awful school loo roll in my knickers and pray it would hold the knicker lava at bay for the rest of the day. We only had RE and maths to get through and then that was the day done. But why did I have to start on the last day of term when we had the disco? What if . . . well, there was no way Ryan was going to put his hand down there anyway cos me and Kel had made that pact. But still.

*Anyway, Mam's been really cool about it actually. She didn't make a fuss or anything and told me how to stick the sanitary towel inside my knickers. But when I was asking her about the colour of the blood it turned out Ben was at the door listening in cos he started snorting and laughing. Mam told him off but he yelled something about girls being gross and that we were like something out of a horror movie. Mam told him not to listen in then but then she quietly told me that I maybe shouldn't talk about the **actual blood** in front of boys because they couldn't handle it. I said I thought that was silly cos boys are always on about how they're harder than girls so why can't they deal with a bit of blood. Mam laughed at that, she said that I was right, perhaps boys aren't as hard as they make out. She can be all right* sometimes. But I still wondered, if half of the people in the entire world had to have periods, why did the other half like to pretend it never happened?

I still went to the disco tonight. But I had to tell Kel that I couldn't do the routine. Cos there was no way I was dancing in the middle of the room and then risking an outpouring or whatever. So I kind of danced at the back like some kind of ladgeful idiot. Imagine if Ryan saw blood on my bum.

I kept going to the loo every ten minutes to check on the leakage at the leisure centre. It wasn't leaking, but it didn't stop me panicking. Like when I got my ears pierced and I kept checking the studs were still there because I couldn't feel them and I was convinced they might just fall out of my ears. Mam said the towel would keep everything in check till I got home but I wasn't sure. So we didn't do the dance and I made Kel promise not to ask for 'Hollaback Girl' but then they played it anyway and you won't believe what happened?

CAROLINE TAYLOR.

I was LIVID. She got up ON HER OWN and did a full routine to 'Hollaback Girl' (which I swear she must've copied from us cos some of the moves were EXACTLY the same). And guess who was watching? Ryan. Then they disappeared OUTSIDE and that can mean only ONE THING.

I went home and then I cried and now here I am writing this. All tears and snot and BLOOD all day. I feel like nobody will ever fancy me now. Maybe it's just **my** period that's all dark and brown? Maybe other girls have prettier pink blood? I feel disgusting. I hate Caroline Taylor.**

I hate my life.

I don't really **hate Ben but he really really really really really really really really **really** annoys me.*

**I proper legit hate Caroline Taylor.

9

'Can you just . . . push your bum downwards, into the bed
. . . that's it. There we go. Now then . . . where are you hiding?'

I squirmed awkwardly, trying to follow her direction. 'I
think they once said it was tilted.' I offered.

'Most of them are.'

'Really?'

'Oh yes. It's rare I go in there to find one wearing a party
hat and waving at me.'

'Oh.' I let out a not-quite-giggle.

'Yours just . . . doesn't seem to want to play today though
. . .' she said, audibly breathing out through her nose as she
continued prodding and poking.

Meanwhile, I lay there helplessly, legs akimbo, staring at
the rusty-orange mark on the tiles above my head, wondering
if somebody had in fact launched a wet tea bag at the ceiling
at some point.

And if so, why?

'It's a tricky bugger . . .'

'Sorry,' I said, mindlessly as I was pulled away from my
ceiling tea bag mystery.

'Sorry?!' The nurse suddenly snapped her head away from my well-lit vaginal vantage point and stared straight at me.

'Oh. Hehe. I said, I'm sorry,' I smiled.

She didn't . . . smile that is.

'I know you did. What are you sorry for?'

'My um, my cervix . . . '

'Why? Did you design it?' she said, her face now back to its original position, eager to coax the little pink donut from its hiding place.

'I . . . '

'It's a cervix, Charlotte. Not a naughty child.'

Her tone made my cheeks hot and angry. I hadn't felt more like a naughty child since getting caught by the headteacher doing that disastrous Britney routine on the school desk.

I could feel the cool plastic speculum pushing down, up, across, up again, waggling around in desperation. She wasn't particularly gentle, but then again it didn't exactly hurt either. I was impressed by her strong, skilled performance.

My eyes moved back to the random tea stain on the ceiling, meanwhile my mind began obsessing about the appearance of my nether-regions. You don't need to vajazzle for a smear test, it's not like your invite from the National Health Service ends with the words 'Black tie and evening dress' – but you want to be smart at least. You want to show that you play an active role in the health of your . . . fairy. You're a modern woman, you know your own body inside and out, and you're certainly no stranger to the old portable mirror.

Unfortunately, I couldn't for the life of me remember when I carried out my last trim and edge.

I wasn't sure which was worse, obsessing over the uncomfortable handy work that was going on deep inside my lady bits, or obsessing over my lackadaisical gardening skills.

There's nothing worse than rogue spiders legs.

I hate spiders.

Oh God, I bet it's like a scene from *Arachnophobia* down there . . .

'Aha! There it is . . . ' she said, interrupting my train of self-conscious thoughts and clearly delighted with her work. The plastic contraption from hell finally stopping still for a moment. 'And there we go. All done.' She removed the swab and released the speculum, allowing it to flop back out from its unwanted intrusion.

'Oh. OK, thanks.'

'You can get dressed now Charlotte,' she ordered.

Before I could let out my customary sigh of relief she'd turned on her heels, the white curtain whipping unapologetically behind her as she left my private little clinic of cringe.

I just apologised for my cervix.

'I'm guessing you know the drill?' she hollered back to me, interrupting my stream-of-consciousness embarrassment.

'Oh, um, yeah, I'll only hear if there's a problem, right?' I said, balancing precariously on one leg as I forced my spotty sock into my Converse All Star high tops. It's a simple rule that I always forget – never wear lace ups for smear tests, clothes-shopping and promising first dates.

'All looked nice and healthy in there anyway. Nice and pink,' she added, without any change of tone.

'That's good,' I said. I could hear the controlled snap of her latex gloves coming off and the clatter of the bin lid as she disposed of the now toxic items.

That's the thing with anything gynaecological. Because of all the latex and the throwaway paper towel bed sheets and the toxic waste disposal, you automatically feel as though you're leaking bad bacteria everywhere. Like you're some kind of STI storage facility – even though you've not had sex in, fuck, what is it now, six months or something? Feels like it anyway.

Better sort that trim and edge before Friday night . . . I'm sure you give off stronger fuck-me vibes when your bits are preened and polished.

'That's good,' I said of the pink report, cautiously pulling back the curtain to find the nurse sitting at her little corner desk, typing whatever it is they type into the system following a routine procedure. For such a slight woman she had some serious presence!

I had to wonder if my procedures were ever considered routine, though, given how much time they have to spend rummaging around in there. I've often wondered if they automatically book me a double appointment when they see my name crop up on the patient register.

It's that one with the difficult cervix again. Better book a double, and warn Nurse to have a KitKat and a cup of tea before starting . . . she's got a long shift ahead of her . . .

'So, no other issues? Bleeding after sex? Bleeding between periods?'

'No. Just the awkward cervix,' I joked, sitting down on the grey cushioned chair.

'Yes, about that . . . ' She said, looking me straight in the eye. 'Never apologise for being a woman.'

There was a brief silence. Her words took me by surprise. 'Oh. Yes, right,' I mumbled. What was I meant to say? 'Sorry,' I added, immediately regretful.

She sighed and turned back to the computer screen.

'Baby One More Time' started playing in my head as those awful school memories of my Britney impersonation came flooding back.

Charlotte Thomas! What on earth do you think you're doing. Turn that racket off, tuck that shirt in, and see me in my office in thirty seconds!

Climbing down off that wobbly desk, hair in plaits, school shirt tied high to show off my new belly button ring (which I knew would be brought up as part of my telling off), I was mortified.

I had been found out.

Just like I had right here in the nurse's room.

And this time it was much worse than being shown up as a poor imitation of Britney Spears.

This time, I was a poor imitation of a feminist.

I left the doctor's surgery with the nurse's words spinning around in my head, and not in a funky Kylie-in-gold-hot-pants-disco-diva kind of way. I felt like an idiot. An absolute fucking idiot.

'Stupid old bint,' I muttered under my breath. 'What does she know anyway?' But then, in my heart of hearts, I realised that I was only angry because I knew she was right. Maya had been saying the same to me for weeks. And then, right then, in that moment, it hit me.

I did, literally, apologise for everything.

Everything!

And what good did it do me?

Last Monday I apologised for being late back to the office . . . after being ordered to take a detour and pick up a flat white for Jamie. And yet he still spent the rest of the day in a huff with me.

And I apologised for daring to suggest that we might not want to get up close and personal in a muddy puddle for a staff away day . . . So Jamie went and booked it anyway, because apparently, signing off with 'no worries if not' can be taken literally. Who knew? Then there was espresso martini girl. Plus cheese-gate. And I said sorry to TimTok for not wanting to share saliva.

And now, now I just apologised for my cervix.

I suddenly felt sorry for my little pink donut thing. All it had done was ask to be left in peace. I mean, nobody wants to be woken up by a brusque nurse waggling a pointy thing at you under a harsh spotlight.

I got out my phone and texted Mush as I walked to the Metro station.

```
I just apologised for my cervix.
What did it do?
It went into hiding.
I've no idea what you're talking about Char,
but I'm really not keen on discussing your
fanny with you.
```

```
   The nurse told me I should *never* apol-
ogise for being a woman.
```

I didn't let him reply before sending another blurting out of all the anger I was feeling . . .

```
   And TimTok . . . why couldn't I say it?
Why couldn't I say I'm just not that into
you . . .
   Stop apologising then. Simples.
   Is it though?
```

I put my phone back in my bag with a sigh and headed to the platform. The Metro station was heaving. Why did I have to get an appointment in the middle of bloody bastard rush hour?

The screen was showing one minute for the next train to town so I wandered as far along the platform as I could, hoping I might be able to grab a seat in a quiet carriage.

As the rumble of the train got louder and the wall of hot air hit my face I walked towards the edge of the platform. The train screeched to a stop and I stepped into the carriage, managing to grab a seat all to myself.

Aaand relax.

But I couldn't . . .

Never apologise for being a woman.

It wouldn't stop whirring and whirring on repeat . . .

Never apologise for being a woman.

I was a poor example of a modern woman. A terrible feminist. A disappointment to all little girls who were preparing to take on the world as engineers or mathematicians or footballers. They were going to follow their rightful destiny as warrior women . . .

Meanwhile, I was apologising for my fairy. No, for my vagina. My vulva. For my actual female anatomy.

God fucking designed it! He's meant to be a fucking he!

The train pulled to a stop at the next station and, to my utter disappointment, a big crowd piled on.

I took out my phone, ready to distract myself with Wordle, when I felt a looming presence next to me.

I refused to look up, clearly not being in the mood for morning chit chat, but I noticed him waggling his gigantic man bag to fit it on the floor in between his legs, which in turn pushed his right leg into mine.

I immediately felt my muscles tense up . . .

You know, I get that it's not exactly inappropriate touching, not in this context, but, on another level, it *is* inappropriate touching because it's my. Personal. Fucking. Space!

God that was all I needed today. The fucking king of manspreading.

Livid!

I tried to take a moment, to pause, it's only somebody's knee after all. Deep breaths Charlotte.

But as the train jolted forward and his thigh knocked hard into mine, I felt adrenaline coursing through me like a gazillion high speed racecars on spaghetti junction.

''Scuse me, but would you mind moving your knee a little.'
I said, still staring at my screen, jaw clenched, as if attempting
to hold in every shade of emotion.

He didn't say anything. And he didn't move, either. I felt
the bile rising up in me. Fifty fucking shades of putrid threatening to expel from my very core.

'Sorry, but could you just move a bit.' I repeated, still
determined not to look at him.

Nothing.

FFS. Just moments ago I apologised for my skewed
womb-junction and now, now I've just said sorry to a
manspreader for daring to ask him to stop his ignorant
man-spreading into my rightful personal space on the Metro.

I was a one-woman sorry machine.

Emmeline Pankhurst, Oprah Winfrey, Meghan Markle . . .
Madonna! It's like I'm undoing all their good work, piece by
piece, day by day. What if there are others, like me, who
apologise simply for being a woman. For taking up teeny tiny
amounts of space?

And who apologises for having a fanny?!

I could feel a rush of anger getting stronger. My foresisters
were calling me. It was time to rise up. It was time to take
my rightful place. It was time to unapologetically be . . .

Before I knew it I was out of my seat. Standing up on the
crowded train, facing my nemesis – who was acting deter-
minedly oblivious – looking down, staring at his phone,
smiling, even.

Prick!

My heart was racing, my mouth opened and, before I knew it . . . a screeching, scratching, hollering sound came hurtling from the depths of my stomach, releasing twenty-nine years of non-stop apologising.

'WILL YOU MOVE YOUR FUCKING LEGS OUT OF MY PERSONAL SPACE?!'

He looked up at me.

His eyes locking into mine.

Blimey . . . oh God. He was fit. With a capital F . . .

No, Charlotte! It doesn't matter. He ignored your polite request. Twice! His looks do not excuse him. Stay focused.

He smiled up at me, a warm, gentle smile. My stomach bile morphed into butterflies . . .

And then, he removed his AirPods.

Fuck.

'Sorry? Is it your stop?'

He had no idea. He hadn't heard me.

He hadn't heard my polite requests.

Maybe he hadn't heard my banshee scream either?

Maybe this could be an opportunity. I could save this moment . . . think . . .

'Um. I . . . '

'Are you OK?' he asked.

I detected an edge. A tone in his voice. Was he patronising me? Was I letting his blue eyes distract me from standing up for myself?

Was I going to apologise for being a woman? For deserving to have my own space after enduring a fucking smear test. It's not as if *he* has to do that. Or give birth, or, or . . .

'Well?' he asked.

'Did you realise', I said firmly, eager to push on despite his now obvious resemblance to Paul Mescal, 'that you've been taking up all my leg space, that you've been . . . manspreading your legs wider than mine were at my fucking smear test just now. *And* I've got a tilted cervix,' I added, just as the train slowed down enough for my last words to boom out louder than the station announcements.

He laughed.

He fucking laughed.

Jesus, Charlotte, what are you doing? It doesn't even make sense. Stop talking. Stop. Right. Now.

'I'm sorry to hear that,' he said, desperately trying to stifle laughter. He moved his legs and gestured to the space next to him. Our eyes locked momentarily as I stood there swaying with the rhythm of the train, blood draining from my face in horror. What do you say next when you've just yelled 'CERVIX' at a stranger's face?

His smile diminished as I did everything I possibly could to avoid looking at him. 'Well,' he said. 'It was nice chatting to you.' The train moved off again. He put an AirPod back in his ear and looked back down at his phone.

He was the epitome of calm. Meanwhile I, unbeknownst to him but very obviously known to the rest of the train, had just screamed like a particularly poor impersonation of Courtney Love, before announcing to half of Newcastle, and Paul Mescal incarnate, that I'd just had my legs akimbo for fanny prodding.

I realised at that point that the entire carriage was staring at me.

But no. Not just staring at me . . .

I spied a camera phone being held in a wobbly fashion at the end of a skinny arm. The wobble was caused by the laughter. The laughter was emanating from the arm holding the phone . . . and the small group of teenagers surrounding said phone.

Hundreds of pairs of bemused eyes. And an iPhone. No doubt on record.

Fuck.

I'm going to become a meme. A fanny meme. A fucking . . . minge meme.

Oh God what have I done?

The train started to slow once more. I was still three stops from mine. I couldn't bear it.

I sat down then immediately stood back up again. And I legged it.

As I made my way off the platform and up the escalator I was hit with daylight. An open air breeze that made me realise I was about a mile from the office. Shit.

I was going to be late again.

But I'd started something now.

And there was no way I was turning back. Not after that. I was filmed on the Metro talking about my fanny. I had to own it.

There was no way I was apologising for being late.

In fact, I decided there and then, I was breaking up with 'sorry'.

10

I walked into the office feeling like something monumental had shifted. I'd destroyed the kryptonite that threatened to ruin me. I was Supergirl. No, I was an Avenger. I was Jessica Jones. I was smart and unapologetic. And I was not afraid to show it.

I popped my coat on the multi-coloured coat stand, took my seat and turned my laptop on. It was 9.13 a.m. I was almost forty-five minutes late. But after what I'd been through, the internal prodding for the sake of female health and therefore the future of actual humanity, I decided I didn't care. Plus, I was investing in my future contribution to the office – by taking care of my wellbeing . . .

Jamie came wandering over and hovered at the end of our bank of desks. He was wearing a garish new wine-red suit with tight trousers. I think he wanted us to acknowledge it or something.

'Morning J-Team,' he said, glaring at me while adjusting his matching tie. Nobody wore ties in the office. I think he thought it was like a 'boss' uniform or something. Funnily enough, the actual boss, Harriet, was usually wearing Converse and jeans.

I always thought their choice of dress said a lot about their inner confidence in the roles they inhabited. To be honest, Jamie should have a touch of imposter syndrome about him given how he was practically parachuted in by a family friend. They were like the media-buying monarchy. Although not quite at palaces and gold carriages level.

As Jamie stared at me expectedly, I felt an undeniably strong compulsion to spill the 's' word from my mouth. I gritted my teeth. I needed to re-programme my brain if I wanted to make it through the day without saying sorry – never mind an eternity.

He stood stock still, waiting . . . but it didn't come. I couldn't let it. Not less than forty-five minutes after deciding that I was never to utter that word ever again.

'Morning!' I said, as cheerily as I could, feeling strangely liberated – even though I was probably about to get a bollocking.

He looked up at the stupid funky wall clock dramatically.

God, this was going to be harder than I thought. Aside from apologising being a thing that we all do, especially as so-called 'direct reports' to the boss, I'd set a personal precedent. I was the queen of apology. It was as natural a behaviour to me as baking is to Mary Berry.

I thought hard. What was the most unapologetic thing I could say . . .

Then it dawned on me.

'Just been for my cervical smear,' I said, brightly.

Jamie's face turned redder than period blood. 'Right,' he said, before skulking back off to his office.

Job done!

I spun my chair back round feeling pleased with myself and focused on my desk, but I could feel eyes on me. I looked up and spotted Maya, beaming like a proud mother bear. Meanwhile, Pete shifted uncomfortably in his seat, refusing to look me in the eye before offering to make everyone a cuppa.

Pete never offered to make cuppas.

I checked my emails. There were a few unopened ones, including something from Stanton Housebuilders, no doubt about that bloody awful ad they wanted to run. She must've returned from her few days off.

Oh, and one from Harriet.

I clicked on the email from Harriet. Stanton could wait.

Dear Charlotte,

Thanks for your email, which I received with interest.
*   There is indeed some movement planned within the struc-*
ture, and I'd be very happy to discuss opportunities with you.
Can you give me a couple of weeks, then perhaps you, me
and Jamie can get together to discuss further?

Best,
Harriet.

The rogue email kisses obviously didn't cause offence after all. This was intriguing . . . and positive. She was a woman of few words but I'd say that collection of words in an email was designed to encourage me. We exchanged a couple more emails and, within the last one, she asked me to start to pull together a mini presentation based on some examples of campaign content that I liked. Anyway, whatever was happening, whatever the position, these were definitely good vibes.

All I had to worry about now was dealing with Jamie. He was making out that I needed him to get an in with Harriet – but that was clearly not the case. Although, I still had to play it carefully, because if he was going to head up both the J-Team *and* the new content team, wherever I ended up, there was apparently no escaping him as line manager.

Still, I was buzzing. Harriet seemed genuinely interested in exploring my options. This could be life-changing.

This could even make the broadband affordable again.

With a renewed confidence firing through my veins I opened the email from Stanton.

Charlotte

Can you please confirm that you placed the ad as discussed the other day.

Nicola.

No, I thought, I can't confirm it because I never placed their stupid ad.

I started typing back . . .

Nicola
I'm sorry . . .

Delete . . . God it's like some kind of compulsion.

I can't confirm that, unfortunately, because I felt unable to place the ad for you. It felt, if I'm honest, a little bit racist. Not all people of colour like reggae. It feels somewhat stereotyped.

I therefore didn't feel able to place the ad using that content as I felt I would be endorsing a trope that would ultimately be bad for society, bad for your brand and not deliver the results we pride ourselves on.

I'd be more than happy to chat through some alternative ideas with you though?

Best wishes,
Charlotte

I pressed send just as my phone pinged. It was Mush.

Sorry about before. Boss was hovering. It's been proper stressful in here. How many times have you apologised so far today then?

I haven't. Not since this morning.

At all?

Nope. I'm never apologising again. Well, I'm having a month off at least. Like Dry January. But for apologies. Easy.

Yeah right.

Seriously. I mean, I've got through it this morning and it already feels good. In fact, forget a month. Let's say, no apologies for a year!

115

OK, while you're geared up to kick ass and
stuff, can you call the broadband people?
FFS.

I rolled my eyes and put my phone back on the desk upside
down – as if not looking at the screen was going to somehow
stifle the notification alerts. I knew, however, that there was
no getting away from it. I guess it *was* my turn to call the
thieving broadband company. Mush had made his own fruitless
attempt – although I wasn't convinced he'd hung on for as
long as I had.

As Pete plonked a cup of tea down next to me I saw an
instant message ping through from Jamie. I'd never felt so in
demand, it was like Piccadilly Circus.

Drinkies tonight? X

Now some people would find the 'X' the suspicious part of
that message. But 'drinkies'? I was on red alert before I even
got to the 'X'.

I mean, this was not on. Not at all. Why did I need to go
out for private post-work 'drinkies' to be in with the chance
of getting a job. Why were so many job opportunities and
client networking opportunities laced with booze? I needed
to stop looking for excuses for Jamie's behaviour.

I guess, deep down, I knew why. And as much as I didn't
really believe that Jamie had any specific or deep desire in
me as girlfriend material, I also knew he had been single for
a while and made it *very* clear at all staff nights out that he

was most certainly on the lookout for, as he put it, 'fun times'. And I guess me, being – as he sometimes put it – 'directly beneath him', made me an easy target.

I shuddered just thinking about it.

But then I remembered. I was liberated now. I wasn't in debt to him – or anyone in this office. So I drew on my inner Jessica Jones. I wasn't going to do it. And I needed to say why. Because, at the end of the day, I wasn't just doing this for me, I was doing it for any other poor female colleague who he decided to wear down with drinks invites linked to promotions.

In fact, I was doing it for every other girl or woman who was ever inappropriately propositioned in return for a leg up in the workplace.

A leg over for a leg up.

Gah. It dawned on me just how *entirely* inappropriate it actually was. It was bordering on reportable, surely? Mush was right. There was the whole power dynamic thing. One minute he's giving me grief for being late, the next sending me messages with kisses on them about having drinks with him.

I decided he didn't warrant my urgent attention, so I'd make a quick call to the broadband company before replying. I slurped my tea while the hold music got louder with a static crackle.

'Hello can I help you?'

Crikey. That was quick.

'Hello. Yes, I, my name's Charlotte Thomas. And I . . . '

I hadn't thought this through, how was I going to get them to change our broadband package to something . . . less expensive than flying into space with Elon Musk . . .

Ah! I remember what Mam always said, if you need something to change, just say . . .

'I need to cancel my broadband account please.'

'I'll just put you through to the right department. Please hold . . . '

Hmm. Not phased then. Maybe that department will pull their finger out and give us a better package.

I took another slurp from my mug, and, before I could swallow the offensive tea . . .

'Hello how can I help you?'

Stay resolute Charlotte.

'Yes, hi. I'm seriously unhappy about the way we have been treated by your customer service team, and I'd like to cancel our account with you please.'

'I'm sorry to hear that, can I ask why?'

I started relaying all of the boring details, the difficult conversations I'd had, the fact Mush couldn't get through when he called, the mind-blowing direct debit amount . . .

'Oh, let me see, I'll just pull up your notes from your last communication with our team.'

I shared our postcode and address, turning up the volume on the 'unsatisfied loyal customer' vibes. 'We've been with you for three years you know. It's not on at all, making us pay for an old package that doesn't even exist anymore.'

'OK, let me just. Right, oh.' There was a muffled sound. And I swear I could hear the guy giggling on the other end of the phone.

'Something funny?' I asked.

He was doing it again. Letting out uncontrollable snorts. 'No, not at all. Let me just . . . '

More snorting.

'So we'd like to cancel please,' I said, now adding a massive dollop of impatience to my tone.

'Were you . . . ' he was snorting again, like it was almost choking him, like his life depended on not snorting but he couldn't help it.

'May I ask what's so funny?' I said, upping the haughtiness in my voice. Honestly, if I wanted to sound like a Jesmond type who shopped at Waitrose, I totally could.

'Was there, um.' He was barely holding it together now. 'It seems it was perhaps an inconvenient time last time you spoke to my colleague. Maybe we can. . . ' He took a breath, clearly trying to compose himself. 'Maybe we can sort something better for you now.'

'An inconvenient time? I'm sorry but if your customer service lines are open as advertised, as a *loyal* customer, I never want to be told that I'm being an inconvenience,' I snapped.

'Sorry, no.' He pressed on, 'I meant, an inconvenient time *for you.*' I heard more muffled breaths. He was obviously covering his phone up and sniggering.

What the hell was so flamin' fun . . . ahhhh fuck. I was on the loo wasn't I?! That bitch queen from hell I spoke to from the loo must've made a note of it on our files. All that trying to hold on and she *still* outed me for pissing on the phone. Well, not literally on the phone. But . . .

I was mortified.

'How dare you?!' I yelled.

'Ahhhh I'm sorry,' he sighed, and I could almost see the tears of laughter rolling out of his eyes. He was probably sitting in an open plan office too – call centres usually are, aren't they? I wouldn't be surprised if he'd put me on speaker phone. Maybe I was on speaker phone last time when I was on the actual loo. He composed himself – briefly. 'Right, um. Look, there's no need to cancel. I'm sure we can work something out for you. We'd love for you to just, hold on . . . ' More snickering.

'I'd like to take your name please,' I demanded.

'It's, it's Lou,' he spluttered.

'Right that's it. I'd like to speak to your manager.'

'One moment . . . ' He was literally crying with glee at his pathetic little joke. I'd show him. I'll be telling his line manager all about this . . .

Then the line went dead . . .

For fuck's sake!

No further forward with that then.

More livid than ever, I went back to my emails. Specifically, Jamie's indecent proposal . . .

I began typing back.

```
Jamie.
I'm sorry . . .
```

FFS! Delete!

I'm afraid I can't come for drinks with you to discuss the promotion opportunity. I'm not sure it's appropriate in the circumstances.

I thought about how to make this land a little, well, a little less harshly. But then I thought, why did *I* need to tread on eggshells? I was being forced to respond to inappropriate drinks offers from the boss. The boss who we all knew had separated from his other half six months ago. And that definitely had something to do with the work's Christmas do last year and that girl from accounts who left not long after. God, what if he had something to do with Tina leaving too? No, *I* shouldn't have to tread carefully. *He* should be the one treading carefully.

He should be the one apologising.

My chest expanded with a sense of righteousness. And I pressed send – without adding any unwarranted niceties.

Damn. That felt good!

11

'Mush. Mush!'

'What?'

'Can you get online?' It was a few days later, I was mind-lessly scrolling through my apps when I realised nothing was refreshing.

'What?'

'Can you get online?' I repeated, wondering why I felt a rising sense of panic over not being able to immediately satisfy my desire for hedgehog videos and dodgy dance routines.

'Char I can't hear what you're saying. You'll have to come up.'

'But you're on the netty.'

'So wait till I'm done.'

I shrugged and continued fannying around with my iPhone. Switching in and out of airplane mode.

On.

Off.

That usually did it.

No joy.

I looked over at the router. It was flashing an orange light. That didn't seem right . . .

'Char!'

'What!' I hollered, picking up the router and trying to figure out the best course of action. Sometimes, it would just pick itself up and come back on – and if you turned it off it could take an age to get back to that green light again.

'Char!'

'What?!'

'Has the internet gone off?'

I rolled my eyes at nobody. Duh! 'That's what I was trying to tell you before.'

'What?'

Mush never went to the loo without his iPad. TikTok or Facebook reels usually. I mean, I was never in there with him, but the ridiculous sounds that I could hear coming from the bathroom more than hinted he was flicking through ridiculous stuff on there.

I sighed. Nothing seemed to be making any difference. Switching things on and off, airplane mode, unplugging and plugging back in.

Mush walked in and, as I replayed the call I'd made earlier that week, it dawned on me what had happened.

'Mush. I've a confession to make . . .'

The broadband company had clearly called my bluff. With nothing else to do now we'd been cut off from the world and all forms of contemporary entertainment, once I'd told him the sad tale of my failed attempt to be some kind of consumer warrior queen, we headed round the corner to our favourite coffee shop for a hot chocolate. It was a little independent one in a converted residential terrace. It had a teeny tiny downstairs with nothing but a counter and a couple of stools lined up next to a wooden bar, full of flyers and local what's-on mags. Upstairs the cafe was spread out over a couple of small rooms with wonky floorboards. We grabbed a table by the window to watch everyone from up above.

'You told me not to take any shit,' I said, grabbing the wooden stirrers and serviettes.

'Aye, but saying you're going to grass him up to his line manager.'

'Did you not hear what I said? He was taking the piss.'

Mush burst out laughing.

'Mushtaq!'

'I know, but it *is* funny.'

'Whatever.' I dipped a stirrer into my extra long glass of chocolate, whisking the bottom of my drink frantically while the whipped cream and marshmallows on top somehow remained intact, albeit balancing precariously. 'Honestly, Mush. I didn't even cancel it. I never got that far. They bloody hung up. And I didn't say anything out of order. And you know what, we're gonna be screwed for telly now as well. No Disney Plus . . . '

'But. . . ! The Mandalorian!'

'Exactly. No Star Wars.'

'You better get it sorted then.'

'Your turn!' I said, scooping all the cream and melting pink mallowy stuff onto my stirrer carefully and slurping it.

It was pretty late when we left the cafe, and the streets were starting to fill with the evening's drinkers. We were close to turning onto our street corner when a couple of worse-for-wear lasses almost took us out. They must've just come out of the pub – the one that has locals in the front and students in the back – and God forbid you sit in the wrong area. It was like an unwritten rule. They definitely weren't students. I let out an involuntary sigh as we passed them.

'What's your problem?' one of them spat.

Me and Mush stopped in our tracks, standing side by side. Fuck. I braced myself for what was to come, biting my bottom lip and letting my eyelids engage in a long blink. We didn't need to say anything to each other to understand the enormity of this.

Perhaps if we just ignored it? We must've both decided we could start to walk off and began putting one foot in front of the other. But then . . .

'Aa was fuckin' talkin' to you!'

My heart started pounding. Strongly. Not in a fluttery way. Not like when you watch programmes about Vikings or Birmingham gangsters on the telly. No, this was definitely not positive exhilaration.

Then I felt something shoot through my body, as though my heart was suddenly pumping liquid wrath through my veins. I couldn't say sorry. I'd promised myself. And once again, this would be precisely one of the scenarios in which it absolutely wasn't my fault and yet I was being forced into a corner.

No. I was taking no more shit! And this was going to be a real test of my resolve.

I swung round and the words fell – no, projectiled – out of my mouth. With all the confidence and conviction of Bruce Banner before his alter ego emerged.

'Yeah and I was minding my own fucking business before you barged into me.'

Mush kicked my foot with his. I glanced up at him, his eyes were now pleading. He couldn't do much in a situation like this. He was a bloke. So getting into a fight with two lasses – regardless of how much they resembled extremely pissed WWE wrestlers – was simply a no-go.

Within seconds, girl number one, with her dyed black hair and over zealous mascara, was right in my face.

Mush tried to take control of the situation. 'Look, we're sorry, we didn't mean . . . '

'I don't give a flying fuck if you're sorry,' girl number one spat, staring directly at me while delivering her words of terror. 'I want to know if she's sorry.'

'She's?!' I said, feeling brave. Or at least, trying to feel brave. Because it was either be brave or fall at the first 'don't apologise for a year' hurdle. I couldn't do that to myself. I had years of non-stop apologising to make up for. I was being tested by the goddesses from above. I had to overcome this without apology.

'What did you just say?' She was now so close to my face I was being showered in angry spit and sweet boozy fumes mixed with cigarette smoke. Girl number two, meanwhile, was glowering over her shoulder, arms folded and a menacing smirk spread right across her face.

I was momentarily frozen, just staring back at them. Unsure what to do. I'd never gotten into a fight before. Not since junior school anyway. Was I about to shatter my street fighting hymen? Was I about to go down in a blaze of glory, be written about in the Chronicle as the brave Newcastle girl who refused to apologise to the drunken bullies. Would there be a grainy photo of my face – black, bruised and bloodied – head resting on a hospital pillow, but giving a thumbs up nonetheless because I had gotten out of this situation without saying the weakest of words?

It didn't feel like a very positive outcome if I was honest. Mush gently elbowed me in the ribs.

But this wasn't my fault. None of this was my fault. The broadband going off wasn't my fault either. And now here I was, a consequence of a chain of events linked to not saying sorry. Was this how the world was going to be from now on?

It hadn't dawned on me before just how much of the compulsive apologising was linked to other people's behaviour. It's like what they say about driving isn't it – it's other drivers you have to look out for. And I realised in that moment that it wasn't about me fucking up and needing to apologise – it was about soaking up the guilt that psychopaths lacked and projecting it back onto them.

I was having no more of it.

I could feel the tension building inside me. My legs were starting to shake. If my body was going to let me down I couldn't let my voice seal its fate. Everything in the street around me was one colourful, neon, chaotic blur of people and takeaway shops and voices and girl number one's angry, constricted pupils. I tried to puff my chest out, I took a deep breath, I pursed my lips and I said . . .

'Get. To. Fuck.'

I felt Mush's presence retreat slightly. He knew what was coming.

And with that I was pushed backwards, falling helplessly into Mush, whose poor body became the crash mat on which I landed. Awkwardly. Ungraciously.

I tried to steady myself by putting my hand out to find the pavement, to get myself up off my long suffering best mate.

Ugh.

A tepid mushy substance enveloped my fingers. I looked down. A swirl of beige, brown and green. A discarded tray of chips, gravy and mushy peas. Half of it stuck to my hand.

Without thought, I stood up, held my gooey fast food-laden fingers in the air, and flicked them hard at the floor right in front of girl number one.

I raised my gaze from her freshly splattered shoes to her face which now raged with the kind of venom I hadn't seen since I made a new year's resolution to stop watching East-Enders. Then, just as she lunged forwards again, she was grabbed around the waist by two figures in black and removed from my personal space.

She was screaming, 'Get the fuck off me.'

It was the police. 'Calm down and you'll get your wish,' one of them said, impatiently. 'At this point she clearly realised who had hold of her as her struggling seemed to subside . . .

I could hear faint pleading. Arguing the toss. Meanwhile, the other police officer asked me if I was OK, just as Mush, brushing himself down, looked absolutely mortified at our current state of affairs.

'Um. Yeah. I think so,' I muttered.

'I'd get on your way if I were you,' the officer said to me, her face a clear description of pity.

I nodded and we left the scene of the crime, heads hanging low, shuffling along the path towards our little terraced street.

'Didn't say sorry though, did I?' I whispered to Mush, a grin beginning to spread across my face when I felt that we were safely out of the zone.

'No you fucking didn't,' he said, his head down and shoulders hunched.

'Wait up will you.' I was struggling to keep up with his pace.

'I'm not taking any chances. You've become an overnight liability.'

'I've become an overnight hero,' I said, beaming.

'If those coppers hadn't turned up, we'd be . . . '

'We'd be what?' I asked defiantly.

He gave me one of his looks. 'We'd be really fucking sorry!'

12

As the little green kettle shook violently on its stand I stared into the rising steam and pondered . . . my sorry project was not getting off to a particularly flying start!

No broadband. A half-hearted street fight. Mushy peas and soggy chips. And gravy. I mean, who mixes gravy with mushy peas?

But surely this poor start was more to do with feeling my way? And it hadn't all been bad. I'd said no to Jamie. Perhaps, the more I *didn't* say sorry, the more accomplished I'd be at it? Or maybe my face and body language would be so much more confident that I wouldn't find myself in these ridiculous situations in the first place?

I jolted myself back out of thought and poured the water into our two chintzy Mr and Mrs mugs that Ben bought me and Mush for 'a joke' when we first moved in. He really couldn't get his head round why his little sis would want to flat share with someone of the opposite sex on a purely platonic basis. For all his youthful 'philandering' – as me mam called it – he settled down pretty swiftly in his early twenties. I still wonder if it was because he needed to be looked after.

Which in all honesty wasn't his fault. Mam still picks his socks up off the floor after him when he stays at home over Christmas or whatever. Even though he's thirty-two.

He couldn't have found someone more averse to running around after him though. Carly was pure class. And my brother was a better man for her. I kind of liked him these days.

I let my tea stew for that little bit longer as my phone rang. It was Mam.

'Hi lovey.'

'Hi Mam.'

'I sent you a text but it hasn't gone blue.'

'Oh, you mean it's green? Yeah, broadband's off.'

'Oh no! How come?'

'Because . . . ' I couldn't be bothered with going through the whole sorry scenario. 'We're just having a dispute with the provider.'

'Eeh, you should get Mush onto that, what with his legal knowledge,' she said powerfully, as if she'd just had the best idea in the world. I knew she thought the sun shone out of Mush's arse and it still exhausted me. The amount of times she hinted at how best friends sometimes make 'the perfect partner' and that I better realise it soon 'before it was too late'. But regardless of her mother-in-law fantasies, I'd told her a million times that Mush worked in employment law specifically and, not only that, he was a digital comms specialist, not a legal specialist. I let it pass this time.

'What were you calling for anyway?'

'Haven't you seen my text?'

'Um not yet no, you know the signal's dodgy sometimes. And anyway, I'm on the phone to you so I can't really . . . '

'I just wondered if you were coming round for your continental breakfast on Saturday.'

Me mam always did what she called a 'continental breakfast' on a weekend. It was just croissants and a cuppa with some posh orange juice which was always reserved for weekends. I think she thought it was a big treat for me, like I was still a young student living off cold veggie pasta every day or something.

'Yeah, that'll be nice,' I said.

'OK well if you can get to us a bit earlier this week. Your dad and I are off to the travel agents to book a holiday.'

'Has your broadband gone off too?'

'No,' she said, as if I'd missed something obvious. 'We always go in to book. It's part of the fun isn't it?'

I personally couldn't think of anything worse than sitting for what felt like hours in a travel agent's. They used to drag me and Ben along as kids, like it was a family fun day out. They'd take in their glossy brochure, jam-packed with page after page of multi-storey modern hotels and swimming pools. They'd have the top corner of the pages downturned on their favourite resorts. They'd always go with a shortlist but the travel agent still usually managed to sway them towards something else. I think me mam always thought that they were getting a really great tip – I think that was another reason she thought booking in person was the way to go. But in reality, they were probably just trying to up-sell the less attractive holiday packages that weren't doing so well online.

I remember Dad was livid when one year, instead of sunning ourselves by the pool on an all-inclusive, we'd gone rural and ended up in some shabby cottage in the mountains. The views were nice, but the dead bird in the bedroom that I came face to face with on arrival didn't set us off to a good start. My screams set off a load more flapping too as pigeons seemed to leave the roof in a mass exodus. Dad kept muttering something about 'legionnaires' and I had visions of them getting the army in to clear up the mess.

I think my parents found it tough entertaining us kids 24/7 too with no holiday club to speak of and a poor supply of *las patatas fritas*. They often tried shoving us out into the street to play with the local kids but, given our Spanish vocabulary wasn't particularly advanced we always seemed to rub them up the wrong way. We didn't know what they were saying but it didn't sound friendly.

'Where you off to this time then?' I asked.

'Italy. The Amalfi Coast. I let your dad choose this one. He's got surprisingly good taste you know.'

'Ah well, he married you didn't he?' I joked.

'Why yes! Anyway lovey. See you Saturday.'

'See you then.'

As I walked through to the lounge with the hot steaming tea I noticed Mush lying on his stomach on the carpet, his head stuck in the TV cupboard. He was frantically clattering around the contents of the cupboard. 'What you doing in there?' I asked, placing the 'Mrs' mug on the coffee table for him.

'Looking for . . . aha! There it is.'

He reversed his head and shoulders from the cupboard and turned round with a smile, excitedly waggling an old copy of *Star Wars* on DVD in front of him.

'Nice one,' I said, falling back into the sofa and grabbing the throw to snuggle underneath.

We hadn't played a DVD in as long as I could remember. In fact, we didn't even have a proper DVD player. We just used Mush's PS5 if we needed to. But I think the last thing we played on that was his high school play. His mam had made him a copy for Christmas last year – much to his dismay.

I think he was meant to be one of the three shepherds, but he gave the role a touch of Justin Timberlake by singing each of his short lines in a melodic high pitched voice.

Today, as one of Foo Fighters' most dedicated fans, he did not like to be reminded of his early Timberlake influences . . .

Still, the memory reminded me that the twelve days of Christmas had passed a good few weeks ago now.

'Think we should remove the last remnants of Christmas?' I asked, slurping my tea while eyeing the explosion of fairy lights we had merrily placed all around the living room.

'Nah. They're universal. They'll see us through till Easter those.' I wondered why I hadn't thought about that before. It's not as though Urban Outfitters isn't festooned with fairy lights all year round. It was perfectly acceptable. I mean, one day, we might even be adding tinsel to the all-season interior design edit. I noticed a rogue piece we'd missed hanging in an unsymmetrical fashion around the framed pic of us both at Whitley Bay amusements. I whipped it off and shoved it in the wooden magazine rack that contained no magazines. It was like a gigantic letter rack – now with added tinsel.

Mush got the DVD menu up on screen and wandered over with the controller in hand. 'Budge up'. He picked his tea up from the coffee table, pulled a face at the mug I gave him then settled back into the sofa, pulling half the throw off me to cover his legs.

As the film's famous music filled the room and the credits started to roll on screen, my phone pinged. I leaned forward to grab it from the coffee table and put my mug down in its place.

It was Maya.

```
You're a social media sensation girl.
```

I scratched my head.

Mush paused the DVD. He didn't like to waste a second of *Star Wars* – not even the credits. 'What is it?'

'It's Maya.' I text back using one hand and picked my tea back up.

```
What you on about?
```

'Work chat is banned.' Mush said, waving the controller in my face.

I showed him the text and he immediately picked his own iPhone up and started flicking his thumb up and down on the screen. 'What does she mean?'

'I don't know,' I said, just as my phone pinged again.

The screengrab.

None the wiser I text back, What screengrab?
Has it not come through?
I scrolled back up through her messages in case I'd missed it
earlier. Then I realised.

Sorry no broadba . . .

FFS!
I deleted my knee-jerk response and began again . . .

No broadband. Can't get media. 4Gs dodgy
round here. What is it?
See TikTok.
I can't get on TikTok.
Fuck.
What? What is it?

Mush was looking at me impatiently but I couldn't think
about *Star Wars*. All I could think about was what was so
important that Maya had to screengrab it. And how was *I* a
social media sensation.

'I didn't post anything while we were out did I?'

'You had one of those fancy hot chocolates. You always
Insta those hot chocolates. Maybe you've gone viral?'

'Ahhhh maybe. That must be it. Weird.'

I put my phone down on the arm of the sofa and shifted
uncomfortably in my seat while Mush pressed play and let
the credits continue.

'Why would my hot chocolate pic go viral on the night I ended up almost getting in a fight, though?'

'Algorithms. They're a law unto themselves. Just like you.' He held his mug out and I clinked my 'Mr' mug against his 'Mrs' mug and tried to settle back down. But something was still niggling at me. I picked my phone back up and tried all the apps on my phone but simply couldn't get anything to refresh. No TikTok, no Safari, no Instagram.

Then my phone pinged again. It was Ben.

`Mortifying.`

'Right this isn't just a posh hot chocolate. Ben's text me now.'

'Ben?'

'Yep.'

Mush sighed, clearly bored of the *Star Wars* intrusion. 'Look, it was a hot chocolate. Maybe he's just mortified because—'

'Because what?'

'Fuck, I don't know. Maybe . . . maybe there's some pervy guys going wild over your profile pic. Just put your phone down and watch the movie, there's nothing else you can do now anyway.'

'I dunno. I just can't help but think there's something to do with that altercation.'

'Altercation? Big word.'

'What if I'm internet-famous for falling over in chips and gravy?' Given my track record, I was much more likely to become a mushy pea meme than a hot chocolate influencer. Something still niggled though.

'Ah get over it man. It just means you can tick one more box on those Facebook quizzes.'

'What quizzes?'

'You know, when you get a score for each rebellious thing you've done . . . cos let's be honest, I reckon you'd've been scoring a big fat zero up until now.'

'Bullshit. I've . . . ' I thought hard. No tattoos. No arrests. No illegal drug taking . . . unless you count that time I picked a half-smoked joint up off the floor, inhaled and immediately puked up on the pavement. He was right. Perhaps even if it was the 'altercation', it was the closest I was going to get to having an 'edge'.

'Just give me two ticks,' I said, causing Mush to huffily pause the DVD again.

'If you're not back in literally thirty seconds I'm watching without you.'

I raced out into the kitchen and through the back door into the yard to try to get some signal. It just flickered in and out, but clearly wasn't strong enough for multimedia.

Damn those 5G conspiracy theorists.

13

I could hardly catch my breath. Being late for work wasn't really an option now I couldn't apologise for it. I needed to be on time. *Every* time. And I stupidly forgot to set my alarm. One of the only things on my iPhone that was actually working since broadband-gate last night. And without my iPhone to distract me last night, I'd got properly into the crime documentary Mush ended up watching after our movie and stayed up far too late.

As I raced through to the platform, I heard doors beeping shut and, as I rounded the corner, the train was pulling away. Shit!

I sloped back towards the wall and let my shoulders slump into it, wafting my shirt to let the air circulate. I was dressed appropriately for winter in my funky patterned shirt, A-line skirt, thick tights, docs and vintage sheepskin coat.

I was not, however, dressed appropriately for a 200 metre sprint to the Metro.

I pulled out my phone to see if there was even a hint of a signal. Nothing. Maybe I should've got the bus today? But then you're always clock-watching and tutting whenever some old dear gets on and has to count their change before the bus can pull away. I might have been late if I took the bus, but at least I'd have been able to see what the hell Maya and Ben were on about last night.

Images of mushy-pea-slinging on Chilli Road were racing through my head. If they'd caught the police in the pic as well . . .

Shit! I could end up on *Police, Camera, Action.*

I'd never live it down.

I wasn't sure rebellion was my bag in all honesty. Funny how not saying sorry immediately throws you into the realms of attack rather than defence when, in reality, it should just be neutral. When you've got nothing to apologise for anyway.

I looked up at the board to check the train times. It was due in two minutes. Thank fuck.

As I continued to reread the messages from Maya I felt two pairs of eyes on me. I glanced up as discreetly as I could. It was two women huddled tight together. They looked away quickly so I wondered if perhaps I'd imagined it. But then I heard sniggering.

I glanced back over, feeling indignant. I mean, if they'd seen me hurling a chippy tea at someone surely they could see I wasn't someone to be messed with!

It seemed to work. One of them bit down on their bottom lip and swung round to face the other way, but I could see the uncontrollable laughter shaking and jerking its way through her body. They *were* laughing at me. This wasn't paranoia.

Or was it? If you're paranoid, how would you know?

I was starting to feel a familiar sense of foreboding. The kind you often feel on a Saturday morning after post-work bevvies get out of hand. But I hadn't been drinking. And I hadn't been lairy. *I'd* done nothing wrong.

If you can't sip a posh hot chocolate and walk down Chilli Road minding your own business . . .

I sighed and unlocked my phone to text Mush but quickly remembered there was no signal. I typed the words in anyway, hoping it would automatically send the moment we moved out of the underground and back into civilisation.

Something's def gone online from last night. People are staring. And laughing.

As a soft rumble grew louder and a rush of warm air engulfed me I put my phone back in my bag and approached the platform, surrounded by eager commuters and high school kids all desperate to get to classrooms and offices on time. A waft of perfume, pastry, meat and sweat hung heavy in the air as we all stood far too close for comfort in a bid to get to the vacant seats first and avoid falling into each other as the carriages rattled at full speed.

The train pulled to a stop and opened its doors. I half walked, half floated on board, packed as tightly as a moving tin of sardines. I was relieved to have been successful in my quest for a seat so I didn't have to risk more sweating while crammed shoulder to shoulder with half of Newcastle.

Thank fuck for patterned shirts. Nobody else need know my well insulated back had the equivalent volume of Byker baths running down it for the duration of the journey.

I finished adjusting my long, heavy coat in my seat, pulling it out of the aisle, and pulled my bag onto my lap as the train started to race ahead. I was sitting next to some young lad who had been happily chatting to his mates in the seat behind him when I dared to sit down. My presence had forced him to turn back around in his seat so I could take the vacant spot next to him. He looked like a deflated party balloon exhaling disappointment.

Aside from my increasing paranoia, and the fact that everyone around me appeared to be either irked or highly entertained by my presence, it felt like a standard morning.

No, it felt *nothing* like a standard morning.

Sure the usual free papers were being read, AirPods were delivering all kinds of sounds into pairs of ears, and groups of mates in school uniforms were chattering incessantly. But aside from that, there was definitely something making me feel as though I was completely naked on a train.

I noticed a couple sat diagonally ahead to my right. They were maybe in their thirties, and dressed for the office, but quite clearly a couple, not just workmates. They were leaning tight into each other like loved up teens, whispering and giggling like crazy. But they weren't giggling to each other. The whites of their eyes kept meeting mine, and at one point, the woman had to hide her head in the guy's coat.

I had that familiar feeling of dread. Of desperately needing to check everything about my appearance. You know, when you start thinking you've not blended your blusher and you've got two massive clown cheeks. Or where you think you might've stood in something without realising and everyone else can tell that the stench is emanating from you.

I instinctively checked my shoes, even though I knew that the reason people were looking had nothing to do with my shoes. Or a make-up malfunction. What I *did know*, however, was that if my cheeks weren't burning as brightly as my flame red lipstick right now they would be very soon.

What I *did know* what that some kind of social media catastrophe was just waiting to greet me the moment I got my 4G back.

I was going to be that crazy person on the cop show. Chucking mushy peas at another crazy person. You wouldn't be able to distinguish between good and bad. I was part of a very public altercation attended by the police. And I wasn't even drunk.

The heat in my face began rising as fast as the Metro was racing and I patted my top lip with my forefinger.

I was sweating again.

This was getting unbearable, and the gaps between Metro stops seemed to be taking longer and longer.

As the train slowed down to a stop, a bunch of people piled off, only for new passengers to take their seats. I wafted my top again as I was now so hot I was close to meltdown. I started checking my coat pockets to see if there was a hair band, even just an elastic band, anything to get my thick, heavy hair off the back of my neck. But then things got much, much worse.

Sitting down on the chair facing me, directly facing me, was manspreader guy. Hot manspreader guy. God . . . why was God doing this to me?

He paid no attention at first. But there was no hiding. I couldn't stand up and move, there was nowhere to move to and no reason to switch seats. No reason I wanted him to know about anyway. But then, as I fidgeted, moving my head around like a demonic doll, his gaze caught mine and it dawned on him. A smile began to spread across his face. No, it was more of a smirk. It was definitely a smirk. He was laughing at me.

In that moment it was as though we were on a stage, the spotlight on both of us, like we were in some kind of TV prank and I was the butt of the joke. It hit me then that it wasn't the mushy peas that got everyone texting me. No, it was far, far worse. I shook my head to try to wipe the memory of the girls filming me the other day on the Metro but it was no good. Everyone around me laughing and smirking and pointing at the sweaty girl who clearly fancied the man she'd previously screamed at like a crazy witch.

I glanced down and awkwardly grabbed my phone from my bag, even though there was nothing I could do on it without a signal except for play some stupid bloody game. I felt as though I was drowning in embarrassment.

Flashbacks of five year old me doing cartwheels in the beer garden came flooding back.

My mam, noticing the problem immediately, raced over to me and scooped me up in her arms, straightening out my skirt and firing my dad the angriest look of disappointment she could conjure. '*Oh Peter!*' she cried, shaking her head as if he were one of us naughty kids.

My dad, trying to piece together exactly what had gone wrong during the morning's military operation of *getting the kids ready* while Mam was at the co-op had a sudden dawn of realisation wash over him.

'*Oh God, Janet, I left her knickers on the chair.*'

Poor Dad was absolutely mortified. And, from that day forward, Mam only ever left outfits consisting of trousers or shorts when it was up to Dad to get me ready for going out.

But while he was absolutely mortified, I was frozen. With red-faced shame.

And right then, in that Metro carriage, I was frozen with shame and dripping with sweat. It was like showing my fairy to the world all over again.

I tried a surreptitious look back up to see if he was still smirking, peering out from behind my dark hair. I was glad I didn't have a hair band to tie it back after all . . .

He was still smirking at me.

Bastard.

My stomach started whirling around. The butterflies were not so much fluttering around in there, they were having a full on rave in my belly. Frustration mixed with lust mixed with embarrassment mixed with feminist angst. I resolved not to look at him again – manspreader, source of my shame.

He looked down and back up, shaking his head, smirking away. Now I felt angry. Proper angry.

But the way his wavy fair hair fell in his eyes and he had ... oh God no ... he had dimples. Oh this guy was everything I wanted and everything I hated all at the same time.

I was *such* a sucker for dimples on guys.

He glanced out of the window smiling. Proving my point. He *must've* been a wanker, there was nothing to see in the window except your own reflection. We were underground. He was Mr Vain. He was Mr Wrong. He was Mr Manspreader. Hot or not, it didn't matter. He. Was. A. Wanker.

Then I noticed the couple. The loved-up sniggering couple. They were pointing at fit manspreader guy, then looking back at me, then trying to hide their giggles behind collars and scarves.

I sat back into my seat and it felt as though more and more people in the carriage were glancing at both me and manspreader.

Then I heard it. The words finally confirming what my useless mobile phone was incapable of communicating to me.

'It's that tilted cervix lass!'

It came from a small group of blokes who were not in any way trying to hide the fact that they were staring at me, and then at manspreader – who, incidentally, was still staring out the window and chuckling to himself.

I felt my throat tightening up as flashbacks from that day on the Metro played at a thousand miles an hour, hurtling through my brain, with each image making me feel more and more nauseous and my face now burning as angrily as a cluster of giant alien wasp stings.

His knees. His smile. His hair. His *obviously* long legs. My outburst. My realisation he was wearing AirPods. My words, my . . .

Oh. My. God. My brother's heard me screaming about my cervix. No wonder he feels sick.

But if my brother knows . . . Mam. Dad . . .

Oh God. Poor Dad! Not again!

My anxious thoughts took me away from the reality of the Metro carriage briefly, and before I knew it the doors were opening at my stop.

I have never legged it so fast.

I raced through the crowds to the entrance, my heart pounding. The memory of cervix-gate had been buried until now. Hidden beneath broadband problems and boss problems and near-misses on Chilli Road. I'd forgotten all about that little shit with her iPhone camera.

As the fresh air hit me and I emerged onto street level I pulled my phone out and sank onto an empty bench.

Ding.

Ding.

Ding!

My home screen was bombarded with notifications. Messages. Messenger. Instagram. TikTok . . .

I took a breath, feeling paralysed. What to look at first?

I decided to leave my mam's message. I had visions of the words 'disappointed' and 'unbecoming' and 'your poor father' hitting me with shame. So instead I went back to Maya's message to find the screengrab and see exactly what had been put out there.

As the image downloaded, a grainy picture emerged. There I was. Like some kind of shady criminal caught on camera, towering over fit manspreader. Pointing. Talking. Shouting.

I checked the name of the account that shared it and quickly opened TikTok. But I didn't need to hunt the account down – my DMs were full of links.

Knowing the imagery alone wasn't the issue, I grabbed my AirPods from the little zip pocket on the inside of my bag, pressed them into my ears and winced.

Play.

And there it was. In all its glory.

'Did you realise . . . that you've been taking up all my leg space, that you've been . . . manspreading your legs wider than mine were at my fucking smear test just now. And I've got a tilted cervix.'

Tilted cervix. I'd told the world (at top volume) that I had a tilted cervix. I had told the whole of social media that my fanny was unnavigable to medics.

No longer did my tilted cervix belong exclusively to me. It was . . . a hashtag. No, it wasn't just a hashtag . . . it was an appeal with a hashtag. It was an appeal with a hashtag that had been picked up by *The Poke* and covered in a multi-media page of horror.

#FindTheTiltedCervix

Shit. How the hell was I going to get out of this one?

14

23rd May 2008

Something happened last night, in my sleep. It was like, all of a sudden, there was a heartbeat in my pants. I don't know how it happened but it felt nice which makes me think it was bad.

I told Kelly on a text and I really, really, really wish I hadn't. Cos Kelly says its masturbating and I told her it couldn't be cos I'd never done that but she reckons I must've done it in my sleep and woken up and now I'm literally MORTIFIED. Like, could my fairy just do . . . whatever it just did . . . like, without me having any control over it. And would other people be able to tell by looking at me if it did?

I deleted the texts so nobody else could ever find out but now I know I can never fall out with Kel cause she knows AND she has a right mouth on her sometimes.

I don't know if people can tell if you've done it but when I walked into the kitchen and Ben was there he pulled a face at me. Ben always pulls faces at me but it's a bit of a coincidence isn't it that he decides to pull a face at me the morning after I did my first . . .

I am NOT typing that word again.

I know that Ben does (which is frankly the MOST HORRIFIC thing in the world) cos when he had his mates round they were all joking about it, like it was really funny to wank off and stuff. Gross.

But I've NEVER heard a girl say it. Ever. I'm not sure I'm meant to do it. But it wasn't on purpose so maybe I shouldn't feel bad?

Perhaps that's even worse? What if it happens in my sleep again when I'm at a sleepover or something? Or what if I make a noise and someone can hear me?

This is the single most awful and ladgeful thing that's ever happened. I'm never staying over anywhere again now.

I've decided that tonight, before bed (and really, really quietly) I'm going to pray to God and apologise for my sins and promise that it will not happen again.

In fact I'm never going to do it again. Ever.

It was quite nice, though.

15

The applause was rapturous. The whooping on a par with floor eight's morning warm up. And I just stood there, frozen to the spot, surrounded by the doorway that felt twenty times smaller than it usually did.

'Nice one Charlotte!'

'How's your cervix this morning?'

All I wanted to do was hide in the loos, but I had to get this over with. I was late . . . and . . .

I was a minge meme.

Feeling more mortified than an adult being sung happy birthday to in a restaurant full of over enthusiastic waiters, I contemplated my next move.

I was all over the internet. I was a social media sensation. I was viral . . . for all the wrong reasons. Maybe I needed to ditch this whole 'not apologising' thing?

But then I remembered . . .

Never apologise for being a woman.

I could either let the world run away with my cervix, or I could own it. I could show them all how proud I was to be a difficult woman with an elusive entrance to my womb.

My reproductive system was perfectly imperfect. And besides, I didn't want to be like one of those God awful politicians, caught out for getting drunk when they shouldn't have or shagging their special advisor and reading out a heavily scripted, emotionless apology that basically just told the world they were sorry they got caught – no matter how good an act they believed they were putting on.

The 'fuck it' vibes began to charge through my body, revving me up for a boldness that I didn't know I had. Feminist queens – eat your bloody hearts out.

I took one step forward . . . and kept going.

The applause got louder.

'All right, all right,' I said, lifting my palms in front of me but smiling uncontrollably. 'Give me a break.'

Something strangely exhilarating shot through my chest and my chin rose higher. I had done something sensational. I had found my inner banshee and let her loose to wreak hell all over the internet. And I wasn't sorry. Not one little bit . . .

I sat down on my swivel chair at my desk and switched my laptop on. But I was instantly surrounded by increasing pairs of bewildered eyes and toothy grins.

Maya, being wholly unapologetic herself, plonked herself down on top of my desk. She was holding a paper bag stuffed with pastry. 'You don't seriously think we're not going to dissect your new-found celebrity status do you?' she asked, carefully studying her vegan sausage roll, yet seemingly oblivious to the flakes she was dropping on my desk.

I brushed them onto the carpet. 'It's hardly *my* new-found celebrity, is it? It's my cervix that's famous. Not me.'

'Aye,' she said, continuing to devour her breakfast. 'But there's a campaign and everything now. You wanted content Charlotte. Now you've got it. And it's pure fucking gold.'

'Technically' I said. 'It's pink.'

'What?'

'My cervix. Thankfully.'

'Right.'

'And it looks like a donut.'

'Perhaps you can get Krispy Kreme to sponsor it?' she said, finishing the rest of her pastry and licking the remaining flakes off her fingers.

'I can hardly brand my cervix up can I. The nurse had trouble finding it with a torch and a speculum. I'm not sure it's a prime spot for advertising.'

'Hey Charlotte.' David, iPhone in hand, leaning over the desk divider, was unusually vocal today . . . 'That awful TV presenter's gone and tweeted about you.'

'Which one?'

'That one who reckons all women should wear high heels.'

Maya looked like she was about to dramatically puke her vegan pastry back up. 'Literally cannot *stand* that man.'

'I don't suppose anyone can.' I sighed, although inside I was really starting to enjoy my new-found infamy.

'Ooh Charlotte.' David continued to chatter away like an out of control Furby. 'What if you went on his TV show?'

'To do what?' I asked, frowning.

'I don't know. To . . . you know. To *give* it to him.'

Maya's ears pricked up. 'Give *what* to him, David.' She could tell David's initial bravado was flailing and she wanted to be the one to catch it, roll it up between her thumb and finger and flick it towards the bin.

'You know. To . . . to . . . put him in his place.'

Maya chuckled contentedly and I noticed the entire accounts department making their way over to us. I mean, there might only have been four of them, but you rarely found them outside of their own habitat. Especially if we were less than eleven months away from financial year end.

They were *always* too busy.

'What's going on?'

'Who's going on telly?'

'Was that *really* you?'

I knew at that moment that I could sink in a pool of cringe, or I could take proud ownership. And, given the fact that the pool of cringe was going to be so deep it was practically a bottomless lake to hell, I decided to opt for the latter.

Without a second to reconsider my next move, I was up on my desk, rising above the rest of the office like some kind of warrior shield maiden.

'Yes. It was me.' I pounded my chest with my fist proudly. 'It was *I* who screamed like a banshee at the inconsiderate manspreader and it is *I* who has a tilted cervix.'

'Not sure about your grasp of the English language there, Charlotte.' The voice came from the doorway.

Fuck.

I immediately scrambled back down from the desk.

'Harriet,' I muttered, sitting straight back down onto my brightly coloured swivel chair, desperately trying to scramble

154

out of the deep pool of cringe I was now kicking around helplessly in.

'Charlotte.'

I couldn't apologise. I simply couldn't. I needed to keep my resolve. But I had to acknowledge that this content wasn't exactly the kind of content she'd be encouraging.

'I . . . er . . . I know it's not exactly professional'

'Your grasp of the English language as I walked in certainly wasn't professional,' she said, her face hard like steel while my chest felt like it was about to collapse in on itself. 'Perhaps instead you could try *it is I – I am the proud owner of a tilted cervix*,' She imitated my stance while chuckling to herself. 'Damn, lady, you gave him hell didn't you?'

She was actually . . . well, proud might be a long shot, but at least I knew she wasn't angry. I breathed a huge sigh of relief. Then she walked towards me. 'Reckon you can get that mini presentation we discussed ready by next Wednesday?'

She was talking about the content role. 'Sure,' I said.

'Great. I'll send you a diary note.' As Harriet wandered away to her office, everyone else took this as a sign to get back to work.

When the crowds around my desk died down I checked my phone notifications again.

There were dozens of red circles emerging from the corners of my apps, all containing at least double numbers. Twitter, Facebook, Instagram, TikTok . . .

I had no idea what I was going to find but I decided that not knowing wasn't an option.

I tapped the TikTok app and was met with hundreds of new followers and messages.

WTF? How did people even know it was me in that video clip? I mean, people who *knew* me would obviously know, but how could, like, 357 people or something know?

I opened my DMs feeling paralysed – which message to open first. Then I spotted a familiar name in there.

I opened Mush's message. It was a link followed by the word '*sorry*'. Oh fuck. I clicked the link and there he was, TimTok. He'd stitched a video onto my viral Metro film and he'd outed me with a tag! The bastard! I'd been so kind to him when I turned down his offer of a third date. Hadn't I? God, even blaming myself wasn't enough to placate him.

And surely he knew better than anyone how awful it was to be humiliated in public. Maybe he blamed me for the stand-up night stage fright all along? OMG I think he duped me. He's clearly a shit.

I was starting to wish I'd told him what I *really* thought of him. That his patter was pants and our chemistry was as electric as a power outage.

I watched his little stitch-up, he'd tagged me and, surprise, surprise, described me in chocolate terms.

With a tilted cervix apparently I was like the limited edition Twirl Orange. Hard to find.

Was that the best he could come up with?

Actually, it was quite funny . . . why couldn't he have been that funny in real life.

I'd never felt so full of regret at being so calm and collected with someone. I wanted to tell the world what happened to

156

him on stage at the comedy club. To out *him* as the most boring man I'd ever met. I had thought he was sweet, nice even, but now . . .

My face prickled with unease. What else of mine was on the internet? Everything felt so out of control I felt as though at some point I might even find footage of myself having a shit on the internet! I mean, anything could happen. Facebook listens to you after all – even when the app's closed. How else would it have sent me ads for the new fish 'n' chip shop in Byker after I had shoved my hand in a pile of mushy peas?

Impatiently, I moved away from TikTok and ventured into the fiercest of all social platforms. I had to get Twitter over with.

And there it was. Bobbing around in the trending feed. #TiltedCervix.

Nice one, internet.

Grainy pictures of me were everywhere. There I was, wrapped in my scarf and winter coat, standing over manspreader, and you could just make out a look of regrettable defiance on the side of my face. Mush's mum had bought me that scarf for Christmas from Fenwick's. She'd made a point of telling me that it was real cashmere. I was certain she never intended for such a sophisticated accessory to be associated with my now highly public vaginal features. I bet she's thanking the Lord that mine and Mush's relationship is wholly platonic right now.

It had seemingly become a Twitter challenge to find the most perfectly curved phallic object to satisfy a tilted cervix. There was even a GIF overlaid with white text that said: PASS ME A BANANA.

And David was right, that terrible TV presenter had tweeted his unwanted views. Apparently discussing your cervix in public is 'unbecoming of a woman'.

Prick.

I fucking hate the internet.

But as I scrolled through there was more – and, rather refreshingly, the tone wasn't consistently bad. Women were sharing the hashtag and pic and talking about what it's like to have a tilted cervix, there were even nurses sharing top tips on making the smear test less uncomfortable. Some good was coming out of my social nightmare. Women and girls were relating, tweeting that they didn't know why sex and smear tests were so difficult, but that perhaps this was the answer. Perhaps they would ask about this. They were going to take action.

I fucking love the internet.

I decided at that point to go for it. To be bold, to stand up and be counted. To be one of those women who dare say it first. To start a movement. Even though, admittedly, whatever I had started was entirely by accident.

I screengrabbed the GIF and began to carefully compose a tweet. Then I quickly changed my mind and went back to terrible TV presenter's 'unbecoming' comment.

I was going to respond directly to the problem.

I began typing. *'If a cervix is unbecoming of a woman . . .'*

I paused. I didn't want to say anything about sex. I wanted to prove that there was nothing unbecoming about a cervix. But then why is sex considered unbecoming.

I guess sex with *him* might be considered unbecoming.

I continued . . .

*'If a cervix is unbecoming of a woman in 2023, then life on earth
would surely cease to exist.*

Get over it or climb back inside.

Yours

#TiltedCervix'

My finger hovered over the 'tweet' button for a moment.
Dare I?

Never apologise for being a woman.

Yes I double dare. I hit Tweet.

Then I quickly closed the app to hide from the anticipated
backlash and switched to Instagram, checking my DMs.

There were a few of those *'Hey. We like your style. We think
you'd be a great ambassador for our jewellery / new smoothie range /
sports leggings.'* I knew to ignore those. But one of them stood
out. It was written a bit differently.

Charlotte,

*My name is Angie and I work for Lunar Cup. We're launching
a new menstrual cup and I'd love to chat to you to see if you
might be up for an ambassadorial role.*

*If you're up for having a chat, please just drop your email
or number below and I'll give you a call to discuss. And here's
our website so you can check us out before you do.*

Ange.

A new menstrual cup? Maya uses one of those. But why?
Why would I be a good ambassador for a menstrual cup?

I replied with just my email address – I didn't want to appear keen in case it was a hoax. I certainly didn't need any more embarrassment. But I couldn't help but be intrigued.

As I clicked send, however, I felt a presence hovering.

'Charlotte. A word.'

It was Jamie. And he'd walked off, gesturing for me to follow him, before I could even reply.

Shit was going to hit the fan. I could just tell.

I walked into his office and, without looking at me, he told me to close the door.

Closing the door was never a good sign.

I took a seat.

'We need to talk about your behaviour online.'

Fuck.

Don't. Say. Sorry.

'Yeah. Bit of a mare,' I said.

'Bit of a mare? Charlotte, Stanton Housebuilders have already been in touch with me about your demeanour. And now this.'

There was a visible shake in his hand as he held his pen. I don't think Jamie was used to confrontations, not really. And I don't think my drinks rebuttal helped matters.

Not only was he forced to deal with a professional conflict, he felt personally slighted. It was obvious. I'd never seen him this tetchy before. He'd usually laugh stuff off, take the piss out of you in front of everyone else if you'd fucked up. That was his way. This . . . was different.

'I. Well, you know, I didn't ask to have my private business shared all over social media.'

'Yet you shouted about your private business on a busy Metro.'

My heart started pounding – quickly, angrily. 'Well, technically I guess I did. But I mean, there's far worse things being said on a work's night out. I was just unlucky to be filmed.'

'Might I remind you that we've got your appraisal coming up?'

I hung my head. 'I know. Absolutely. I know.'

'This isn't the content I want coming from my team.'

I almost started to tell him about Harriet joining in with it all. But I thought better of it. Whatever happened, whether or not there was really a job for me, Jamie was going to be my line manager, not Harriet.

How the fuck had I got myself into this mess? Was it wrong to turn down drinks? Was that why he was so angry with me? Honest to God, I heard him trying to impress Maya and the new girl in admin with his 'feminist' views the other day. Saying how Britney was standing up for her rights by posting nude pics on Instagram.

I'd've almost believed that he thought those things, if Maya hadn't pointed out that she heard him on the phone calling Britney 'unstable' for the very same reason.

I wished I had more Maya energy. I might not have been saying sorry, but Jamie's response to me wasn't exactly what I'd hoped for. In standing my ground, in turning down his offer, and in not apologising, he'd apparently become my office nemesis. Perhaps I needed more conviction?

After all, Maya simply couldn't hide what she thought of him, and for some reason, that meant he left her in peace most of the time. Either that or he'd try desperately to impress her.

Why couldn't I elicit that kind of response from him? I felt angry at myself.

'It won't happen again.' I muttered, still determined not to apologise for something else I wasn't responsible for.

'Good,' he said. 'I've apologised to Stanton on your behalf and informed them we'll be placing their ad. Racist? Honestly Charlotte. You're getting bogged down in all this cancel culture nonsense. No more, you hear me? Not on my fucking watch.'

As angry as he was with me all I could think about was how it didn't really count as an apology if it never actually came from me.

16

So much for not letting it happen again. There were interview requests for local radio, the health editor had written a piece in the *Chronicle* about making smear tests more bearable and, according to my mam, who heard it via my grandma, even a phone-in discussion with the resident doctor on mid-morning television.

Mam was, weirdly, beaming about it all. You'd've thought I'd won an Olympic Gold medal or something. Popping round for a Saturday morning cup of tea and a raid of their bakery cupboard (she always got the posh croissants in on the Friday night big shop) she was proudly informing me that her work-mates had nominated her to lead a new women's wellbeing group.

'Honestly, Charlotte. I've never felt so popular,' she said, placing the entire packet of croissants on a rack and popping them in the oven to warm. She must've felt in the mood for celebrating, I hadn't seen this many pastry goods being offered up in one go since our extended family trip to Brittany. 'Did you know that one in five women have a tilted cervix? Did you know that? That's like, well, it means that one of the

Spice Girls has a similar internal build to you. Eeeeh isn't that just great?'

'Well, given the nature of my smear test appointments I wouldn't say . . . '

'But that's the thing,' she interrupted, grabbing the butter from the fridge before continuing in campaign mode. 'Everyone's talking about how you can make your smear test more comfortable. About how you can make *sex* . . . ' she mouthed the word without saying it, 'more . . . enjoyable.'

I winced. I really didn't want to discuss enjoyable sex with my mam.

'What's all this Janet?' Dad breezed in, clearly oblivious to the topic of conversation.

'I was just saying how brilliant it is. Statistically, Charlotte has the same reproductive composition as at least one of the Spice Girls.'

Dad stopped in his tracks, considering this statistical 'fact', mouth downturned, eyes pointing upwards towards the window, before finally giving us a nod and then sticking his head in the fridge.

My mam, undeterred, continued in her praise of my accidental campaign. 'You could make a real difference, you know. You could save somebody's life talking about smear tests. Oh Charlotte. Imagine. You could end up being an ambassador for the health service or something.' Mam was clearly ecstatic that details about her daughter's minge were doing the rounds on social media. Meanwhile Dad sloped back off into the lounge with a glass of orange juice in hand which, given the smell of butter and pastry emanating from the oven, demonstrated that our kitchen banter had clearly put him off his breakfast.

'I can't exactly take credit for it,' I said, sitting down at the table, desperate for a croissant to halt the flow of vaginal discourse. 'I had absolutely no intention of talking about it on social media.'

'Yes, well. You've owned it lovey. And me and your dad are incredibly proud of you.'

I smiled. Although I had a sneaking suspicion that my dad would be wishing none of this had ever come to light. Poor fella. He'd be mortified. I had images of his workmates giving him grief as he rocked up to the factory of a morning.

My mam turned back towards the oven, pulling the door open. A waft of steaming hot air made her crinkle up her face as she removed the croissants with her chunky oven mitt. But before she presented me with the mouth-watering French treats she paused. 'One thing to consider though,' she said looking me in the eye, balancing a dozen tempting pastries on a red hot tray. 'Don't go into detail with your brother. You know he's a bit meek when it comes to *women's bits*.' She mouthed the last two words again instead of speaking them. It was as if giving certain words volume might burn her mouth and force her to do three Hail Marys or something.

'Has he been whingeing?' I said, grabbing a croissant and immediately ripping an end off, pastry flakes coating my fingers and sticking to my teeth. 'I mean, it's not as if he doesn't sleep next to a cervix every night.' I was aware of the stray flakes that flew out of my mouth but Mam didn't seem to care.

Ben was happily settled down these days. Which made a change. His previous exploits in town on a Friday night meant that I could never understand my mam's over-protectiveness when it came to Ben. If she knew what he used to get up to she'd have zero qualms about discussing *women's bits* with him. From what I could gather, he'd seen more than enough of them in the wild.

I think Ben just wished that his sister didn't own the very same things he adored in other women.

Mam carried on pouring the tea. She didn't seem to be in any hurry to eat a croissant herself. Standard.

'Posh!' she proclaimed, while grabbing the sugar bowl and placing it in the middle of the table.

'Posh what?'

'The Spice Girl most likely to have a tilted cervix.'

'Why would . . . '

'If it's only one in five women, then it's more exclusive, more, you know . . . '

I rolled my eyes. 'I honestly don't think it's anything to do with class mam. I've got one after all . . . '

I couldn't believe that my mother had now positioned my cervix according to her skewed idea of a class system.

After finishing breakfast, I said my goodbyes giving them time to get sorted and head to the travel agent to book their dream trip to Italy. There was a bus stop just two minutes from our house, where I used to catch the bus to school, so I waited for the next one to arrive. I decided it might be worth treating myself to something new to wear for Monday's appraisal. I mean, don't get me wrong, I wasn't trying to impress Jamie. God forbid, he didn't need any more encouragement. It was more about making a statement. About reminding him that I was a professional, this was a professional exchange and *he* was *supposed* to behave like a professional. I didn't want to give him any opportunity to tear me to pieces. And I certainly didn't want to crumble if he did. So I needed something to instil the right vibes – warning him off any more inappropriate behaviour, and instilling a sense of kick-ass in myself. But I had to strike the right balance and not look too dissimilar to my usual self.

Shopping wasn't exactly my favourite thing to do on a Saturday, so I gave myself a cut-off point of 12 p.m. by arranging to meet Mush for lunch at our favourite little coffee and sandwich shop, just a little wander down from the Theatre Royal. He hadn't come home last night, which made me think he'd got lucky, meaning we would have a full debrief to run through. That'd take my mind off things.

With little more than an hour to kill, I decided the department store was going to be the most fruitful. A concentrated collection of different brands and styles. There had to be something in there.

I walked in past the menswear and the waft of perfumes, all sharp scents mixed with delicate florals and musky undertones. Everything was lit in artificial light and it was rammed with shoppers pacing around not knowing what they wanted to look at but seemingly impatient about getting there.

I was beginning to regret not planning this shopping spree earlier.

I made my way onto the escalator and headed to the first floor towards the womenswear. There were always two distinct sections. They weren't sectioned off as such, but you didn't exactly need a trained eye to know which half of the floor was for me, and which half was for the more 'elegant' lady.

On one side you had concessions full of bright clashing colours and patterns, daring you to make a statement, brushing up against more muted colours and fabrics cut into edgy streetwear and smart casual pieces with a touch of something new.

On the other side there was an air of formality; silk shirt dresses and wrap skirts hanging out next to country casuals for the fashion conscious with plenty of disposable income.

I headed past the strikingly loud concession towards the brands I knew I could rely on. I wanted something that had a lot to say, but not in colour. I needed to emanate confidence, professionalism and 'don't fuck with me'. So I needed to stay on the statement side of the shop, but my mission was to find something that was just cut a bit differently. Something that gave me an edge without trying too hard.

I was furiously flicking through rail after rail, conscious of the little time I had but not really concentrating on the task in hand, when I heard what sounded like a child sobbing.

I moved around to the other side of the nearest rack, but I couldn't see anyone. At first, anyway. Then I glanced down to the bottom of the rail and saw a little girl, knees up to her face, her cheeks burning brightly . . .

'Hello there, have you lost your mammy?' I asked. She lowered her head further, burying her presence behind her knees, her nose sniffling furiously accompanied by sharp little intakes of breath. 'Can I help you find her?' I asked as gently as I could.

'My mammy's not here,' she said, looking up at me with huge, blinking blue eyes, her eyelashes wet with tears.

I was just about to open my mouth again when I felt a presence behind me.

'Gracie! Gracie? Ah thank God. You had me so—' then he looked at me. 'Worried,' he continued, a smile spreading across his face as the dawn of realisation hit him.

Oh. My. God . . .

It was him. It was the fit manspreader. With this impossibly cute child. He was smiling or . . . was he laughing? Was he laughing at me again?

My feet seemed to work on autopilot, reversing me back behind the rail, to the safety of the other side. A barricade of sorts. Just as little Gracie was hiding behind her knees for comfort, I was hiding behind . . .

Jesus Christ. It was the knicker rail. I was attempting to hide behind barely-there lacy thongs. I hadn't even realised I'd wandered into the lingerie section. But before I knew what was happening, I was keeping myself busy by flicking through the impossibly tiny pieces of material that were trying to pass as pants – as though I was here on a mission to prepare for a hot date.

'Hi,' he said, and I noticed the little girl had stopped crying.

I didn't *want* him to think I was going on a hot date. I wanted him to think I was single. I *am* single. And I'm *not* going on a hot date. But hang on . . . this was manspreader.

This was . . . everything came flooding back, piercing my consciousness like a recurring nightmare.

And here he was. In real life. Smiling at me while my hands continued flicking through the overpriced wares.

I stopped myself. 'Hi,' I replied, a squeaky kind of whisper leaving my lips uncertainly.

Why was he staring at me like that?

I didn't know what to do. So I started flicking through the rail again, casually picking up a hanger and studying the price tag . . . before realising it was a . . . oh . . .

I was holding what appeared to be a bright red piece of dental floss. I immediately tried to wrestle the hanger back onto the rail, but in my panic I dropped it. I swooped down to retrieve it but, from the other side of the rail, he beat me to it. We were now crouched down on the floor, facing one another, eyes locked. And worse, he was now holding a pair of knickers that even Christina Aguilera wouldn't've worn in her dirtiest days.

'Nice,' he said, holding them back out for me, as little Gracie, still in her hiding place, albeit looking slightly more at ease with her legs sticking out in front of her, wrinkled up her nose as she clocked the offending item.

I grabbed the hanger back off him and, as I did, I caught his hand with my fingertips. His skin felt warm. I immediately felt a flutter in my chest and had to catch my breath. I stood up, exhaling as I did, to try and relieve some of this pent up . . . what even was it? It certainly didn't feel like anger . . .

But this was *the manspreader*. I had a right to be angry with him. Didn't I? And surely if I fancied him just because of how he looked, when he obviously thinks he deserves All the Space and women deserve None of the Space that makes me the worst kind of feminist . . . and as shallow as a frying pan.

But he had his headphones in. He hadn't even heard my polite request asking him to move. And he had a cute child. And he was hot. He was so, *so* . . .

'Well, at least you're not shouting at me today,' he said, chuckling, his dimples appearing in his cheeks.

'I . . . um . . . ' I was lost for words. I couldn't exactly say sorry now could I? I'd only just made the big unapologetic promise to myself. And he was the man that started it all. Or was it the smear test? Either way, he played a significant part in my resolution to never say sorry again. And I wasn't about to fall at the first hurdle. No matter how bloody fit he was.

'Daddy. Daddy . . . ' I tilted my head to see around the side of the rail and noticed Gracie holding his hand and hopping about in her little green wellington boots. 'Daddy . . . I need the loo. *Now*, Daddy . . . '

An inexplicable sense of anger struck my core and I felt my jaw tighten.

If he was Gracie's daddy . . . then Gracie has a mammy and fit manspreader has . . . a wife. Or a girlfriend. Or a husband. But whatever, he wasn't exactly looking available right now. And that realisation seemed to reignite my rage. It gave my rage every excuse it needed to rear its ugly head.

'Well at least, for once, you're not taking up my space,' I snapped, muddling my words and immediately hating myself for being a bitch. His smile dropped, and his cute dimples vanished.

'For once?' he said.

'I . . .'

'Daddy! Now. I need to wee *now*! Please Daddy.'

'I have to go,' he said, his face unsmiling and his eyes no longer sparkling.

'Sure,' I said, as nonchalantly as possible.

He looked down at his little girl, then back at me. 'Come along Gracie. Let's leave this lady to it.' And off they walked.

This lady. He was making it very clear that I was never going to be more than a stranger in the lingerie department. Or a crazy woman on the Metro screeching at him.

Oh fuck. Oh fuck oh fuck oh fuck. *Why* was I so rude? Again!

I stomped off from behind the rail and headed to the next one, concentrating as closely as I could on the pairs of pyjamas that were now hanging in front of me and flicking through the hangers once more.

After I thought it was safe to lift my gaze I watched them walk off. His little girl skipped and hopped along by his side, pulling him in the direction of the department store loos. And just as they reached the door, he looked back over his shoulder. Mortified to be caught staring, I dropped my head and concentrated on the swirly pattern of winter forestland on the pyjama bottoms in front of me. Foxes and deer and rabbits and . . .

An unwelcome yearning hit me.

I clearly had a screaming crush on the very last person I should ever have a crush on. Someone who I now knew I would never stand a chance with. Even if he was single.

Nice one, Charlotte. I'd behaved terribly.

I headed to the escalator, giving up on my shopping mission in the hope that Mush might be a few minutes early. I needed to debrief him on this hellish encounter without delay. I needed reassurance. For what, exactly, I wasn't sure. I guess I just needed to know that I wasn't a bitch queen from hell.

Or was it that I just wanted to have an excuse to talk about him and pretend it was anger driving the conversation and not some kind of love/hate fantasy.

As my feet hit the bottom of the moving escalator, taking me by surprise onto the static shop floor, I realised my thoughts had been completely lost in the dimples his smile forced into his cheeks. Dimples that, I was starting to realise, would probably never reappear in my man-repelling presence.

17

'Right then.' Jamie was sternly flicking through papers in front of him as we both sat alone in the little glass pod at the end of the office. 'I take it you've completed your forms.'

'I have,' I said.

'Right. We'll chat through them, starting with your objectives, and then we'll move onto the values.'

The atmosphere was below freezing. This didn't bode well.

We both looked down at the sheets of paper in front of us. These appraisal forms always reminded me of some kind of game show. Like *Play Your Cards Right* or something. Is your manager going to score you *higher* or *lower* than you scored yourself?

The first objective was about the profit we were making on our accounts. Had we hit our commission targets? I knew this one would be a breeze because you couldn't argue against it. The numbers were there in black and white. But had I met or exceeded my objective? Because I knew that some of the other objectives might come under more scrutiny given his behaviour lately, I decided to be bold. I marked this one as exceeded.

Was it a match?

Computer says no. Or rather, Jamie did. 'Remember Charlotte, for an objective to be considered as "exceeded" it needs to be exceptional. Wouldn't you agree that going ten per cent over target isn't exactly exceptional?'

I felt my chest flush, and I was so relieved to be wearing my old high necked top. It ended up being a blessing dashing out of the shop without any new clothes the other day. I realised that, if only I washed everything in the washing basket, rather than just continually picking off the top layer of dirty clothes, I'd have an entire second wardrobe.

I knew, however, that I wasn't flushing with embarrassment. It was more a rage. It was as though my body was just building up for conflict. I'd never had an appraisal like this. Fuck, I'd never had a meeting like this. Jamie was being purposefully harsh. I knew it. And all because . . .

As I looked up from my papers and towards my boss, I felt my eyes deaden as an image gatecrashed my angry mind. I was Jessica Jones. Leather jacket clad, super human Jessica Jones. I jumped up onto the desk, leaning forward, grabbing him by the throat and picking him up out of his chair, his legs kicking while he spluttered and cried and . . . then . . .

'Charlotte. Wouldn't you agree?'

I shot upright in my seat to ground myself back in reality. 'Um. No . . . not really.'

'I'm sorry?' He appeared shocked. Surprised that I wasn't just going along with whatever he said, I guess.

But by now I'd already said it. I told him I didn't agree. So I had to give him a reason.

I gave myself a mental talking to. *Just stay objective, Charlotte. Stick to the facts. Don't get emotional.* 'Last year,' I said, as calmly as I could. 'Most account handlers were unable to retain commission at a rate equal to the year before. Business has been tough. This year I increased by ten per cent. Which is exceeding my target, is it not?' I leaned back in my seat, putting the ball in his court and feeling pretty pleased with myself. It was as though I'd just served up an ace.

'You are *expected* to exceed your target. That's the whole point of the objective. So, with that in mind, you've met it.'

He began filling in the sheet, adding a massive 'M' in the box. I couldn't back down now could I? 'What if I disagree?' I asked.

'That's fine, I'll make a note that you disagree and you can sign to that effect.'

This was not going well. After what I thought was a powerful start I felt deflated. No more was I Jessica Jones, making stealth moves like some kind of warrior goddess. No, I felt more like Serena Williams at the Open that year, smashing my racket because nobody was listening to me.

I had to keep my cool.

'Moving on,' Jamie, the Umpire with all the power, shuffled the papers around some more, as if they gave him an extra kind of power surge.

Unfortunately, he really did hold all the power at this point in time. I couldn't believe he was being such a dick about everything just because I'd turned down his drinks offer. I mean, that's all this could be about, surely? I wasn't arrogant, but I knew I'd done well this year.

My heart started thumping in my chest and I wondered how to try to slow my breathing without him noticing I was so wound up in the first place. I took a slow drink of water from the glass in front of me, but saw my wrist shaking as I did. I put it back down again.

'OK,' he said, still not looking me in the eye. 'So, objective. Number. Two.'

It was as though he was trying to prove he was actually a consummate professional beneath all his bullshit. But he obviously felt in order to do that he had to be a total bastard. No jokes, no smiling, tons of criticism.

I looked at the next section. The objective was to, *Support the reputation of the brand through professionalism at all times and in all transactions.* I'd marked it as 'met'.

'So,' he said, placing his papers down neatly in front of him. 'How would you score yourself in this section?'

He still refused to crack even a hint of a smile. I'd never seen him behave so coldly. Was Mr Freeze my nemesis? Was this his superpower? Showering me with shards of ice cold criticism?

'I marked this one as met,' I said.

'Really?' he said, his eyebrows raised, as though he was goading me. I refused to get my back up. 'I think it would be pretty difficult to even mark this one as a "partially met" objective. He looked around the room as he spoke, still refusing to look directly at me. 'You've caused a fair bit of outrage on social media. And I wouldn't say your response to Stanton was entirely on brand. You weren't living the values there.'

'Excuse me?' I couldn't believe he was bringing this stuff up. Especially the first comment. The number of times he and Danny have gone out on after-work benders and ended up in some rat-arsed mess in public.

I remember one time, John, the CFO, who was always in early because he's finance and they're always very organised aren't they, well he found Jamie asleep on the sofa in our reception, a wastepaper bin next to him. It was a few years back now, but he got away with it. It was when his uncle was still a consistent presence in the office. I mean, judging by the tone of his voice that day and the look on his face when he hauled Jamie into his office he wasn't exactly happy about his nephew being caught dribbling on the sofa after a few too many Jägerbombs in town, but nothing bad ever came of it. It was as though he was immune to the consequences of his actions. It made me sick.

He took a deep breath and the muscles in his face began to relax, like he was in his element being able to tell a member of his stupid 'J-Team' that they'd fallen below par. 'Did you ever stop to consider what impact your social media storm might have had on the business?'

'I did, yes, but as far as I can see, there has been no negative impact.'

'Well you're obviously not looking hard enough.'

'OK, so what *is* the negative impact?' I asked, feeling emboldened. Because how could he possibly come up with a fair response. No harm had been done.

He shifted uncomfortably in his seat. 'Reputation is hard to quantify, but the damage has been done.'

'What damage?'

'Negative brand association.'

'But—'

'It's not good for business.'

'Hang on a sec. But what negativity has there been? OK, one of my social accounts made it fairly obvious I worked here. So yep, there was association, until I deleted it, but how was it negative?'

He opened his mouth to speak but by this point I was enraged.

'Also,' I added, with a growing level of assertiveness in my voice. 'Wouldn't you say *I* was more a victim of the social media content than the company? Nobody asked me how I was coping with it?'

'You shouldn't have—'

'But I didn't, did I? I didn't post it. I didn't ask for it to happen.'

'But it *did* happen. And it was wholly inappropriate screaming like a bunny boiler on the Metro about your, about your . . . ' he stumbled over his words and waved his hand in front of himself as if hoping to catch it.

'Cervix,' I finished. I didn't have the energy to challenge the ridiculous bunny boiler comment as well.

'Honestly nobody needs to hear about your bodily functions.'

'Excuse me?'

'It's lewd, Charlotte.'

I could hardly believe what I was hearing. After the shit he subjects us to in the office, and he's trying to tell me I can't use the word 'cervix' in my own time because it's 'lewd'.

179

'Cervix is not a profanity, Jamie.' I couldn't believe I just used his name with that tone. It was as though I was talking to a toddler. But oh my God – it was as though I was talking to a toddler. One that wore a tie and had control of our departmental budgets and, at this moment in time, my career and livelihood.

'Well it's not something I want to hear about,' he said. 'Moving on.'

I couldn't believe it. I'd never had a poor mark in an appraisal before. I was consistently at 'meets' and 'exceeds'.

The rest of the appraisal continued in much the same vein. It didn't matter what I said, or what evidence I had about meeting my targets, he found things to pull me on. Things that were out of my control. Like placing a campaign with a magazine we always used that went bust – leaving the client out of pocket. How was I to know? They were on our approved list. Seeing into the future, sadly, wasn't one of my superpowers.

If it was, I would have never gone to the pub for post-work drinks that night when he got far too close for comfort.

But it didn't matter. This had got personal. He wanted me to be apologetic. To assume responsibility for every shitty thing that had gone wrong. I knew that the social media stuff was troubling. But even Harriet was cheering me on with feminist sisterhood vibes.

'So,' he said, tapping the papers on the desk to straighten them up. 'I'll get all this typed up and emailed over to you. Of course, if you want to lodge a formal appeal against the gradings – as you seem to be heavily hinting that you disagree with them – it's your call.'

He stood up and walked out, leaving me sitting there miserable like some kind of bad date in a restaurant. I was left surrounded by my own papers covered in my overly enthusiastic notes.

I hadn't even thought to ask him what this meant about my upcoming content presentation. It wasn't a low enough score to kick off a performance improvement plan or anything, but I'd never scored this badly. My work was my pride. And it was all too much of a coincidence. The timing of the appraisal.

I had to wonder how he would have scored me if I'd agreed to have those drinks with him.

18

'We say sorry for saying sorry too much, then we say sorry for not saying it enough. And we say sorry simply for being alive. We can't win. We are just massively apologetic people and refusing to acknowledge this is like . . . it's like . . . '

Mush finished my sentence for me. 'It's like Disney refusing to acknowledge how cute Baby Yoda is.'

'Exactly.' I picked up my iced tea, before changing my mind and putting it back down onto the wonky wooden coffee shop table. 'Can you believe how much of a dick he was?'

'Baby Yoda? Well he did eat all that—'

I rolled my eyes. 'Jamie!'

Mush sighed. 'Well, yes. Because he's always a dick. He's a full-time, permanent dick. He couldn't be made redundant from being a dick if he tried.'

'And can you believe he thinks the word cervix is lewd?'

'Yes.'

'And can you believe he marked me—'

'Yes!' Mush snapped impatiently, shaking another packet of sugar and frantically pouring it in his tea. 'Yes, yes, yes! He is a full-time dick, Charlotte. So I can't imagine there could ever be a time when he's OK.'

'I know,' I said, Mush raising his eyebrows at me as if he's heard it all before. 'I *know*'. I stressed. 'But what can I do? And maybe he does have a point. I only ended up on the internet because—'

'Honestly Charlotte. If you're penalised for one morning's worth of commuter rage . . . '

'I know, I know, but it makes no difference does it. If I'm penalised for it, whether that's right or wrong, it's done isn't it?'

'I think there should be guidelines, you know, to put an end to the apology epidemic. To stop people from having to take responsibility for things they had no control over. Besides, even if you begged for his forgiveness, even if you threw your hands up and said yep – I was seriously out of order for showing a little bit of anger on a train, he still would have marked you down for something.'

'Thanks for that.'

'No but he would, wouldn't he. He's personally marked you down for refusing to have a drink with him. So now he's finding a way of translating that into your career. If you start humming and hawing about whether or not you did something wrong, if you start apologising for it, other people might start to see his point. Don't give an inch. Seriously Charlotte.'

I raised my eyebrows. Mush didn't seem to be in the best of moods today.

'You OK?' I asked.

'Just worn out. It's not exactly a breeze over at my place either.'

'I know. I'm sorry. Tell me – what's going on?'

'It's just the culture change since the new boss started.'

'The maternity cover?'

'Aye. Everyone's clambering to prove that they're the best candidate for the job long term.' He drained his mug dry and picked at the last bits of salad from his plate. 'Seriously, you feel as though you have to say sorry if you need to leave on time these days.'

That word again. Being used in situations to cover up other people's bad behaviour. It almost felt as if we needed to reset the whole etiquette thing. But it would be a shock to the system, as so many people were used to hearing you apologise if you couldn't make it to the pub with them on their new job celebratory night out – even though you were actually going to your grandma's funeral that same day.

'This why you had a blowout last Friday night?' I asked.

'Yeah. I guess. Needed to let off steam.'

'Well good on you.'

We'd chatted about the night he never came home over lunch after my disastrous shopping trip. He *had* got lucky. But he wasn't feeling all that great about it. He'd got tipsy and ended up getting it on with someone he dated back in high school. Said he felt really bad for it. But they were both adults, both willingly took part in a one night stand. So what was the problem? And why do we always assume that it's only the blokes who want a one night stand anyway?

There were so many things we needed to stop apologising for. Sex wasn't lewd and neither were our body parts. In context, anyway. And then there are the other types of apologies we make. Like in the professional capacity. For example, when you apologise before sharing a brilliant idea – on the off chance it's not quite as genius as you think it is. And then, when your idea does do amazingly and helps your company meet and exceed its targets, and you're given the praise you quite clearly deserve you're all like, *well, it wasn't all me. I am so grateful for being given the opportunity . . .*

And we needed to stop apologising when we've been on an absolutely excruciatingly awful date with a guy who acts like he'd rather be looking at his phone than having an actual conversation.

It really was an epidemic. It was bad for our health. And it certainly did nothing to level the playing field. I mean, as much as we all say it, I swear it's some kind of inbuilt female thing. I think the apology virus was always more prevalent amongst the women of the world. It's like – I'm so, so sorry for daring to step foot inside the space that you've hogged for so long. I know my place is in the stationery cupboard in the office, or on reception, or in the kitchen, or the nursery, or on your arm, and I should only be seen or heard when summoned to make a cup of tea, type up a letter or give my man a blow job.

Mush stood up to get the next round in and I realised I'd been lost in angry feminist thought for the past few minutes. 'Another iced tea?'

'Make it an espresso,' I said, slurping the last of my peach iced tea – which was now almost tepid and creating a shimmer of condensation around the edges of the glass. 'And could you get me a granola bar while you're at it?'

He sloped off towards the counter and I picked my phone up to check my emails. There was something from one of my favourite labels whose algorithm clearly responds to my online activity in a far too close for comfort sense. They were informing me that the dress I looked at was low on stock. I wanted to berate the lack of privacy but in the same moment I realised how helpful it was.

I resolved to order myself the dress if I could get through the next month without saying sorry.

Then something else popped up. It was from Angela Cooper. It was the woman from Lunar Cup. I'd almost forgotten about her.

I opened the email.

Dear Charlotte,

I hope this email finds you well. If you're still keen to find out more about becoming a brand ambassador we'd love to meet up with you via Zoom at your earliest convenience.

Our new product is due for launch in the coming weeks and we're keen to work with you as part of our North East campaign.

If you're up for it, please click my calendar link below to pick a suitable appointment time.

Best wishes,
Ange

This was serious stuff. It wasn't a free pair of leggings that might never arrive.

Mush wandered back with a tray full of coffee and crumbly tray bakes.

Defiantly, I picked up my espresso and knocked it back as if I was hammering the tequila.

'Woah. Steady on.'

'Fuck the stupid appraisal.' I said, regretting the haste in which I drank my burning hot coffee.

'OK.'

'I mean it. Fuck 'em. There're far more lucrative opportunities on the horizon than staying in my crappy job.' I placed my cup back down in the pool of coffee that had slopped over the side of Mush's cappuccino.

'Like . . . '

I pushed my iPhone under Mush's nose and he read the email subject aloud. 'Lunar Cup?'

'Yeah. I told you about it. Didn't I?'

'Nope. What is it. Something to do with *Star Wars*?'

I nearly sprayed him with granola pieces. 'Um. Not quite.'

I snatched my phone back from him and googled 'menstrual cup' before plonking it under his nose again. He looked none the wiser when presented with my Google image search.

'It's a menstrual cup.'

'I don't know what that is,' he said.

'Well what do you think it could be?' I asked, rolling my eyes.

'Fuck's sake. I don't know . . . a . . . erm . . . ' he leaned forward, squinting at the screen as though he needed glasses. He didn't. 'Is it a . . . a stress toy?'

'No! It's an environmentally friendly alternative to the tampon and sanitary towel.'

'And . . . '

'They need an ambassador.'

'Oh God,' he said, looking towards the door as if desperate to escape. 'Do I really want to know?'

'Probably not, but if it pays enough to get Disney Plus back . . . '

'On that note . . . '

'*They* need to apologise to *me*.'

'Yeah but there's battles to fight and battles to . . . what's the saying?'

'Nothing like that. It's "pick your battles."'

'Yeah. So. Can you *not* pick a battle with the broadband provider? Can you maybe just, I don't know, call them up and apologise?'

After everything we'd just been saying it felt like a right cop out. So I wasn't exactly jumping for joy at the prospect, but upon debating the matter, perhaps Mush was right. Perhaps we weren't *really* compromising ourselves if we knew we were only saying sorry to get what we wanted out of a situation? Perhaps that was a whole other ball game altogether? Manipulative apologising. But then, how will we ever chip away at the apology epidemic if we just. Keep. Saying. Sorry.

Maybe mistaking fit manspreader for an arrogant twat was one of those things too . . .

Perhaps part of this being unapologetic thing was giving myself some slack and allowing myself to apologise when I needed to? You know like how we're never perfect at being body positive. Sometimes, I *do* choose a granola bar over a triple chocolate brownie purely because I want to wear my old bikini this summer – even though I know I can wear a new bikini with those extra inches. And I'd be wearing it more happily because nobody is ever going to be thin and contoured enough to be society's idea of perfect. It doesn't exist. So give me the fucking brownie. That's how it *should* be anyway. But my brain still piles on the guilt sometimes . . .

Also, a total lack of apologising simply couldn't exist. Because if it did, that would mean I'd have to behave perfectly for the rest of my life and never fuck up. And in retrospect, that all sounds a bit boring. Sometimes, just sometimes, we had genuine things to apologise for.

I found the number for the broadband provider in my recent calls and tapped the green button on the screen. I still had a few crumbs of granola left by the time they picked up. 'Interesting that you're never on hold for long when you're looking to renew your contract.'

Within minutes we were back in business. And I didn't even need to apologise. I had it all ready in my head – my compromise to myself. I'd apologise for being rude to them on my last call, but I'd make very clear that they shouldn't treat their loyal customers like dirt. It was how life was sometimes, nuanced. There were grey areas. However, none of that mattered. Because I accidentally gave them my email address instead of Mush's and they took it to mean that we were completely new customers. We bagged one of those introductory deals – half price for six months – and went home happy and primed to watch Disney Plus and stream YouTube on our big TV screen.

As we approached the house I had a thought. 'I'll just nip to the supermarket, grab us some ice cream and beers to celebrate.'

'OK, I'll get our viewing lined up.'

The supermarket was literally round the corner, next to the Metro station. It was one of those mini ones with just a couple of aisles of essentials and the odd ready meal. Useless for a big shop but perfect for a night-in shop. I grabbed a basket and got distracted by the pizzas. We hadn't eaten tea yet so it would be a very welcome move to grab a cheesy feast and a barbecue chicken deep pan.

I was just trying to make a decision without being drawn into studying the calorie numbers plastered all over the front of the pizza boxes when a voice drifted over my shoulder. 'Looks tempting.'

I swung round and I couldn't believe it. It was him. Manspreader. Again. I felt my face flush and my mouth started talking without my permission. 'Are you following me or something?'

WTAF did I say that for? I immediately regretted the words. I tried to finish it with a smile but I had clearly irked him. His tone became sharp. 'I live literally round the corner from here. I could say the same about you.'

My back was up. 'Well, so do I.'

'Well that's not exactly a surprise given that we keep seeing each other on the Metro. Besides, *I* wasn't the one attacking you for no reason.'

'You. You . . . '

'Yeah, exactly. No reason whatsoever.'

I stood there dumbstruck. It had all started with a nice opener. He was commenting on the pizza. He'd sounded friendly. Why did I have to spoil it. Why the fuck do I *always* have to spoil it. He was hurt. And he was lovely. 'I . . . '

'I get the message. I was just trying to be nice. Stupid idea,' he said, turning his back to me.

'Yeah well. *I* . . . was just trying to mind my own business on the Metro.'

'I wish you had,' he said, and then swiftly disappeared out the door. I stood there, cheese pizza in one hand, chicken pizza in the other, my arms deflating and dangling lazily either side of me, no doubt allowing all the delicious toppings to slide to one side of the pizza box. I didn't even care. I'd give that half to Mush.

Why did I do this? God I wasn't usually so awkward around men. Why was I falling to pieces in front of this guy? Well, inwardly I was falling to pieces, outwardly I feared it was much, much worse. I was behaving like a right cow.

Why, after realising I owed that man – that gorgeous man – after realising that I owed him an apology, why did I accuse him of being a stalker? Why, when I was in the company of him did I become a completely incoherent, arrogant, pathetic rambling say-the-first-words-that-come-into-your-mouth twat? Why did I feel the need to either hide behind the knicker rail or hurl abuse from the pizza aisle in these situations?

Was there any wonder I was single?

My heart sank. Anger was trying to compete with disappointment, to make me feel better. But I couldn't pretend any more. That poor man and his cute dimples had done nothing wrong. Not really.

This was the one time I needed to apologise and mean it. And instead I'd behaved like a spoiled brat having a tantrum in the shops. Twice.

19

I booked one of the small meeting rooms via the online booking system, adding a note that it was to get some 'quiet time for planning'. Given we were only a small team we probably didn't need an online booking system, but we had to be at the forefront of everything, whether we needed it or not.

In reality, of course, I wasn't getting some 'quiet time for planning' in at all. I was actually having an introductory Zoom meeting with Ange from the Lunar Cup company to find out what all this ambassador stuff was about. I hadn't even told Maya. There were seeds of doubt growing bigger and bigger and niggling at my confidence about the authenticity of this meeting. What if it was a rip off? A scam?

What if I was about to appear on some kind of 'Top 10 embarrassing jokes played on idiotic women' YouTube playlists?

But I had to find out, because at the end of the day, if things carried on the way they were, with Jamie treating me like some kind of company outcast, an ambassadorship might just plug the financial gap that was growing steadily bigger.

Besides, there hadn't been any real promotion opportunities for the last couple of years, and, as much as we always got our increments, they were rarely much beyond inflation. In real terms, it wasn't a pay rise at all.

I hovered by the door watching two of the accounts team, Sue and Calvin, finish up their meeting.

They pretended they hadn't seen me – even though there was no way they could have missed me flailing around at the window. I watched the clock move to one minute past and decided that was it. I knocked on the door three times. They looked up, blank expressions on their faces and slowly closed down their laptop. I wandered in, managing not to apologise for turning up for my booking on time.

I took my AirPods with me so that nobody could overhear the conversation I was about to have. At least, they wouldn't be able to hear the spiel about the value and benefits of the Lunar Cup.

I never aspired to be the 'face' of women's menstrual products but then again, perhaps my current embarrassment of it was part of this whole apology business. Why on earth should we be embarrassed about how fifty per cent of the population bleeds every month? The world wouldn't exist if we didn't bleed every month.

I resolved to change my attitude and stop apologising for being a woman.

I should only apologise for being a bitch to fit men for no reason.

It was still playing on my mind. Mush reckoned I should just get over myself and put out an appeal on social media to track him down and apologise very publicly. After all, my social media accounts had grown exponentially in the last couple of weeks. But I wasn't really relishing the idea of potentially going viral again.

Not unless I was getting paid for it.

I closed the door behind me and positioned myself in one of the comfy chairs facing outwards so nobody could see my screen. It was still warm from Sue's backside sitting on it for far too long, and the speck of pastry on the seat was a dead giveaway that they were scoffing Greggs pasties in there too.

I unlocked my ipad. I'd kept the calendar open on screen so I could easily click on the Zoom link. As my face appeared on camera, allowing me the opportunity to check my appearance before joining the meeting, I wondered if it was indeed the right sort of face for such a campaign.

But then it hit me. What if they didn't want my face at all? Given the product . . . what if they wanted . . .

No. Don't be ridiculous Charlotte. Although, as I pondered it, at least then they wouldn't know who I was. I'd be paid for getting my anonymous fairy out.

Ha! Can you imagine? Like, if that TV presenter who hated women in flat shoes saw an ad with actual real blood and ably demonstrated Lunar Cup insertion techniques? And *they* call *us* snowflakes.

I decided not to think about it yet. Hitting the 'join' button wasn't committing me to anything other than a conversation. I tousled my hair, checked my face from about seven different angles then hit 'join' and waited to be let into Ange's meeting room.

Ange appeared pretty quickly. She was young, about my age. Late twenties, early thirties. But she had that London-cool vibe going on. The nineties was back in, and Ange was Kate Moss reincarnate. Naturally cool, relaxed, understated. T-shirt and barely there make-up. I could tell straight away she was oozing confidence.

'Hi Charlotte. Just, bear with me two ticks . . .'

'No worries,' I replied, watching as she wrestled the cutest little fluffy dog off her knee.

'Sorry about that,' she said. 'We've got a new pup. Working from home has its benefits, right?'

'Right!' I said, realising that the word didn't fall out of my mouth as naturally as it did for Ange.

Oh God Charlotte, please don't mirror her speech. It was a nervous habit I had developed. I was once asked if I was Liverpudlian just because Ben's uni mate had been staying with us for a week.

Ange wore her sandy hair long and wavy, oozing beach vibes and adding a grungy kind of look. And her plain white T-shirt was punctuated with a two-layer necklace sporting a heart pendant that looked like it had a pressed flower captured within it.

I could bet Ange didn't apologise for being late when she was held up in a queue ordering her boss' morning cappuccino . . .

Maybe she was her own boss?

We started with a chat about their new product. Ange explained that it was designed specifically for women who had a high or tilted cervix. Apparently they – we – needed something slimmer and taller to 'reach the places other menstrual cups couldn't'. She held up the new model – a lilac purple colour with a cute little pink drawstring case to go with it.

'Have you used a cup before Charlotte?'

'No I . . . ' I had to stop myself apologising. If I hadn't used a menstrual cup before it wasn't because I was lazy or cheap or bad or because I didn't care about the environment. I simply hadn't had many conversations about it. Aside from with Maya – but then Maya is the kind of girl who can snort a condom and pull it out of her mouth as a party trick. If Maya could do it . . . it didn't necessarily mean that I could. It was something I'd read about, but I didn't know too much about how they worked. 'I don't know too much about them if I'm honest.'

'OK. So, you take your cup like this . . . ' Ange was holding the little purple cup by its base between her thumb and forefinger. 'And you kind of fold it in on itself like this . . . ' She folded the cup almost in half. 'And then you insert it like you would a tampon . . . but you don't leave too much stem outside of you.'

I was slightly wary. 'So how do you remove . . . '

'Yes, that's the bit some people struggle with. At first. Once you've got the knack, honestly, it's easy . . . 'Ange explained that you don't pull it by the stem, you push your fingers up around the cup itself and sort of 'pop' the rim away from you, releasing the seal. Apparently, if you pull on the stem in the wrong way, you can weaken your pelvic floor muscles – so that's a definite no-no.

'I'll pop one in the post to you today so you can give it a whirl.'

'Thanks,' I said, desperately hoping I'd given my home address and not the office one. After all Jamie had said about my apparent 'lewdness' I didn't want my menstrual cup being opened by the admin team first thing.

After the demo we talked about what the ambassador role would involve. Firstly, a trip to London for a photo shoot – all expenses paid. They were working with a few different 'real' women, of all different ages, from all different regions, to promote the new cup. I was assured it wouldn't be an 'invasive' photo shoot (what was I thinking? I was hardly signing up to go on *Embarrassing Bodies*!) and that it would simply involve a pic of me, holding the cup and saying something about it.

However, due to my own social media furore, they wanted to capitalise on my social media 'equity' and use the now infamous hashtag – #FindTheTiltedCervix.

Of course, for their national campaign they also had a celebrity lined up – the actress from that show where two of the characters talked about period blood after having sex. That was a scoop! And she would appear with us all on a photo collage of 'real women' who were using the cup. We were to become a tribe, Ange said, of women who knew their bodies and cared for the planet.

I was quite warming to the prospect. Particularly now I had been reassured that I wasn't obliged to be a constant user of the cup. I just needed to try it, be able to use it, and 'believe in its value'.

I could do that.

The shoot was all expenses paid but even better, use of my image was going to land me a whopping £10k fee! That covered my monthly salary like three or four times over or something.

It would be a big fuck you to Jamie. With three months' wages in my back pocket, I needn't take any more of his crap.

I felt both relieved and empowered. That tricky little pink donut sitting high in my vagina was at last being respected. It had nothing to apologise for. And neither did I.

20

The dreaded team bonding day came round before we knew it. And the ordeal was only made worse thanks to Floor 8's invite. It started with a photo shoot. We stood there, donning our brightly coloured branded headbands looking awkward as fuck — an aura of dread radiating off us all. Then, to make matters worse, Jamie had smuggled in a surprise bag of J-Team T-shirts. He was really going to town with this.

He was even in high spirits around me today, which, on reflection, made sense. When I thought about it, he hadn't changed the way he was with me on the office floor. It was only in one-to-one meetings when that nasty streak really came out. It made me angry to think about it. Like, he must've known the way he was speaking to me was all kinds of wrong, or he'd do it in public too. But clearly, he didn't want any witnesses.

Each T-shirt he had brought us to wear was white (typical — at least me and Maya could layer up — we'd already considered this risk factor) with an army style font on the front that screamed *J-Team Army*. Honestly, his lack of self-awareness was really something to behold.

Jamie had asked one of the event staff to take our pic while he positioned himself centrally in the shot, his arms around our huddle as if we were all mates together. 'Right then comrades. Game faces out for the snaps.'

Then he stuck his thumbs up so we all followed suit with an air of resignation.

Our over enthusiastic photographer counted us in. 'On three, two, one, all shout – warriors!'

We echoed her, struggling to hide our reluctance. We couldn't've sounded less like warriors if we tried.

I couldn't believe Jamie was actually making us go through with this. On one side you had us, the J-Team, desperate to just get this over with and have a cup of tea. On the other, competing against us, was floor eight, almost literally chomping at the bit.

Danny was at the front of his 'gang', posturing like a peacock. 'Eat dust loserrrrrrs!'

'The fuck we will,' Jamie retorted, and I could hear more than a hint of nervousness in his voice. I'd learnt to detect it.

We were never going to win at this. We didn't even want to be here. And deep down, Jamie knew it.

Maya elbowed me in the ribs, 'Wonder if *his* team are aware of how fucking cringe he is?'

'Not sure,' I said. 'I think they actually look up to him.'

Although she complained relentlessly in the weeks running up to it, Maya seemed unshaken by the whole event. I think she was keen to get stuck in to be honest. I don't think doing the Warrior Mud Challenge was ever her problem really, I think it was more about who she was being forced to hang out with. Particularly since she'd seen the piggy back challenge on the website. We all got on, sure, but we weren't exactly relishing the idea of getting up close, muddy and personal with one another.

And the idea of being paired with Jamie made my stomach jolt.

I still hadn't told Maya about my appraisal. I was still digesting it all, and every fibre of me was desperate for the get-out clause from Ange and the Lunar Cup photo shoot. I'd pre-booked the time off as holiday, copying in HR to the initial email request so Jamie had no wriggle room to make up some excuse as to why I couldn't take it.

I glanced over to the rest of our gang.

We had mountains to climb, ice baths to submerge ourselves in and, of course, the signature mud to flail around in. Maya and I made sure to wear black – and layer it up. As Maya put it 'there's no way he's turning me into his warped fantasy. Especially not on my own time.'

We were doing it mid-week, but, unlike floor eight, we were having to use a day's flexi to take part. Apparently, due to the cost of the event itself, and the fact it was an 'opt-in' activity (on paper it was opt-in, in reality – it really wasn't), we had to endure J-Team hell on a day's leave. I mean, it just got better and better.

We started off with a scramble over the world's tallest netted mountain. We were timing ourselves – the full team – and keeping score. We had to complete it as a collective more quickly than floor eight, and, frankly, that was never going to work. We watched floor eight tackle it first. Predictably, they performed some kind of Geordie Haka prior to setting off. As the air filled with the cries of *hawayyyyyy*, the first of the participants legged it up the netting like spiders up a drainpipe. They didn't make it look easy as such, we weren't witnessing finesse, more a dogged determination not to come second to us lot.

Trainers were frantically scrambling through the holes in the net, legs and arms getting entangled, then, as they got to the top, they expertly manoeuvred to the other side by grabbing the netting and flinging themselves over in some kind of mid-air flip.

High fives were thrown enthusiastically as they landed on the other side and whoops were screeching through the air.

All of a sudden it was our turn. Rather than a ceremonial dance, we just kind of looked at each other nervously, tried to laugh off our awkwardness and then hurled ourselves at the netting on the blow of the whistle.

Jamie went first of course, accompanied by Maya who was climbing side by side, simultaneously. I bit my lip as I watched them go, seeing Maya take the lead and, even though we weren't officially competing against each other, Jamie would be taking note and brimming with hostility towards anyone who did better than him.

As space opened up the rest of us lurched at the steep wall of net, and I discovered that trainers weren't really made to easily slip in and out of netting. But I guess that was the point. I climbed up at a fair rate, feeling pleased with myself as I flung my legs over the top and descended with relative ease.

Perhaps this wasn't going to be as bad as I thought.

We moved through mud and electric shock wires and weird balancing things that relied on teamwork to ensure the obstacle didn't topple.

Then we came to the mud pool crawl. Under caged wire. It seemed to go on forever. You had to submerge yourself backwards in muddy water, and pull yourself along by wrapping your fingers around the cage. Meanwhile, because the caging was so close to the surface of the water, you barely even had your full face out of the water – almost every part of you was submerged bar your nose, chin and eyes.

As we prepared to go through we were lined up in two, again to go simultaneously side by side. I was paired with Jamie. Deep joy. At least this one didn't involve physical contact.

Walking backwards into the muddy water we both prepared to crawl to safety.

As I started pulling myself along, the ice cold muddy water completely enveloped me. I had to concentrate hard not to give way to a bubbling claustrophobia. I found counting each pull on the caging helped keep my focus, but it certainly wasn't pleasant. Where were these endorphins that were meant to be surging through us?

As I moved along I could see that Jamie, who had initially raced ahead of me, had all but stopped.

'Charlotte,' he gulped as I pulled up beside him. 'Charlotte.' I tried to turn my head to look at him but it was almost impossible without submerging half of my face in the cold water. I turned my face backwards and paused momentarily. Was he trying to get me to slow down so he could burn me off?

'Pretty hardcore this one,' I said, trying to make conversation in the most bizarre of experiences. I'm not sure why I was being pleasant to him after the way he'd behaved recently but something compelled me to be given we were 'on the same team'.

He wasn't smiling though. 'I. Charlotte. I . . . ' He seemed to be gasping as he spoke. I couldn't understand what he was trying to say.

'Are you OK?'

'I feel like . . . like I can't breathe,' he managed.

This was . . . unexpected. He was always so full of bravado I really wasn't prepared for this. Vulnerable Jamie. I mean, what if he was winding me up. I wouldn't put it past him.

'You can do it,' I said, my tone being non-committal to any level of sincerity.

'I can't do it. I can't breathe.' He spluttered again and I noticed he was bobbing up and down a bit in the water, flailing in the most uncoordinated manner. He *was* struggling. 'I think I might be . . . ' he gulped again.

He was *really* struggling.

'Are you having a panic attack?' I asked as calmly as I could. I'd seen Mush struggle with them on occasion. Especially after a big night out.

I remember one particularly bad one. It was while we were at uni doing the things students do. We'd started drinking at about 12 p.m., as soon as the campus bar had opened, which seemed OK given that it was an especially big day in the uni calendar. It was the BUCS sports league and we were hopping from venue to venue watching volleyball and netball and basketball, before hitting the rugby ground in the evening.

By the time we got seated at the rugby we were both feeling pretty out of it, still supping our beers regardless because, well, that's what students do, isn't it?

Long story short, the next day we were sat in the lecture hall and I noticed Mush fidgeting around next to me. I nipped his arm to check if he was OK but he didn't smile, or pinch me back, which was odd. Instead he just . . . looked like he was standing in front of an oncoming train. That was the only way to describe it.

At one point he kind of half went to stand up but then sat back down again. And I could hear his breathing, fast but stunted. I knew something was wrong. Mush was always the life and soul, drunk or sober, and if he wasn't joking around when he was at uni it was a little unnerving.

I scrambled around for my phone in my bag and opened my texts to compose a message. I typed the words are you OK? Do you need to leave? He nodded in response.

We grabbed our stuff, chucked our bags on our backs and ran down the stairs out of the hall. As soon as the door was shut behind us Mush started almost gasping. I was terrified. I had no idea what was happening. But he managed to tell me he was having a panic attack. He'd had them before, he said, but often, in public, he was able to sit on them, to hide them from view. But not this time.

Not after a night of vodka and Red Bull! The caffeine mixed with the alcohol mixed with the endless ciggies we'd smoked (even though we didn't actually smoke) was wreaking havoc with Mush's brain.

We wandered outside and sat on the cold concrete and chatted about daft things, letting him catch his breath and calm back down again. Which he did – eventually.

When it was over I asked him how it felt. He said it was like he was suffocating. Said it was even worse given the fact he was usually so talkative and outgoing. He said it made it even harder to hide it. That people didn't expect 'somebody like him' to have panic attacks.

But Mush was naturally outgoing. He was confident in a kind of relaxed way, if that makes sense?

Jamie on the other hand . . . well, he was always putting on a front. He was keyed up confident with a bucketload of caffeine and a boatload of ego. So I wasn't exactly sure how to handle this . . .

'Jamie?' I pressed him. 'Do you get panic attacks?'

'Don't be stupid,' he spluttered. 'It's not a panic attack.' He was clearly offended by my suggestion but continued gulping and flailing wildly.

'Do you want me to get someone?' I said, wondering if instead he was having some kind of seizure or heart attack or something. After all, we could only really see the tops of our faces, the rest of us was entirely submerged in mud.

'No!' he snapped.

'But if it's not a panic attack . . . '

'Fuck's sake.' His face was almost completely enveloped by the muddy water for a brief moment before popping back out again, that same look on his face that Mush had in the lecture hall. I went to help him but he pushed me off.

'It is. It's a panic attack.'

'But you said . . . '

'Yeah I get them. All right. I just, I need to get out of here!' He seemed simultaneously panicked and angry.

'I'll help you,' I offered.

'But . . . I can't have them all see.'

'Nobody will judge you for it,' I said. I knew from what Mush said that holding a panic attack in when you were in public was a natural albeit difficult thing to do – that it sometimes made everything ten times worse even though it could be scary admitting what was happening.

'Are you kidding? I'll never hear the end of it.' He was shaking so badly at this point he was causing muddy ripples in the water.

'OK,' I said, trying to think about what to do while my boss – the boss I was beginning to develop an innate hatred for – gasped for breath literally inches away from me. But I really felt for him in this moment. I couldn't not.

Luckily we were the last two onto this obstacle so the rest of the team were some way off and probably couldn't tell what was happening, other than realising that we weren't moving towards them at any speed. 'Have you tried counting?' I asked, and moved my right hand while counting *one*, then my left counting *two*, pulling myself along. He followed suit but he was still spluttering. 'One, two.'

'You can do it.' I let him catch up with me then counted us again, we counted and moved in unison. 'Three, four. Five, six.'

He began flailing less and moving more smoothly in the right direction, and we continued counting together, 'Seven, eight.'

It felt as though the bank wasn't getting any closer, because the voices of our teammates still called out as though they were in the distance. There were occasional whoops and 'come on my son' being yelled — which was probably Danny — but the counting just seemed to go on forever.

'Nineteen, twenty . . . '

Jamie seemed calmer as he got in his stride, at least, the water around us felt calmer. I couldn't properly turn to see his face so it was the only way I could really sense what was happening. This wasn't a challenge that was fun for anyone, surely even the toughest of participants would be overcome with claustrophobia doing this. I had had to kick my own mind into gear before I even realised Jamie was in trouble, so when he was thrashing around next to me, chucking more muddy water over our faces, it really wasn't helping anyone.

As we approached the other side of the muddy pit I could hear the team cheering us on.

'Almost there now,' I said, trying to reassure him.

'Aye,' he replied, with slightly less fear and slightly more disdain in his voice. His anxiety had clearly abated somewhat now the end was in sight. And I wondered if being able to help him made him more angry with me, not less. As though there had been a tipping of the dynamic.

We reversed ourselves up and out of the water once the metal railing above us had cleared, opening us up to miles of fresh air and sky. As we clambered up the banks, dripping wet, Jamie grabbed my wrist, holding our hands up in the air in a victorious fashion. I turned to look at him but he kept his face forward towards the cheering crowd.

His game face was well and truly painted back on now.

21

By the time the little coach pulled into the parking space at the front of the train station the sky was a deep petrol blue, illuminated only by street lights and pub signs.

The bravado on the coach had rapidly quietened – a mix of exhaustion, cold and sheer disappointment of coming second to floor eight. Even Jamie was quiet. I could only assume he was contemplative. And David had fallen asleep on Maya's shoulder in the seats in front of me which prompted Maya to relentlessly push him off with a huff every five minutes.

We were like a bunch of kids who'd been taken out for the day to tire ourselves ready for bedtime. The thought made me smile. I guess we did need to rid ourselves of all our pent up frustration, anger and resentment . . .

As the coach doors folded back on themselves making a noise as if they were exhaling in relief, David sat up with a staggered start, blinking and looking mightily embarrassed about where he'd laid his head. Maya was quickly up and out of her seat, impatient to remove herself from J-Team hell, but still blocked in by a sleepy David.

As parkas, rucksacks and puffer jackets were pulled out from the bag stores above, the coach slowly emptied and I felt relieved to feel Newcastle's cold night air on my face.

Thankfully, nobody was hanging around to make the ordeal last any longer, and one by one my colleagues disappeared into the night, some heading to the station, others hailing cabs or wandering up the hill towards town for a nightcap. Jamie, however, hovered uncomfortably by the bus doors as I stepped down onto the ground.

'Have you got a moment?'

'Um, yeah, sure.'

He thanked the driver and the doors fan-folded behind us, letting out another mechanical exhale. We both waved the driver away as he indicated and pulled out into the dual carriageway amidst the city's stream of cabs, cars and tipsy pub goers staggering obliviously across the road.

'I just wanted to say thanks. You know, for before,' he said it quietly, as if he didn't really want the words to come out of his mouth.

'Oh, right. No bother at all,' I replied. 'These things happen.'

'Well, not to me!' His words were abrupt, but then he softened his tone. 'I mean, well, it happens sometimes. But it's not something I want people to know.' He was staring at his feet by this point and I was starting to squirm on his behalf.

'It's OK,' I tried to make light of it. 'It was only a panic attack. Honestly, it happens to the best of us.'

'You get them?' he asked glancing up at me sideways.

'Um, well, no, but a friend does. Honestly, it's nothing to worry about. Well, I mean, it's clearly something to worry about because that's the very point of a panic. I mean . . . it's nothing to be embarrassed about.'

He cleared his throat then took a deeper tone, holding his chin taut. 'It's just that it's not me. OK. I'm not scared of anything. I think, really, it's probably a problem with my bloods or something. Some kind of vitamin B deficiency or something. Probably all the gallons of booze me and Danny get through, you know.' He tried to laugh but it was stunted.

He was re-engaging his primary state of arseholery just as someone jabbed him in the ribs. 'Y'alright fuck face!'

Jamie flinched before realising who it was and firmly pressing his bravado button. 'Evenin' squire. Hahaha, nice one. Yeah . . . Have one for me son!' His attention was taken for a few more seconds as he watched his well-oiled mate swagger off towards the pub by the station. Then he turned back around to face me, a hardened look on his face. 'Yeah, so, I'd appreciate it if you didn't tell anyone about today.' His tone was purposefully unfriendly, but there was a hint of shakiness in his voice.

'OK,' I said, wondering why he felt the need to revert to being such a nasty fuck right at this moment in time. I mean, I could've just left him there, flailing about in the mud, then everyone would have seen because somebody would've needed to fish him out. But, as big an arse as he is, it's not his fault he suffered a panic attack.

He raised his eyebrows impatiently. 'Don't worry,' I said gritting my teeth. 'I won't mention it to anyone.'

He straightened up slightly, lifting his chin. 'Good. Cos it's boss's orders. And you can hardly afford to drop more marks on your appraisal,' he said it with a chuckle before adding,

'Just kidding . . . or am I?' He winked at me then started walking off.

I couldn't believe him. This was beyond the pale even for Jamie. 'Night.' I called, trying to highlight his sheer lack of courtesy.

He waved his hand in the air without looking back.

If there was one thing not saying sorry had taught me, it was that the people who *should* say sorry, the ones who have good reason time and time again to say it, are the ones who are never going to.

Had I been making up for other people's mistakes all this time by uttering that fateful word and letting them know I was a pushover?

I was grumpy, cold and tired, so instead of walking to the Metro I flagged a black cab at the station. After playing dodgems with a few more groups of lads and lasses who seemed to be coming at the cars in random formations from every direction, I was thankfully home in less than ten minutes. I could see the TV flashing through the horizontal blinds in our big bay window and could just make out the fairy lights sprawled lazily over the fireplace. Mush was home.

'Evenin!' I hollered, being hit with a welcome wall of centrally-heated air. I let the door slam behind me, kicked off my shoes and dropped my bag of muddy wet clothes on the doormat.

'How was it?'

'Wet. Muddy. Cold. How was your night?'

'Just got in. Been out for a beer with a couple of the lads from work. Needed to decompress.'

I could tell he'd had a few. He always had a slight light-hearted drawl about his voice when he'd been drinking. He'd been making post-work drinks more of a regular thing recently.

'Tough day?' I asked, nodding to his glass of wine. 'Any more where that came from?'

'In the fridge.'

I grabbed my rucksack and took it through to the kitchen to unload into the washing machine. Everything was so disgustingly wet and slimy I decided to turn the rucksack inside out and wash that too. I lobbed in a ton of fabric softener, a couple of tablets and hit the start button. Then I grabbed the cold bottle of wine from the fridge, poured a glass and took the rest of the bottle into the front room to make the most of what was left of the evening.

'Budge up.'

Mush reluctantly folded his knees to make room for me on the sofa.

'What're we watching?' I asked, grabbing the throw to curl up for the night.

'Not sure,' he said, continuing to flick through every channel and category on every app.

'Just stick some funny YouTube on or something. I could do with a laugh.'

Instead Mush clicked on the TikTok app and, after watching a couple of 'How Brits cope in snow' and 'signs your cat is trying to kill you' funnies, we were greeted with a new video from TimTok. He was reviewing Australian confectionery this time. TimTams or something. Apt name. He reviewed them with some kind of haughty British accent – the joke being that he was pretending they were not a patch on English chocolate, but his face couldn't hide his orgasmic delight. We were both transfixed. I just couldn't equate the two Tims – the one I was watching on screen right now, and the one I saw freeze on stage at a comedy club.

He'd only just uploaded this new video, but already had thousands of likes and comments.

'I feel bad,' I said.

'Why?' Mush asked, topping his wine back up. 'Fancy him again now you've seen his popularity soar.'

'No! I'm not that bloody shallow.'

'For what then? For apologising?'

'No, no! I mean, well yeah, I feel bad for apologising – bad for me! But I mean, it shouldn't have ever got to that stage. I should never have gone on that second date with him just to be nice.'

'People pleaser!'

I chucked a cushion at him almost knocking his wine from his hand. 'Steady on!' he said. 'Anyway, speaking of nice . . . any updates since you last saw your man?'

'Who? Fit manspreader?'

'No, Ed Sheeran. Yes fit manspreader!'

'No. Not seen him since I was a cow to him in the supermarket.'

'Like I said, why don't you track him down on social?'

'I could give you ten good reasons – no, make that 100 good reasons – why that's a seriously bad idea.'

'Go on then.'

'Well, firstly . . . ' I had no idea what to say. Because, while I was relentlessly embarrassing myself in front of this insanely gorgeous man, he *was* insanely gorgeous. And I couldn't deny how much I desperately wanted to snog the face off him. And not only that, I think he was trying to be nice to me before I messed it all up by behaving like some kind of up-myself idiot. But I felt like I should probably admit defeat with this one. 'Well, firstly,' I said, 'he's obviously got a family.'

'Ah but you don't know that. She might have been his niece.'

'She called him Daddy.'

'Oh.'

'Secondly . . . well, I mean, I screamed at him about my smear test and inadvertently turned both of us into unwanted social media sensations.'

Mush opened the packet of tortilla chips that had been sitting idly in front of him waiting to be devoured. He crunched one loudly in his mouth. 'Not strictly true that . . . '

'How do you mean?' I asked, snatching the bag off him and stuffing a handful of crisps into my mouth. I pulled a face and put them back on the table. They were triple-cheese flavour. Not exactly the best accompaniment to Pinot Grigio.

Mush swiped them off the table again. 'If you think about it, you could only see the back of his head. He kind of got away with it.'

'I'm not sure if that makes me feel worse or better. I might have a sponsorship deal out of it. What's he got?'

'Haha you're like some kind of influencer now.'

'I know. A fanny influencer.'

'Ha. Well, whatever it makes you feel, it means you don't need to feel bad for him. Well, I mean, not for the memes and that. You can still ask him out.'

'Er point number one Mush,' I said, chucking my half of the blanket over his legs and standing up. 'He has a kid.'

He tilted his head to one side raising an eyebrow. Then he shifted. 'Just remembered. You've got mail. It's out in the hall.'

I jumped up off the sofa and walked into the hallway, fully expecting a pile of dull letters with typed addresses. Instead, however, I was greeted with a neat lilac package with a hand-written address and the word 'Lunar' stamped discreetly along the bottom. It was the Lunar Cup!

I ripped it open, keen to see what it was I was going to be contending with the next time I got my period. There was a note from Ange.

Here's the model in question. Give it a try – let us know what you think.

Ange x

PS – there's an instructional YouTube video avail-able, just scan the QR code on the leaflet.

I put the packaging down on the stairs and resolved to give it a whirl the next day.

When I got back to the living room Mush was sitting with my iPhone, 'What're you doing with my phone?' I squealed, throwing my arm out to grab it but Mush turned away, protecting it at all costs.

'Nearly done . . . '

'Nearly done with what?'

He was sticking his tongue out in concentration, hitting my screen, obviously typing something out. I wasn't feeling good about this. 'There you go,' he said. 'You'll thank me for this.'

I retrieved my phone, which was still unlocked from whatever he was doing. He'd been in my Instagram.

'What've you done?' As I checked my grid I could see a new post . . . the video. 'But that's already been shared like, a million times . . . ' I said, confused but also slightly relieved.

'Keep watching . . . ' I don't think I realised just quite how tipsy Mush was tonight. Whatever he thought was a good idea now he better be hugely apologetic for the next day.

As my Metro tirade started to filter out from the screen, graphics popped up, an arrow pointing to the back of manspreader's head. #FindFitManspreader.

A familiar haze of dread and mortification quickly toured through my body. 'Mush!' I was livid. He, on the other hand . . .

'You love it.'

'I certainly do not. You're proper pissed aren't you?'

'So? Who're you, my mother?' He chuckled incessantly to himself, like some kind of cartoon dog, while picking his glass back up.

'How much have you had to drink?' I asked, wondering how my so-called best mate had just put me in this hugely embarrassing predicament with a brand new hugely embarrassing hashtag. He had form for it. I'll never forget him tweeting my ex once when we were both drunk in town and I'd nipped to the loo. We'd been reminiscing about past relationships and I made the mistake of suggesting I might have regretted ending my three month romance with Joe from uni.

'I'm gonna delete it,' I said, my fingers poised to make the defensive move.

He jumped across me, sticking his hands over my iPhone. 'No! Seriously. You'll regret it.'

'I doubt it!'

Mush tried to wrestle my phone off me. 'Seriously. When was the last time . . . you've not even . . . your last shag wasn't even . . .'

He was right. I hadn't had sex or a boyfriend in as long as I could remember. Maybe the slightest prospect of either was worth the embarrassment. Besides, I think I was getting immune to it all now. The embarrassment that is.

Unfortunately, I wasn't growing immune to the charms of my unrequited love. And even though inside I felt kind of cringe about what Mush had just put out there, I decided it could stay. *Just in case* there was a chance of making contact again.

22

3rd January 2011

Kel asked me for ALL the details. But where do you start? Kel just kept saying 'start from the beginning. What did he say. What did you do. Who touched who first.'

I tried to shrug it off. I wasn't sure how I felt about going into all the gory details. Besides, now I'd done it, I wasn't sure I felt all that different after all. If anything I felt kinda flat.

I didn't tell Kel that. I'd never live it down. Plus, I think that would make Liam sound bad wouldn't it. Like he was rubbish or something.

I wouldn't know if he was rubbish even if he was. I wasn't sure what it was meant to be like.

It definitely wasn't like it is on the telly. But they tell you that in sex ed. And we definitely weren't doing all the horrible things Cosmopolitan *tells you to try. Maybe those positions they always feature are for more advanced people. Like, when you have your driving test, then you have your advanced get-on-the-motorway driving test.* Cosmo *should make it clear. They shouldn't assume everyone has been doing it all their lives and keep telling them about how to do things like anal or 69ers or whatever when some of us are just learner drivers.*

Had we even done it properly?

I didn't have an orgasm.

He did.

It was his first time too. I know it was because he told me and because I know the other lads were teasing him about it. If he had done it there's no way he would have pretended he hadn't to them.

I'd gone round to his when his dad was out and his sister had a shift at the pub. It was weird when I got there. Because I'd been going round for like four months or something, but this time it felt kind of formal. Because I was there for a reason. A big reason.

I was there so we could both do it.

When I got there he offered me a drink. I asked for a cup of tea. But then realised I probably wasn't meant to do that. So I went to kiss him to distract him from making the tea. I didn't want to snog him after drinking tea anyway.

What was I thinking? I never drank tea at Liam's. Not ever.

It makes everything feel a bit weird doesn't it. Knowing you're going to do it for the first time.

He said we should go listen to some music. In his room. When we walked in he closed the door behind him, like properly shut it, and I couldn't help but think he was doing that in case his dad or sister came home early. My face felt a bit cold at that thought.

I sat on his bed that I'd sat on a thousand times. The same stripy duvet cover that I'd hidden underneath when we mucked around doing everything other than this. Today, getting onto his bed felt like a portal into another world. A grown up world. I lay back and tried to be cool. But my mouth was dry and I wished I'd asked for some water.

Liam put Green Day on and I had to wonder how we were going to have sex to 'American Idiot'. But I didn't say anything.

Then he sat on his bed. And I didn't know whether to say anything or just be quiet. Perhaps if there was an awkward silence we would just get on with it?

We looked at each other and giggled, which led to a kiss, which led to a snog . . . He was lying on top of me but it was like he wasn't letting all his weight press into me this time. As though he was holding off or something. I think he was trying to take it slowly, because I know he came once when he was fingering me and obviously that couldn't happen this time or it would be really embarrassing.

We never, never spoke about that. I pretended I didn't notice.

We snogged for ages, I think because we were both not sure when to turn it into the actual moment. When to commit to going in. But there's so much preparation. Why doesn't Cosmo tell you things like, the best way to take off a boy's jeans? Because it's not romantic. Like, you undo their fly, and then it's a right fanny-on trying to get their legs out the bottom of them. Then they've still got their socks on, which looks odd, but should I take them off or should he have taken them off?

Nobody thinks about these things. In the past, we'd just stuck our hands in each other's jeans. But we couldn't exactly do the sex like that, not comfortably anyway. Cosmopolitan and co really needed to get real and stop banging on about the Kama-bloody-Sutra. We had socks and condom wrappers to deal with before we progressed onto doggy style.

222

Once we'd got nearly everything off, and we were just in our pants, we just lay on top of each other snogging for a bit more. It was nice, actually. And I could properly feel myself getting into it (if you know what I mean) cos from what I've read, you have to be wet otherwise it would just be painful. Like going down a metal slide at the park with bare legs.

I asked if he had a condom and he then had to lean back out of bed to grab the jeans we chucked on the floor and get the condom out of the jeans pocket.

He took his boxers off and he was all hard and this was the first time I'd actually seen one. I mean, not a cock, obviously, but a hard one. I'd felt it under his jeans before, but we'd never actually had it out fully naked in the open.

Once the condom was on we kind of looked at it in its pink rubber overcoat for a moment. Sitting there all good to go. And then we lay back down and he kind of wriggled into position. It hurt a little, but it was nice too.

Liam was dead nice though and he kept asking if I was OK but then almost straight away he came and that was it.

We lay there together, but I could feel him getting smaller inside me and then he just kind of flopped out.

We were both dead silent for what felt like ages. Then he asked if I had come too.

I didn't know what to say. I mean, I hadn't. Had I? I'd know if I had. Surely. I didn't have that hot wonderful pulsing feeling down below. But then again, I wasn't sure if you're meant to on your first go. That's something Cosmo *definitely talked about – G-spots and how to reach them. Like even some blokes who are in their thirties and that can't find them cos people write in complaining about it.*

So I probably didn't have an orgasm. And I think that's probably normal. So I said, 'I don't think so, but I think that's normal on your first go.'

But he looked so hurt, honestly. At one point I thought he was welling up. So I said I was sorry. I told him that it was nothing to do with him, just that my body wasn't used to the sex and it might take a little practice. But then he asked what he had done wrong so I told him nothing. It's me. I just need more practice.

But then I thought – so did he. He needed more practice just like I did. But I didn't have the heart to tell him that. I mean, I was certainly no Angelina Jolie in the bedroom, but he wasn't exactly Brad Pitt either. And it only lasted like a minute or two. And I'm sure that's normal too, for boys on their first go.

Anyway, I decided not to tell him. I thought if I blamed myself, we were more likely to do it again. And I really wanted to do it again.

23

'Charlotte. Char. You up?'

'Huh? What? Mush?'

'You awake?'

'Clearly am now. What time is it?' I yawned and stretched my feet and toes out underneath the duvet.

'5.30.'

'What?' I jolted upright. 'What's happened?'

I tried to open my eyes slowly and focus on something. It was still pitch black outside so I couldn't see much other than the vague dark shapes of the furniture in my room. But Mush had burst in, two cups of tea in hand and plonked himself down on my bed.

I shuffled myself backwards to sit up, still feeling dazed and more than a little confused. He handed me a hot mug. He seemed happy so clearly nobody had died. Nobody we liked anyway.

'Thanks. But. Hang on, why are . . . ?'

'Wait till you see this.' He pushed his phone under my nose but I couldn't make anything out, my eyes were still adjusting to the room, which was shrouded in that miserable winter morning blackness, aside from the landing light that was pushing through the crack in the door.

'What do you mean?' I said, reaching over towards the bedside table, struggling to find the switch for the lamp along the cord that awkwardly hung behind the headboard. The light came on and I instinctively squinted.

'This is big, Charlotte. This. Is. Big,' he said grinning.

'I bet you were a right nightmare on Christmas Day,' I said, taking his phone from him to see what he was getting so excited about.

He had Instagram open. A ton of reels on the grid. All of my viral video. 'What the . . . ? Mush!' Then it all came back to me. I remembered how he'd started it all up again last night after a couple of glasses of wine too many. My heart sank.

'I really wish you hadn't sent that stupid hashtag out last night. I'm trying to get a promotion right now.' I shuffled myself backwards into the pillows to prepare myself for the worst. How bad had it got this time? 'Plus, what if I do something to fuck up the ambassador thing. I mean, remember Kate Moss got caught doing coke and lost those sponsorship deals.'

'Bit of a different league don't you think?'

'Cheers for that.'

'Anyway, I'm not sorry. Not if there's a chance you might find him. You've been proper sulky lately. You need something to put a spring back into your step.'

'Yeah well I can tell you now, you waking me up at 5.30 a.m. is certainly not going to put a spring in my step. Anyway, I haven't been moody.'

'Yeah, right,' he said, picking his hot mug up without holding the handle and flinching. He blew on his tea.

I picked my own phone up and noticed a ton of DMs in my Instagram account, a load of TikTok notifications and a similar amount in Twitter.

'Jesus Christ,' I said, my brain quickly waking up. I showed Mush my home screen with the number of red notification flags on it. My heart was pounding. On the one hand – oh my God. If I had managed to live it down the first time around God knows how I was going to cope with phase two of viral gate.

Mush fidgeted excitedly, slurping his tea. 'Well go on, see if he's there.'

'We've been through this. He's clearly married – or at least shacked up playing happy families.' I sighed. 'And besides, you're forgetting I fucking screamed at the man like a total idiot on a train. I am a train wanker, Mush.'

'But your total idiocy is what makes you so endearing.'

'I'm not trying to be some kind of modern day Bridget Jones you know.' I let out an audible huff and opened my Instagram. 'Ah Mush, see. It's just a ton of fake accounts pretending to be him. Like the guy on the Metro would happen to have an account called Metro Manspreader.'

Mush took it off me and flicked through more of the messages, 'Manspreading Love', 'Manspread4u' – oh my God. 'ManspreadNo1'. Fuck. Perhaps I do owe you an apology.'

'You think?' I snatched the phone back off him. 'And for waking me up at ridiculous o'clock.'

'I'll make another cuppa.' He grabbed our mugs and sloped off, trudging down the stairs clearly deflated, while I went through my DMs deleting and blocking as appropriate. I heard the kettle gearing up for a boil and the cupboards and fridge door being clanged. At least I was getting more caffeine out of it. I'd need to be switched on to deal with this mountainous disaster.

More than anything I was worried what this might mean for my job prospects. I mean, he'd sent the message from my account, well, as a reel from my account. So given that I was trying to keep a low profile in terms of 'tilted cervix gate' he wasn't really helping matters. It looked like I was just stoking the fire. Not letting it lie. In some ways, I was glad the appraisal had taken place before Mush decided to let the world know I was in love with some stranger I'd relentlessly and consistently bawled at in public places.

But as much as this concerned me, and compromised my professional integrity, part of me was exhilarated. Even though he was clearly unobtainable.

There was something urging me to find him, though. To at least apologise. To help me sleep better at night. He, alone, deserved an apology.

That's what I was telling myself anyway.

As Mush's feet padded back up the stairs carpet I had already deleted around ten DMs from ominous accounts, including dick pics.

'The shit you get on the internet as a woman.' I grumbled, while taking the fresh cup of tea which was uncomfortably hot in my hands. I quickly placed it on the bedside table to cool a little and wafted my fingers.

'Dick pics?'

'And the rest.' I showed Mush a link to a Tinder profile belonging to a guy called Steve.

The profile pic was kind of hot, but it wasn't verified. 'Probably a catfish,' I tutted. 'But look at the description. Who does he think is going to go for that? It's like those stupid bloody emails asking you to enter your details in return for a reward from your long-lost uncle from Estonia or whatever.'

'You only know of Estonia because of Eurovision.'

'I was shite at geography,' I laughed. 'Moldova. Azerbaijan.'

'Eurovision.'

'It's the best geography education I ever had.'

Mush grabbed my phone to read the offending profile out loud and winced. 'Generous of heart and cock. Guaranteed to make you smile and scream. Looking for female who can return the favour.' He made puke noises. 'I'm embarrassed at being the same species as blokes like that.'

'I know! And look at his passions.'

He listed photography, reading, movies and spectator sports. Mush wrinkled his nose. 'He's clearly just a big porn fan who just wants some IRL porn. Dick.'

'Exactly,' I said, deleting him. 'I'm not gonna be anyone's pervy fantasy.'

'Cept fit manspreader's.'

'Fuck off.'

'Hang on.' Mush was giggling. 'How can you even view porn fan's profile – unless you're already logged in on Tinder.'

'How can you know that you can't view a Tinder profile while logged out unless you're already on Tinder.' I snapped back.

'Fair play.'

'Oh hang on . . . ' I was deleting several notifications when I came across a normal looking message. 'Who's this?'

Mush leaned in and we both read the DM. It was from a guy called Greg Lancaster. And when I looked at his grid I could see it was him. 'Oh my God. Mush, what do I do?'

'Suggest we read the message before I answer that.'

I flicked back into the message.

Fit manspreader eh? :-)

My heart was pounding. I was raging with excitement, but, even though I was sitting with my best mate, I felt nervous. I didn't want him to know just how hot and bothered this man had got me. 'Seriously. What do I do?'

'Reply.'

'Doh! Course. But I mean, saying what?'

We tossed a few ideas around. Did I want to be nonchalant? Did I want to be excited? Did I want to be apologetic – even after my commitment to never apologising for anything for the rest of the year . . .

'Go into his profile. Find out more about him. Like, is he actually single? Or married? Oh and. . . ' Mush seemed more excited even than me. 'And see if he's said anything about you, you know, from the day it happened.'

'There's not too much on his grid though, he probably uses stories, you think?'

'Aye maybe. Hang on, is that the kid?' We both leaned forward and squinted.

'Yeah. That's the one. Gracie. Isn't she adorable?' I clicked on the picture and read the description.

I frantically searched through more of his pics to see if there was any mention of a wife or husband. I was transfixed. There were pictures of him shielding those blue eyes from the winter sun, holding his little girl up in the air – the blue sky behind him making the scene picture perfect, but there was nobody else in there. No perfect family pics. Just him, him and his mates, him and his daughter . . .

I went back to the most recent picture of them both. And I read the hashtags he'd used. Then I leapt out of bed excitedly in a pyjama-clad power pose.

'He's a hashtag single dad!' I squealed. 'Honestly, that's better than being a cat dad or whatever. Like, he's gotta be a good guy?'

'Why?'

'I don't know,' I said. 'Looking after a kid on your own and all that. Single mams are superstars so he's gotta be too hasn't he. He's a hashtag single dad, a hashtag single dad,' I sang. Mush jumped up to join me at this point, high-fived me and then we performed our dance – the silly one we did when a new episode of *Succession* dropped or one of us got a new job or something. It was broadly reminiscent of some Beyoncé moves crossed with *Saturday Night Fever*.

'Right' I said panting slightly and sitting back down. 'Compose yourself Charlotte.'

I decided to have more of a nosey through Greg's profile – which brought with it much more joy now I knew he was a #singledad. 'Ooh, some reels' I squealed, and Mush moved in to take a look.

I clicked on his most recent reel. 'Guitar player.' Mush said. 'Aye, say what you see, Mush.'

'Yeah, but I mean, it's good isn't it?'

I unmuted the clip and heard Greg clear his throat. He looked kind of shy as he started quietly strumming away on his acoustic guitar. Mush and I both listened intently until we worked out what he was playing.

'It's, it is isn't it . . . ? It's Foo Fighters,' Mush yelped. 'OK, my approval has been granted.'

I elbowed him in the ribs. 'Shh. Listen.'

Greg was playing the opening to 'Times Like These' and, if it was even possible, I fell even harder. 'He's pretty good isn't he?' I beamed, just as Greg missed a note, looked straight into the camera and said 'Oops. Try again.'

'He seems canny,' Mush said.

'He does doesn't he? OK. Let's do this,' I said, navigating back towards the message I'd received. I began typing out a reply . . .

My mate Mush . . .

Nope, I thought. Just own it. Who cares. Delete, delete, delete . . .

I just wanted to say . . .

But what *did* I want to say? Was I really about to break my sorry commitment. No, I couldn't go there yet. But how could I broach this conversation? I mean, he'd added a smile, which was a good start.

> I just wanted to say hi. Properly this
> time. I was just a little shocked in the
> shop the other day. Felt a bit caught
> off guard. Anyway, hope you're enjoying
> the newfound social media fame. Oops x

'Think the kiss is too much?'

'Nah. You said it yourself, you need to be more straight-forward. Especially with people you like.'

He was right. For far too long I'd been the kind of girl who waited to be invited. Who only returned the gaze rather than catching the eye in the first place. 2023 wasn't a time to be shy, it wasn't a time to sit on your arse waiting for Mr Right. I mean, what a load of old shite that was. I was in my prime and I needed to have more fun. On my own terms.

I studied my messages carefully . . . all of a sudden, the word 'seen' popped up and my heart raced. Then, a laughing emoji. OK, this is good, this is friendly.

Then another message pinged through.

> It was certainly a surprise ☺

I typed back . . .

> Was quite a surprise to me, too. X

We both sat around my phone, slurping our tea and watching until he'd seen my message. Daylight started to tease its way into my bedroom but by this point we were too engrossed in Greg Lancaster to worry about getting ready for work.

He typed another back. And then another. We exchanged a few of them and I told him I felt bad for the way I behaved. They were the words I opted for instead of the out and out apology. He said I had no need to 'feel bad' and that we all had off days. He laughed about me thinking he was ignoring me. He had his headphones in. I asked what he was listening to. He added a blushing emoji. He told me it was Taylor Swift though he said he needed to make very clear that he mostly listened to Wolf Alice and Fontaines DC.

This was definite flirting.

I had to go in for the kill. I had to do it.

```
How's about I buy you a drink, to make
up for all the trouble? No worries if
not.
```

Mush grabbed my phone from out of my hands.

'What now?'

'It's one thing saying you feel bad for making the back of his head go viral, but Charlotte,' he pushed the screen in front of my eyes.

No worries if not.

'Oh,' I said, my heart deflating. I was thoroughly disappointed in myself. 'It just came out . . . naturally. I mean, it's not actually the word sorry.'

'Might as well be.' Luckily, Mush had grabbed it off me before I had the chance to click send. I took a breath and deleted those four fateful words. Four words that basically said, here, have a get out. I don't really deserve your time. I'm not worthy. It's clearly going to be a dull experience for you, if not an ordeal. I mean honestly – don't put yourself out.

I did *not* want to go for those vibes. I did not want to give him every reason to say no.

I sent the message minus the get out clause. He either had to say yes or no, end of. And surely we could agree that me buying someone a drink could only be considered a nice thing. A pleasant thing. It wasn't as though I'd asked the guy to marry me, after all.

We sat, guzzling what was left of our tea, watching and waiting for the response to come in.

Sure.

Then he carried on . . .

Need to chat to you anyway. About this newspaper thing.

Newspaper thing?

24

I'd decided on black cropped trousers, Dr Marten's shoes and a crisp white shirt. I felt it gave me the edge I needed while retaining a sense of formality – and an acknowledgement that I was about to endure a grilling and was therefore dressed with an appropriate level of seriousness.

My interview panel – if it even *was* an interview – consisted of Jamie and Harriet. I wasn't even sure why I was putting myself through it. It felt like a pointless endeavour in many ways. But I decided that it was worth letting Harriet see who I really was and what I was really capable of, rather than leaving it all up to Jamie to spin his own version.

When it came to Jamie and Harriet you couldn't find two people more unlike one another. I'd been role playing possible interview questions and answers with Mush, who alternated between the two in his responses.

You know like, if I got the traditional *what's your biggest weakness* question, I'd need to respond in a way that pleased both of them.

Harriet would be over the moon with something like: 'My biggest weakness is my flight of thought. I often think so quickly that I struggle to explain the strategic process involved – but it's always there.' I rehearsed that one over and over – I felt it was a goody.

However, Jamie would probably want to hear something ridiculous. Something he would be happy to hear even though HR would be livid. Perhaps: 'I struggle with my work/life balance. I throw myself so wholeheartedly into my work that boyfriends break up with me, I become diagnosed with a heart condition, I take up heavy drinking at the nearest bar to the office and I keep a duvet under the desk.'

Well. Perhaps not quite that strong but something along those lines. He just liked the work hard/play hard idea – problem was he was only committed to one part of the concept.

My presentation slides were ready to go and Mush had timed me on them. A ten-minute presentation Harriet had said. I'd pretty much got it spot on. It ran slightly over at twelve minutes thirty (Mush averaged it out across three rehearsals) but we figured that would be fine, because I'd probably speed it up a bit if I was nervous anyway.

The interview was due to take place at 9.30 which meant I had an hour of fidgeting and squirming at my desk in advance of the mega-grilling I was about to get in the boardroom.

Maya brought a cuppa over and perched on my desk. 'Nervous?'

'I think so.' I said, readjusting the mug in my hand. 'Yes. I'm definitely nervous.'

'When you're in there, if he's being a dick, just imagine him with his pants down getting his arse whipped by Harriet.'

'Not helping Maya!' I said, sipping my first cup of tea of the day and shaking my head. I didn't want to overdo the caffeine today. I needed to remain calm at all times.

Maya held her hands up and walked off, as though she'd given me the best interview hack in the world. All she'd done was made me feel more nauseous.

I tried to concentrate on some of the emails that had stacked up in my inbox over the weekend. I swear people just scheduled emails to send on a Saturday night to prove they were hardcore weekend workers who never had time off. Jamie was especially good at it.

Then my phone pinged. A text from my mam:

I've just been asked if you and me could do a talk for the whole office. Isn't that wonderful? Xx

What? Why? X

Our new HR lead, Sharon, she's really clued up when it comes to menopause and stuff. She reckons we need more honest conversations in the workplace. With the men too. And she wondered if we could help her launch a series of discussions by giving a talk. Xx

But I'm not menopausal Mam xx

Obviously – but we can talk about how to have conversations about periods and smear tests and menopause. Normalise the conversation she said. X

I decided to let that one hang. I couldn't make decisions about speaking publicly in someone else's workplace while I had issues of my own in my own workplace.

Just then Jamie emerged from his office. 'Ready to prove yourself then?' he hollered as loudly as he could across the banks of desks, alerting everyone to my fate. He was putting on his fake good mood. But letting the wider team know what was coming was the last thing I wanted. The boardroom had glass windows and you had to walk past it to get to the kitchen. It was like an invitation for feeding time at the zoo.

I grabbed my USB stick from my desk and headed into the meeting room. Harriet got there just before me and was already seated. She gave me a brief smile which I returned. I had to wonder what Jamie had filled her in on since the appraisal.

I took a seat opposite and Jamie followed suit, plonking himself in the seat next to Harriet and leaning back in his chair, elbow lazily hanging off the back of it.

'OK,' he said. 'Over to you.'

'I. Er . . . '

Harriet cleared her throat, 'I think we'll start with a little intro to the role first,' she said, shooting Jamie a look. 'I believe you haven't had too much information on what it entails so far?'

Jamie squirmed. Perhaps they weren't on the same page after all.

'Not especially. I mean, I obviously know about how we are expanding into content, that it would be a more senior role and it would report to Jamie.' With that Jamie shifted even more uncomfortably.

'Right,' Harriet said, giving him a sideways glance that he refused to return. 'This will be a new team, *reporting to me*,' she gave him another look. 'It's about providing our clients with more consistency and added value. As you know, many don't have in-house creatives and full service agencies are often too heavily priced. Hence, some of the ads we've been placing on behalf of our clients are . . . how can I put it . . . questionable.'

I nodded, thinking back to Stanton Housebuilders and their reggae themed ad. I wondered if that might have had something to do with all this – although Jamie made it very clear he wasn't happy with me challenging the marketing director on it – and I'd never heard from her since. He had clearly passed the account onto somebody else without even discussing it with me.

'Our brand is on the line,' Jamie added. 'If we associate with clients who perpetuate racist stereotypes, it reflects badly on us.' He raised his eyebrows at me. He knew that *I* knew that this was him sucking up to Harriet and backtracking on his *real* views about Stanton. He'd already given me grief for this. He'd also said before they were one of our most loyal clients and they deserved our loyalty in return. But his eyes were making very clear his position – challenge him and face the consequences.

Suddenly I felt enraged. No, empowered. Perhaps it was both. He had obviously done a U-turn as popular opinion had shifted. I had visions of him bringing it up in the senior management meeting, ready to let rip about how irresponsible I'd been, then having to turn it round when everyone agreed it was in the best interests of the agency.

He was such a slimeball! I decided to ignore his forceful look.

'Yes,' I said, smiling slightly, 'we had an issue like that with Stanton. I informed them that I couldn't place the ad in its current incarnation.'

'*You* did? That's interesting . . . ' Harriet said, another sideways glance at Jamie.

'Yes. And I think that, well, I'm not exactly an expert in content yet or anything, but I do have a good instinct I think. And it just felt very wrong.'

'Instinct plays a big part in creative,' Harriet said, rifling through some papers in front of her. It was a print out of my LinkedIn profile. 'But in terms of expertise . . . '

I was preparing for the ultimate disappointment. She was going to tell me I needed to build up my experience. That she needed somebody who could hit the ground running. I'd heard similar from Jamie in the past so it wasn't exactly going to come as a shock. He said she usually went for new.

'I think you're maybe selling yourself a little short. If we look at . . . '

Jamie, elbow on table, pointed lazily towards me with his finger, his eyes narrowing a little. 'Yes, if you can't sell yourself, how can we be confident in your content selling our clients?'

'OK. Let's move on shall we,' Harriet huffed. And at that point I was wondering why I should even bother with the presentation. It was clear I wasn't going to land the job. It would be one of those slightly encouraging but not *too* encouraging responses, you know like, you're definitely a good candidate for a future role, but not quite ready just yet . . .

'Shall we take a look at your presentation?' Harriet gave me a smile and I definitely detected a tone of apology in it.

'Sure'. I grabbed my USB stick, my voice becoming slightly shaky, and took it towards the smart screen and laptop that were positioned at the bottom of the table. I tried to turn the screen on but then realised there were no cables connecting it to the power socket.

'Problem?' Jamie asked, relishing in the potential hiccup for me.

'There doesn't seem to be a cable,' I said, looking around helplessly and checking the box that it always sits in.

'How odd,' Harriet said, standing up and surveying the room.

'Did you not check the room set-up prior to your inter-view?' Jamie delivered it nonchalantly, but I could hear in his voice that it was definitely something he'd thought about.

'There's usually one here . . . ' I said.

'Yes,' Harriet added. 'It's meant to be kept in here at all times,' she said looking around, clearly irked by the situation.

Jamie picked up his phone and lit up the screen. 'We don't have much time, Charlotte.'

My heart was pounding. This was where I should apologise. This precise moment where an apology needed to float from my lips with authenticity. But I couldn't let it happen. Even though Harriet was now also looking impatient. I'd made a promise to myself. I wasn't going to apologise.

'Perhaps I . . . maybe I could talk through it from memory?' I said.

'Fail to prepare . . . ' Jamie hissed.

'Go for it,' Harriet said, straightening up her notebook impatiently, a bluntness in her voice.

I blundered my way through, remembering the brands I'd picked out, the campaigns. Picturing the imagery in my head, trying to recall the storylines in the ads. It all came flooding back to me.

'Well, that was definitely food for thought. Before we finish up, remind me, have you had your appraisal yet.'

My stomach felt like it was being shaken by thunder. 'I erm . . . ' I glanced at Jamie. He said nothing. 'Yes,' I said. 'I have.'

'Well. . . ?' Harriet looked at me, then at Jamie.

'Go ahead Charlotte.' Jamie put the ball in my court. Bastard.

'It—To be honest, it was OK. I'm not sure it was at my usual stand—'

Jamie put his pen down. 'Her scores have dropped some-what, if we're honest. It might be because she's had her sights set on this role, I don't know. But she's dropped a couple of balls lately.'

I narrowed my eyes. What balls. What was he talking about? The only balls I had any kind of awareness of were the ones under the table between his legs that I desperately wanted to kick right now.

'I see,' Harriet said. 'Right, OK. Well, if you can forward me a copy of the review, Jamie. Then we'll re-group and go from there.'

I knew in that moment, this job was not for me.

243

25

I hovered in the relevant section on the platform waiting for my train. It was the early morning direct train, the one that's always rammed with commuters because it gets you to London just after 9.30 a.m. I watched the coaches fly by me until the train slowed and I could make out Coach C. It moved slightly past the section it was supposed to stop in and I found myself lagging behind a few passengers who were carrying heavy bags or pulling suitcases on wheels.

I was still queuing for my seat as the train pulled away, hovering behind some woman who was fannying around with her bag – putting it in the shelf above the seats, then bringing it back down again to retrieve whatever it was she needed for the journey. I sighed, 'Excuse me'.

The woman turned, gave me a look of irritation and moved into the seat without smiling, allowing me to pass and take my seat three rows down.

I had nothing other than my work bag and a takeaway coffee, so I sat down, got my phone out and tried to relax into the journey. At least we weren't going to be stopping every ten minutes at some other station.

I opened my Instagram account to see a direct message notification. I had been desperately waiting to hear back from Greg since he mentioned this 'newspaper thing' the other day.

He explained that, basically, some journalist had got in touch with him wanting him to sell his story about being called a manspreader. After Mush had put out an appeal to find fit manspreader on my behalf, Greg's account had come to light – one of his friends had tagged him in something. Anyway, this journalist, he said, wanted to write about how *all* men get the blame for *some* men. And there was a fee involved. He would be getting paid for speaking out about being shouted at by a woman for doing something that men are compelled to do – naturally – because of their genital make up. Or something like that. And he wanted to discuss it with me. My heart sank.

All previous thoughts of dates and snogs and taking little Gracie to McDonalds just drained from my mind, leaving behind a stain of bitterness. I'd obviously imagined Greg to be something he wasn't. Then imagined him to be something else he wasn't. Now I was back to thinking I was actually right in the first place and I needed to trust my instincts better. I was gutted.

I texted Mush.

You know this newspaper thing, it's basically a journalist asking him to sell his story. Think I should bail on tonight?

I put my phone down on the table in front of me, waiting for Mush's reply as we hurtled out of Newcastle, the bridges over the Tyne passing by in a blur.

My phone pinged.

```
If he is considering selling his story —
whatever his story is — you need to keep
him onside. You have to go either way. Damage
limitation.
```

The thought of seeing him after the journalist revelation actually made me feel sick. How could he even entertain the conversation if it was all set up to paint women – and me especially – as some kind of ranting banshee, picking on men and their psychologically essential need to sit on a train like they were a cowboy on a horse? But then I remembered I'd already asked him out for a drink – *and* offered to buy the round.

Fuck – what if it was all a set-up? What if he only said yes to meeting me because he had invited a journalist along? Maybe it was all a ploy to get me in a public place and get new video footage of the stupid screaming girl on the train that all of the internet seemed to be either loving for raising awareness of smear tests, or hating on because I was apparently a frigid, man-victimising idiot. Considering half the internet thought I was a hero, and half thought I was 'everything wrong with our snowflake society' I already knew which side any tabloid newspaper was going to come down on.

But it wasn't just my impending doom about meeting Greg that was irking me. I decided I needed to try to get that bloody Lunar Cup in place before the photo shoot that I was due to take part in in precisely four hours' time. I'd tried once or twice at home but then with all the distraction with Greg and the interview and everything I hadn't really given it my all. And the reminders of being a thirteen-year-old awkwardly trying out a tampon for the first time came flooding back. Spending what felt like hours in the bathroom while Ben pounded on the door cos he needed a shit or a shave or whatever.

I decided to have a second cuppa before attempting my awkward insertion in the train toilets. We were just hurtling through Durham when the trolley came round so I ordered myself a cup of tea in a paper cup with three of those little milks because you never get enough – even for lovers of a good old builder's brew.

'Ooh, I'll have some of those choc chip cookies too,' I said, double-clicking the side of my phone to pay.

As the trolley moved along the aisle I poured all three little milks into my cup and tried to squeeze the teabag out with my stirrer, before plonking it in a soggy brown mess on the napkin I was given.

I crunched into one of the cookies feeling like such a phoney. I was heading off to London to take part in a photo shoot for a menstrual cup I hadn't even managed to wear yet. On the two occasions I'd tried I did all the folding-of-the-cup-thing to fit it in, read the instructions back to front and back again and even watched that YouTube tutorial they told me about. But no matter what I did, it just didn't feel right and I panicked and took it straight back out before I'd even got it perfectly in place. Ange said it takes a bit of getting used to, but still. I felt like a failed woman. I mean, we should be totally OK with our own bodies shouldn't we? If I wanted to put something up there and take it back out again I should be the one person who knows how to do it. It was my vagina, my cervix and yet . . . well . . . I realised I was about as unfamiliar with it as I was with the West End of town. I should not feel like an intruder in my own fanny.

I checked the time. I still had two and a quarter hours before I reached London. The weather was miserable, with rain hammering diagonally on the windows as we rattled on past Darlington and through the countryside. I looked up towards the end of the carriage and noticed the green vacant sign was flashing indicating that the loo was free. I knew I had no time to spare to give it another try.

I looked around and asked the older couple opposite if they'd mind watching my stuff then grabbed my handbag and headed for the loo. Once safely inside, I pressed the button to automatically close the door and a sign lit up confirming that it was locked.

I don't know what it is about train loos but you always feel paranoid that the doors are going to swing open and some random will be standing outside staring in at you. I always felt better in a slightly more enclosed space with a good old fashioned dodgy slide lock.

There was nowhere really to store anything so, leaning against the sink to steady myself as the train carriage was jerking along the tracks at high speed, I pulled out the Lunar Cup from my bag, released the drawstring on *its* little bag and held it in one hand. Then, placing the little fabric bag back inside my handbag, I pulled out the lube. Surely, if anything was going to get that thing to sit comfortably against my vaginal wall it was Superslick water-based lube.

I carefully placed a fingertip full of the gloop around the rim of the menstrual cup, then realised I needed to hold onto it whilst unbuttoning my jeans and pulling down my knickers. I carefully balanced the lube on the sink, held the cup in my left hand and did everything else with my right.

Wiggling rigorously my jeans fell to the floor, which panicked me slightly given the fact that I was in a public toilet. But then I grabbed some tissue from the box mounted on the side and placed it carefully on the toilet seat. Then, keeping my back supported by the sink, I picked up my foot, placed my trainer on the loo seat and tried to navigate the purple cup up towards my nether regions – my brain trying really hard to tell my muscles to relax.

It wasn't happening.

Bloody hell.

I tried again. To my surprise, it just went. It slipped in like an oyster slips down a gourmand's throat.

But then I panicked. This was the first time I'd got it into position. What if I couldn't get it out? I'd be worrying about it all day.

I decided to have a practice at removal. Ange seemed to infer that this was the trickier bit. I stretched my forefinger up around the cup and tried to un-suction it. It was so high up. Perhaps if I'd kept up those piano lessons as a kid my fingers would now be strong and flexible enough for such an operation.

Suddenly, I felt it release. But it wasn't a straightforward removal. It came out . . . sideways.

I rinsed the little cup under the sink and noticed that my finger was hurting.

I popped the cup back in its drawstring then washed my hands, before hearing a cautious knock on the door.

'Excuse me. It's staff. Are you OK in there?' It was a female voice. A bubbly female voice with a Geordie accent. It was clearly one of the train conductors checking in. I hurriedly grabbed some towels to dry my hands while she continued. 'We just wanted to check, you've been in there a while.'

'Oh yes. Um. Two ticks, just coming out . . .'

I was mortified. I dumped the paper towels in the bin and immediately opened the door, not wanting to spend any longer than necessary in there. They were clearly suspicious that I was snorting drugs or something.

The short bubbly lady in her train guard uniform was grinning from ear to ear. I was just relieved that the total lack of confidence on my face must've made it very clear I wasn't snorting coke between Darlington and York.

'All good,' I said, my face flushing with heat as I immediately turned to walk back to my seat, moving through the automatic doors that couldn't open quickly enough for me.

I sat back down in my seat and thanked the cute older couple opposite for watching my stuff, knowing they won't have watched it because nobody does, do they, when you ask them to. I mean, what were those little dears going to do if some thief came along and tried to nick my stuff. They looked about ninety.

My finger was still hurting so I bent it and straightened it back up a few times, having to conclude that I'd clearly strained it trying to get the damn thing out.

'We were a bit worried about you,' the lady said.

'Oh,' I said. 'All good, I smiled at them. I guessed it was nice that they cared enough to ask a member of staff to check on me.

I took my phone out of my bag to check my messages and noticed the uniformed train lady approaching me.

'Excuse me miss. You left this in the loo.'

Holding out her hand proudly she waggled my Superslick water-based lube right under my nose. And in full view of the rest of the carriage.

My eyes must've widened like they'd seen . . . the most embarrassing item you could be caught with in a public toilet. 'I. Thanks,' I said, snatching it away and out of sight as quickly as I could.

I hastily shoved it in my bag but couldn't help but notice the little old man watching me, while the little old lady elbowed him in the ribs.

Then it dawned on me. If the whole train knew I was awkwardly trying to insert a menstrual cup in the train toilets that would be embarrassing enough. But that clearly wasn't going to be the first conclusion they spring to.

I sank down in my seat and stared out of the train window.

Why did these things *always* happen to me?

26

The photo shoot was taking place in one of those big modern buildings round the back of King's Cross. It was the kind of workspace that inspired our office and its deck chairs and brightly coloured carpets. But this one seemed effortlessly cool somehow. Maybe because the foyer had so many different things going on and there were so many different companies based inside. There was a reception desk manned by people in T-shirts and jeans and trainers, running around everywhere as though they were on some kind of TV game show mission. There was a little smoothie cart parked up by the floor to ceiling windows, and an endless stream of people coming and going through the main doors.

I approached the reception desk and said I was there to see Talk – the PR agency who were hosting the photo shoot for the Lunar Cup team. They took my digital photo then printed it out, handing me a magenta pink lanyard and case to slip my printed picture into.

I took a seat as directed – apparently Mona would be on her way down to greet me. It was a chance to people watch and try to take my mind off the fact that a whole train carriage of people on the Newcastle to London route clearly thought I'd had a wank in the loo.

Within minutes, my mortifying stream of consciousness was broken as Mona, a small slim young woman in brightly coloured Adidas, black jeans and T-shirt with a graduated dark bob appeared. 'Hey there. I'll take you through.'

I figured her greeting was very much on brand.

I followed her towards the lifts and we went five flights up. By this point I was starting to feel the nerves tingle through me. I was never really a natural in front of the camera, I wasn't even sure why I'd agreed to this. Well, aside from the pay cheque that I definitely needed, of course. But my God, I wished I'd ordered a gin and tonic rather than a cup of tea on the way down. How the hell was I going to blag this.

Mona took me through to a spacious office with comfy seats and people milling around. 'Just grab a seat and I'll let Ange know you're here.'

I sat down and had visions of some photographer telling me to 'work it' in front of the lens. My stomach churned. It was now almost 11 a.m. and, other than that poor excuse for a chocolate chip cookie, I hadn't eaten anything decent since before I got on the train hours ago.

'You made it.' I turned around and saw Ange. I wondered why she was so surprised that I made it to London, but then remembered that the North seems a very, *very* long way from the capital when you don't know it.

'Sure did,' I said smiling, then cringing at my terrible attempt to speak like my interpretation of a creative agency type.

'I used to work here before moving on to Lunar. It's a beautiful space isn't it?'

'Yes,' I agreed, looking around at the trendy army of energetic agency ants, all marching around the floor, each clearly on a creative and important mission.

'Come on through, I'll introduce you to Jen, the photographer.'

I smiled and followed Ange through to another room, feeling relieved that we had a female photographer doing the shoot. I wasn't sure why, but somehow that made me more relaxed. Even though Ange had already confirmed that there would be absolutely no photos of me inserting the cup! The fact I asked was embarrassing enough in itself.

We walked into a spacious studio with a white walled backdrop and lots of camera equipment. There was a rail of clothes and boxes of shoes all lined up towards the front of the room, and cans of pop and bowls of mini wrapped chocolates on a long table.

'We'll get you into make-up first, then Carrie'll help find you the perfect outfit.'

I hadn't realised this was going to be the full shebang. I was starting to feel excited now. This was like a luxury photo shoot that people pay hundreds of pounds for, and instead I was here on an expenses paid trip, being offered pop and chocolate and being paid for the privilege.

I had people buzzing around me, waving my hair, sculpting my eyebrows and contouring my face. They said they liked my signature red lipstick and laid back clothes so that's what they were going to recreate – but obviously they were doing it far more flawlessly than I ever could.

My long dark hair was as bouncy as it had ever been, and my face like alabaster with striking, perfectly lined lips and the odd freckle still peeking through. I smiled at my reflection. I was already feeling far more confident – and secretly delighted at the fact that I would be heading home on the train looking like this and going straight out to meet Greg (who I now hated again but who I desperately wanted to fall in love with me, just because).

'Why don't we keep your Converse, but we'll put you in cropped jeans and a plain black tee.' Carrie was frantically raking through the clothes rack looking for the perfect pair of jeans. 'Here you are. These should fit,' she said, pulling out a pair of cropped boyfriend jeans in a faded blue.

I nipped into the changing area to finish my transformation into . . . well . . . just a more flawless, more stylised version of me, really. I liked it. I had so many visions of them putting me in the most unflattering outfits and painting my face like some kind of doll.

For the shoot, I needed to hold the cup between my thumb and forefinger and smile/laugh at the camera. The photographer made me relax, telling me jokes and stories about some of the models she'd been on shoots with in the past. Nothing mean or gossipy, just fun stories about mishaps and silly dances and eating donuts. I felt like I trusted her to do a good job, to not take pictures that zoned in on my flaws. Perhaps I just viewed them as flaws and she saw something differently? Regardless, she was a real pro.

She snapped away, making me giggle. 'You a cup convert then?'

'Getting there.'

'Been using one for six years. Once you get the hang of it, honestly, there's no going back. Just make sure you break the seal correctly before pulling.' She advised, looking out from behind the lens. 'Sometimes I swear the suction's so strong you could strap menstrual cups to your hands and feet and safely scale Big Ben!'

I giggled. 'Maybe that's the next photo shoot.'

'Perhaps!'

27

The shoot took a little longer than expected and I had to leg it back to the station for my train. Taking my seat feeling sweaty and dishevelled, I was mortified to see the very same train conductor on there who clearly believed I was having a lubricated wank with some sex toy or other in the train loos. The thought of it still grossed me out – I couldn't think of anywhere that would turn me on less. The smell from two carriages away was enough to put you off!

As I settled in for the journey I got a text from my mam, chasing me up about that HR presentation thing at her work.

I just wasn't sure I needed that right now. On top of everything else. I was juggling the day job with this Lunar Cup ambassadorial role. I mean, maybe if I was just all out a menstrual cup ambassador I could join her to talk about that. If the theme of our session was how to talk about bleeding – or not bleeding – then it would totally compliment it. And, although you often saw blokes on Twitter or whatever freaking out because someone mentioned period blood, it was a bit hypocritical. I mean, firstly, nobody had problems talking about giving blood. So it kind of made me think that they were grossed out about where it came from. Yet it comes from the most sacred place of all. It comes from the place of pure joy and wonder.

Secondly, if we didn't have periods mankind would not exist. Period.

Right now, however, although I was getting a decent fee for my Lunar Cup work, it wasn't enough to walk away from the day job. And given I still hadn't heard back about the awful interview with Jamie and Harriet, if it even *was* an interview, I needed to play things carefully.

I was also starting to wonder if I should have told them about this, but how could I have told Jamie? He'd already called me lewd. The prick. There was no way I *couldn't* have done it though because if things went tits up at work, at least I had a few month's grace now with this fee.

I text Mam back to say I was still mulling it over. Then decided to focus on my upcoming date – sorry, meeting – with Greg. I needed a clear head to throw everything I could at deterring him selling his – no, our – story. Having a renewed and intense dislike of someone I fancied the pants off was going to make things difficult. But I needed to keep him onside, to remain friendly to keep things courteous and use my influence – as Mush put it in his latest text.

If all else failed, he said, I could go for the jugular. Thanks to his law firm marketing skills he suggested hauling in words such as 'defamation' and 'women's rights' and 'social media influence' – but I hoped to God we didn't have to get that far.

We were meeting at a bar near the station. I didn't want to go too far after such a long day. I was absolutely dreading it. I knew I was about to be assaulted by a confused mess of emotions.

I felt nervous. And angry that he couldn't be the man I wanted him to be after all this time. The dream I had been savouring for weeks in spite of myself. It still hung in the clouds of my mind, desperate to be true. But reality shone a far different light on the man I should've trusted my instincts on in the first place. I mean, when you consider the circum-stances we met under, and then those highly embarrassing run-ins in the shops, I felt ridiculous even entertaining the idea of romance . . .

But either way, I fancied him like mad. How could I possibly keep that hidden from him?

As I walked in I saw him sitting at a high table on a bar stool. Who chooses to sit at a high table when there are booths free?

I realised I was desperately trying to find reasons to be angry with him. It would help my cause, after all, if I didn't feel confused by my hormones going into overdrive. I smiled and waved, and he smiled back at me from under his fringe, glancing down as though he were shy. Oh my God.

I walked to the bar, shaking myself out of the stupor this bloody man seemed to put me in. It must've been an act. Shy blokes don't sell their stories to the press. He was clearly trying to pretend he was something he was not.

'Dry white wine please.'

'Coming up.'

The bartender turned around to fill a wine measure before pouring it all into a large glass. I wondered if I should have perhaps ordered a double vodka too to keep my nerve. Maybe that would be a bad idea.

As she placed the bottle back in the fridge a thick Geordie voice boomed out from behind me, ''Scuse me love.'

I turned around, fully expecting to see Greg standing there (even though it really wasn't the voice or the words I was expecting) but instead I was met with the flash of a camera that almost blinded me. 'What the . . . ?'

The moment I realised what had just happened the man with the camera was gone and so, clearly, was my picture.

I spun around puzzled and caught Greg out the corner of my eye. Then it dawned on me.

The bastard. He wasn't meeting me for a chat or a date or to 'discuss' anything with me. It was a flamin' set up. I was livid.

'That'll be five sixty please.'

I paid for my wine, picked it up, marched over to Greg, and threw a perfectly fine Pinot Grigio right over his stupid arsehole manspreaderly head.

28

'Sorry Charlotte.'

'I don't even want to hear that word, never mind say it.'

'Sorry.'

'Mush! We agreed.' I slammed my spoon down into my bowl of increasingly soggy cornflakes. 'Nobody should apologise when they don't need to. And there's only one person who needs to apologise to me and he's an actual bastard. And I don't want his apology anyway. He can fuck off with his cheap tabloid story and his stupid long legs and his stupid dimples and his pathetic blue eyes.'

I was livid, and ashamed. Ashamed because, as much as I had vocalised how much of a twat Greg clearly was, a little part of me was grieving the imaginary whirlwind romance I'd created in my head.

What a fool. What a stupid, stupid fool.

'OK. Let's just change the subject.'

'No! You know why?' I was on a roll with my hatred of the man. I grabbed the sugar bowl and sprinkled a full spoonful over what remained of my cereal, as if it was the cereal's fault I'd let it go all soggy and tasteless while being so preoccupied with Greg. 'Because this man deserves *all* the wrath. He's . . . '

'Jesus Charlotte . . . it's doing you no good getting all het up.'

'What do you want me to do? I'm probably going to be in the bloody *Chronicle* or something now. Or the *Sun*! He's gonna be lining his pockets. And I'll not get the job because I've fucked up. Again.'

'Just wait and see. You're seeing her today aren't you?'

'Yeah,' I said, exhaling a rush of disappointment that even sugar couldn't save what was left of my breakfast. I pushed my bowl in front of me and sank into my chair. 'We all know what she's going to say though.'

'You might be surprised.'

'We all know what happens when I get my hopes up. As well as never saying sorry, I'm never going to get my hopes up ever again.'

Mush rolled his eyes and picked his keys up. 'Right. I'll see you later. Positive mental attitude . . . '

'Oh fuck off.'

'Good idea. The atmosphere's dire round here today.'

He gave my arm a friendly nip and headed out the front door. As it slammed shut behind him the house was quiet and I realised I was just putting off the inevitable. I gathered my shit together, pulled my boots on and headed out for the Metro.

I got into the office in just enough time to make a cuppa before my meeting with Harriet and Jamie. Floor eight's feet were stamping hard on the ceiling as I poured water into my cup and today they annoyed me more than ever – their roar making me physically wince.

'Morning Charlotte,' Harriet's voice made me jump.

'Morning. Want a cuppa?'

'I'll grab one, don't worry. You still up for our catch up?'

'Yeah, course.'

'Great. Grab a seat in my office when you're ready. It's just the two of us today.'

'OK, great,' I said, curious as to where Jamie was and why he wasn't joining the meeting. I glanced over towards his office, he was in, so it seemed odd.

I wandered through to Harriet's room, grabbing a pen and notebook from my desk en route, and sat in one of the comfy chairs around the mini coffee table in Harriet's office. Her workspace was so much less 'quirky' than Jamie's. Not in a dull way. It just . . . didn't try too hard to stand out or intimidate you in the work hard, play hard kind of way Jamie's did. She had a couple of nice plants, a stylish desk tidy, and an outfit hanging on a hanger on the coat stand. She was clearly off out for the night. It made me resent her slightly knowing she wasn't going to be emotionally battered by *her* day of work judging by her evening plans.

Meanwhile I planned to go home and drown my sorrows with a bottle of wine.

I was jolted out of my thoughts as Harriet breezed in, coffee in hand. 'Sorry for keeping you waiting,' she said, and I felt that cemented it. There's no way she'd apologise if she was about to deliver good news.

'OK. So. Firstly. let's chat about your experience. You were very apologetic in your interview.'

'Really? But I . . . ' I realised I was about to inform Harriet of my commitment to never saying sorry, but then realised it probably wasn't appropriate so softened my response. 'I mean, I didn't think I had apologised for anything?'

'You can be apologetic without using the "s" word you know.'

'I . . . ' I pondered for a moment.

'Your experience is good, Charlotte. There's no doubt about it. So own that. You don't just need to own your mistakes, you need to own your accomplishments too. You're probably the most experienced person in the agency when it comes to copywriting and social media – especially given your recent exploits . . . '

'Oh,' I said, wondering if now might be the time to actually utter the 's' word. 'About that . . . ' I was fidgeting with my mug in my hands.

'Charlotte, it was bloody genius. I mean, I know you didn't mean to end up all over socials. But you've handled it superbly. I'm impressed.'

I felt my eyes open wide with surprise. 'Really?'

'Yes, really. And I have to ask,' She leaned forward in her chair and picked up her mug of coffee without taking her eyes off me. 'Have you tracked down fit manspreader yet?'

'Well, it didn't exactly go to plan,' I said letting out a sigh of relief at being able to come clean about it, and placing my mug on the table.

'It's become stuff of legend. Maybe you could write a blog about it? For the website?'

'Perhaps,' I said, feeling more relaxed.

I told her all about the messages and the newspaper story and being papped in the bar by some photographer. How she might change her opinion about how good the viral content had been when she sees what the *Chronicle* or whoever it is decides to write.

'But that's my point,' she said in response. 'You can own it. Get the last word in. Stay dignified. You can take this in all manner of directions. I mean, you could be going out there getting us clients in the health sector, or perhaps a new feminist-focused brand. Imagine, Charlotte, if you had a stake in building brands who shared your vision for speaking up, speaking plainly and not being sorry.' Harriet was looking up at the ceiling as she spoke excitedly. I'd never known her to be this animated before. I was starting to feel a little more relaxed, more upbeat, but she still hadn't delivered the news about the job . . .

'So I need to ask you about Jamie,' she said, suddenly looking more seriously. 'What's your professional relationship like?'

'Um, yeah, good, I think.'

'He didn't seem too supportive in your interview. Did you feel that too?'

'I . . . ' It was hard to know how to handle this line of questioning. I mean, on the one hand, Jamie's attitude towards me had changed enormously since I rebuffed his drinks invitation. And she was right, he was off with me in the interview, and the appraisal was a disaster. But then after the panic attack in the muddy water, and his 'boss's orders' comment about not telling anyone, I felt a little bit silenced about anything to do with Jamie.

'Charlotte. Let me cut to the chase here. You can be honest with me. No more pussyfooting around. No more apologetic approaches regarding your value to this company. You need to be able to stand your ground if you're going to join the senior management team.'

'If I . . . the senior management team?'

'Yep. Content marketing director. Do you want the job or not?' she grinned, slurping from her huge oversized coffee cup.

I took a breath that jolted my chest and felt my nose fizzing. 'Oh my God. Well, yes, of course. Thank you.'

'You don't need to thank me. All I've done is see through the bullshit. The things that went wrong in your interview weren't your fault, you do know that, don't you? And besides, you've got talent lady. You just need to be free from the shackles of the current dynamic. Don't get me wrong, you'll have to deal with colleagues being jealous of your new role. Certain colleagues more than others, if you know what I mean.'

I nodded.

'So probably best not to mention this to anyone yet, until I've spoken to Jamie. But I'd like you to lead content, Jamie will continue to lead media buying. In essence, you'll now be peers. And you'll report directly to me.'

I couldn't believe it. I was so happy. My cheeks felt like they were going to cramp with all the smiling.

Harriet explained that she was going to email me a job description which I would review and feedback to her so that I had influence over the function as well as my role. I'd be building my own team with her support. This deserved a celebration.

'Back to Jamie first, though,' she said, her forehead pinching at the top of her nose. 'Has anything happened between you?'

'Between us?' I started to feel sick. I hadn't done anything had I? I hadn't encouraged him? I mean, I point blank turned down his cosy offer of wine and a chat. 'No, I mean, well, how do you mean?'

'I need you to know you can trust me. Somebody's raised concerns. Somebody in the team.'

I couldn't believe it, had somebody actually suggested I had behaved inappropriately with Jamie? Then Harriet added, 'I don't want to speak out of turn but I have to ask. Has Jamie been out of order with you?'

'I, well, Jamie's Jamie isn't he.' I tried to let out a giggle, but it was clear that Harriet wasn't joking around.

'Charlotte. Tell me what happened.'

'Well, I guess I just turned down his offer of a drink.'

'When was this?'

'Before the interview. He said he was going to coach me through it over a glass of wine.'

Harriet raised her eyebrows and shook her head, pointing her eyes at the ceiling. 'And he needed alcohol to do that, did he?'

'I don't know. He just suggested we go for a bottle of wine one evening. Did someone report this? I only told . . . '

'No, actually. It was a concerned colleague who saw Jamie getting a bit too cosy with you at the pub a couple of weeks back. I didn't know this had happened as well. Do you want to make a formal complaint? You'd be very much within your rights to do so.'

'Oh I don't know about that,' I said, wondering how this had become such a monumental issue all of a sudden. One minute it was a problem I was mulling over and over in my head. Wondering if I could carry on working under Jamie. The next it was all about formal complaints. I was going to kill Maya for this! 'I mean, I don't want to get anyone into trouble.'

'But he's perfectly happy to lose you your job by trying to mess up your interview? You don't owe him anything you know.'

'I know, it's just, at the team away day, he seemed so, vulnerable. He was having a panic attack and . . . '

'Look, I'm not being funny, but Jamie's the last person to support anyone else from a mental health point of view. And a panic attack in the middle of a muddy assault course certainly doesn't excuse his behaviour. From what I can gather he made you lot go to that course anyway. I've no sympathy. I mean really, you don't need to apologise for him.'

'I'm not I . . . '

'Charlotte. Please. Think this over. Think about it carefully. You might have got out of it fairly unscathed but it could easily have turned out differently. It could have been worse if somebody wasn't looking out for you. And you're not the only woman in the office . . . '

I nodded and assured her I'd mull it over, before walking back towards our bank of desks, conflicting emotions engaged in battle. On the one hand, did I really want to dampen my job celebrations by raking up all the details of the bad behaviour of my boss.

My *former* boss.

But on the other . . . Harriet was right. It was bang out of order.

As I sat back down at my desk I opened a direct message to Maya.

```
What did you tell Harriet about Jamie in
the pub?
What?
About Jamie being out of order with me in
the pub.
Nothing.
You must have.
Nope.
```

I was confused. Maya would surely just tell me outright. It must have been somebody else who was there. But who? And who would be that bothered. There was only me, Maya, Jamie, David and Pete . . .

I sat in my chair unable to concentrate on anything, peering out across the sea of faces, wondering who it was who had said something. Had somebody else been there? Maybe they came to the pub later on?

Then I noticed a new email from Harriet. Subject header: Stanton Housebuilders.

Shit. I forgot about that. Jamie had said he was dealing with them after I pissed the marketing director off, and I hadn't even considered what that actually meant. Would he blame me? He had finally cottoned onto the fact that what I challenged them on was actually the right thing to do.

I opened the email.

Check out this LinkedIn discussion thread . . .

I clicked on the link wondering what on earth I was going to be faced with. It was a ranty post from the marketing director. She'd decided to complain about her media buying agency. Publicly. And the engagement on the post was through the roof!

Fuck. Maybe I *had* contributed badly to our company reputation?

But I couldn't believe what I found. Bar a couple of replies, it seemed that the whole of LinkedIn were backing us. They said it was time that people stood up to this kind of thing and called it out. And that she should be thanking her agency for sound advice not slamming them on social media. I was over the moon. I should learn to trust my instincts more. Why do I always doubt myself? I realised that anything good I did, I always put down to luck, while the stuff-ups, well those were always definitely absolutely my fault. That had to change.

While I was feeling much more positive about recent events as the day came to a close, I was still no closer to figuring out who had raised the alarm about Jamie. But maybe that could wait. Maybe it wasn't even important.

As I gathered up my bag and coat I decided to try and focus on the positives instead. I had a new job to celebrate! I don't think it had even sunk in yet.

I excitedly text Mush to tell him the news as I walked out of the office, saying goodnight and feeling more uplifted than I had in a while. .

But as I walked into the corridor and hit the button on the lift, I could hear his voice. I craned my body and neck backwards to peer into the stationary room where the sound was coming from.

'Aye. She's been sniffing around for weeks now. Aye. I know. Could totally smash her. Haha. I know. Aye. Honestly thought she was frigid . . . '

It was Jamie banging on about his latest conquest. Perhaps not conquest. Perhaps some poor woman he'd tried his luck with on a night out. He was clearly talking to Danny.

I sighed and looked back up to the numbers on the lift. It was stopped two floors above so almost there. I was desperate to get back home and celebrate. But then I heard more . . .

'Yeah mate. Charlotte's literally gagging for it. Honestly, mate. If I wasn't her boss . . . I know. Ha, I know you would. No, I turned her down. Tried to get me out for sly drinks the other week . . . '

I caught my breath and immediately felt sick.

The lying misogynistic . . . the lift bell dinged and the doors opened, immediately filling the air with the chatter of its human inhabitants, drowning out Jamie's disgusting fairy tale. I stepped in and the doors shut behind me, surrounding me with awkward bodies, nobody wanting to look at themselves in the mirror – or at each other for too long – except for the man and woman from the floor above chatting away about someone they clearly didn't think much of from their office.

I caught sight of my face in the mirror. My mouth was gaping with shock. I knew he was unprofessional, but this? This was something else.

'Cheer up love, might never happen,' It was one of the guys from the floor above, the gap in his conversation about their co-worker obviously inviting him to comment on my face. I wasn't in the mood. I fixed him a stare until he felt uncomfortable and turned back to his female colleague, no doubt expressing what he thought of me with his eyebrows, given the fact she peered around him to get a good look.

I didn't care. This was much bigger. This was far worse than any kind of lift awkwardness.

How could he? Harriet was right. I needed to think carefully about how to handle this. I couldn't just let it go. But at the same time, I had a new job to celebrate. The power dynamic had shifted. And there was no disguising how Harriet felt about Jamie. In some ways, if I just bided my time, I had a feeling he'd be long gone anyway.

But I had a couple of weeks of reporting into him to get through until I started working with Harriet properly. Knowing what he'd said . . . could I really do that?

I decided that, while it needed some careful consideration, tonight there was no way Jamie was going to get in the way of my celebrations. I stopped off at the mini supermarket and grabbed a bottle of fizz and some chocolate.

When I got home, I chucked my keys on the side and presented Mush with a bottle of champagne in the kitchen. He was already boiling the kettle. I switched it off. 'Hey!' he snapped, looking confused.

'We're drinking this, then we're off to town,' I said, grabbing a couple of champagne flutes from the cupboard.

'You've changed your tune since this morning!'

'Guess who got the job!'

His expression immediately changed and he gave me a big hug. 'Eeh this truly does deserve a celebration.' He sat down at the table and popped the cork, filling both glasses half way with fizz, waiting for the bubbles to recede and then filling them slowly to the top as he chattered. 'Tell me all about it then. What did they say?'

'Well, it was just Harriet.' I filled him in on the conversation.

Mush jumped back up and grabbed a big bag of crisps from the cupboard, pouring them into a bowl on the table. I dug straight in and continued chattering excitedly through my crisp munching.

'If we own other people's resentment, or anger, or even just try to diffuse their potential anger, we end up being apologetic when we don't need to be. I can see it all more clearly now. It's like, yes, use the "s" word – but only when you really mean it. And never apologise for being good at something. Women do it too often. It's like we're apologising for taking up a man's role, or being better than them at something. No offence.'

'None taken. I think you're right. I've seen it myself.'

'Right,' I said, enjoying this roll of realisation we were both on. 'We need to make a stand. If we don't realise that we're being apologetic, even when we know we're good at things, or deserve a seat at the table . . . '

'Nothing will change.'

'Exactly.' I held up my glass and we clinked our flutes. Then it dawned on me. Doing nothing means nothing will change.

'Mush. There was something else. Someone told Harriet that Jamie had been out of order with me. You know, with the handsy behaviour in the pub and everything?'

'Not forgetting the indecent proposal,' he added, chucking crisps in his mouth.

'Yep. But the thing is . . . she's asked me if I want to make a formal complaint. And I'm not sure. I mean, it feels a bit . . . formal. And I got the job in the end so . . . '

'You did because you're great!' He raised his glass and we clinked them again. 'But he *did* try and chuck a spanner in the works.'

'Aye . . . ' I lunged my hand into the crisp bowl and scrabbled around, as if I was trying to find a good one. 'I just don't know if I want to be responsible for potentially putting someone out of a job.'

'Look at it this way. You're going to be a manager. You're going to build a team. Imagine if he did it to someone else . . . '

'I'd be livid!'

'Exactly. Be livid for how he treated you. You deserve as much respect as anyone else in there.'

I crunched down on a handful of salt and vinegar crisps, the flavouring stinging the corner of my mouth. I must've been picking at it today. It was a bad habit. A nervous one. 'You know what. You're right. Bang on.'

'I usually am.' He grabbed the remaining crisps out of my hands. 'I think if anything it's a brave move. You got through it, but you're putting your head above the parapet. He needs to be held to account, or he'll just do it again. I mean, you're hardly the first . . . '

He was right on all counts. And that made me feel less anger towards the person who raised it with Harriet. In fact, if anything, I wondered why I'd never raised any of his previous behaviour on behalf of my other workmates. The man was a sleaze.

I knew I had to do it. And somehow, rather than filling me with dread, my decisiveness made me feel powerful. And good. I was going to do something good. I was not going to apologise for the behaviour of my sleazy boss any longer. We'd all suffered because of him. He'd throw any one of us under a bus before he'd take the rap for something. Why had I even hesitated?

'Right, let's go out,' I said standing up and stuffing a few last crisp calories into my mouth to line my stomach. 'I feel like a new woman.'

29

14th January 2011

Today was the worst day in the history of high school. Of any high school. How could he?!

Dumped with a capital D. No, not just with a capital D, with ALL the capitals. I'm listening to 'Don't Speak' by No Doubt as I write this. But then again, I'm not sure I'm sad. I don't think it's sadness. It's a raging anger. And it's not my period – whatever my stupid brother says. Like how would he even know my cycle anyway. And besides, I always sync with Kel and she always logs hers so I know we're not due for another week and a half at least.

We've only just had sex. Not me and Kel – obvs! Me and Liam. I'm not daft enough to think we were in love or anything. But what really, really annoys me is he was the one who was rubbish, if I'm being honest. He was the one who came too quick. And I was left hanging. Like, I was all up for it, then bam, it was over. And there was nothing pulsating for me.

I didn't think too bad of it when it happened. I'd read about it in one of my magazines. There was this whole piece on what men want in bed, and then another on what they don't want to hear.

And in that there was this whole thing about not shaming someone for premature ejaculation. And I wouldn't. I mean, I just wouldn't. Because there are things that happen to girls too. And also, I sometimes felt bad about the embarrassing things that happen to boys. Especially when they get a hard on in the middle of class and then the bell rings and they have to hide their coat over it when they walk out.

There was an awful lot about what men want or don't want in those magazines and not much about what girls want. Typical. I couldn't understand it because they are meant to be girls' magazines but they are like some kind of stealthy boys' magazine when you dig a bit deeper.

Anyway Kel said there's been some rumours that he dumped me because we had sex and I was no good. Me? I might not be Angelina Jolie or anything but come on. It was our first go and I was the one left disappointed. Apparently she was reliably informed that Connor told Becky in the year below because he'd started going out with her and then she spread it round like she had one up on one of Year Twelve or something. I've never liked her.

Me and Liam hadn't even had sex since that first time. I did try to, you know, get him in the mood and stuff. But he just wasn't having it. There was always an excuse. In fact, come to think of it, he'd been avoiding me a bit too. We usually saw each other most nights but we hadn't seen each other as much since then. He was always going swimming or playing football or whatever. Which was obviously just an excuse.

I wish to God I had just said what I really thought at the time. I had been so nice about it all, and he'd got sulky. And yet he's the one shouting his mouth off about our first time.

Maybe I was wrong though? Maybe underneath it all I'm like one of those people who has a high opinion of themselves. Maybe I did everything wrong. Maybe it was something I did that made him come too soon?

I hate boys sometimes. I wish we could just craic on with our mates and lust after fit celebs instead – and not have to deal with any of this shite.

30

When it eventually hit the newsstands, I was prepared. I was wearing my metaphorical hard hat and gloves, and feeling confident in batting away the trolls on social media. Maya had sent me the pic of the front cover and, well, if anything, the photo was kind of flattering. Which reminded me to try and be more relaxed or spontaneous when I knew I was getting my picture taken. It's funny how we try to make ourselves look better by pulling funny faces when in reality, being caught off guard and natural is sometimes a good thing.

What I wasn't prepared for, however, was the headline.

VIRAL SOCIAL MEDIA STORY FAKED

It was in one of the national magazines, which I'd talked Mush into rushing out and buying the moment Maya informed us of the news. I couldn't go after all, I'd have to hide behind sunglasses or something which would just make it even more obvious that I was the girl on the front page.

Yes. They put it on the front page alongside **My brother's ghost had sex with me** and something about a kinky trip to A&E. This was not cool. I wondered if the Lunar Cup ambassadorship might even get pulled because of this?

I tried to understand what the story might be and where it could have come from. How had I supposedly faked the whole thing? What whole thing? Were they accusing me of advertising or something? Maybe because I work in advertising? That must be it. That I had promoted the whole tilted cervix thing with pounds rather than it just being viral-worthy content.

But then why would Greg have sold that as a story? I couldn't get my head around it. Maybe he told them I'd shouted at him on purpose, knowing that somebody was filming? Or perhaps, that the person filming was like a stooge, and I had planted them there. That maybe we were in cahoots and splitting the money from it.

Hang on . . . what money? Why would I fake it? Gah. I just needed Mush to hurry up. It felt like ages waiting to see. And I made him promise not to read it before getting it back home.

When I heard the door open I practically leaped out of my chair. 'You got it?'

'I bought them all,' he said, proud as punch at his approach to damage limitation.

'Mush, that's very sweet of you, but these things are gonna be all over the bloody country. And all over the internet. Anyway, hand it over . . . ' I practically snatched the pages from him, sat down on my chair so hard I got a numb bum, and flicked through the pages furiously, until I found the full story on page four.

Mush was reading it from over my shoulder.

'It's saying I already knew him. Before the video went viral. That it was staged cos I work in marketing. Why would it say I knew him when I didn't?'

'He was there, wasn't he? In the pub, when the photographer papped you.'

'Yeah but . . . '

'So they clearly thought you were out together.'

'Well we were, at least we were meant to be, but why would he tell them that? Firstly, cos it's not true, secondly because . . . '

'Hang on. Are you *sure* Greg sold this story?'

'He said he'd been offered money for his story so . . . '

'Yeah but look here.' Mush pointed to a couple of paras in the second column. 'It says here that you were snapped in the pub together. That you were in it together.'

'So that's obviously what he's told them. Oh my God, Mush, what a dick. He's basically made out I'm a liar just to get the money.'

'Well he is a single dad, perhaps . . . '

'There's no good explanation for it. How dare he? He's made us both look like liars for the sake of a few quid.'

'But would he do that?'

'Oh don't tell me you've still got the nice guy idea in your head. He's already blown that theory wide open. He's a stranger isn't he? We don't know him from Adam. He could be like that Dirty John guy off Netflix. You know, that dude who conned all those women . . . '

'Ha – we'll call him Dirty Greg from now on.'

'Exactly.'

'But Char. It says here that they caught *him* off guard as well.'

'It's all an act. It's all been a set up. This is the fabricated story.' I hit the pages with the back of my hand. 'Not the original one.' I pushed the magazine away from me. It felt like every time I took one step forward with something, the internet or the media – or Dirty Greg – pushed me 567 steps back again.

'But look,' Mush pointed to a smaller pic in the article. It was of Greg at the table. 'See.'

'See what?'

'He looks like he's been caught out too.'

'Clearly a good actor then.'

'Seriously. I don't think your theory is correct. I think he was just as surprised as you to get papped in that bar.'

'But why would he tell me about selling a story.'

'He didn't though, did he? He told you a paper had approached him to sell a story. He never said he wanted to talk to you about actually selling it. He said . . . '

Then it dawned on me. I had put two and two together and made five. Mush was right. He did look surprised. And shocked. And a little angry if I was being honest. Just like I did.

'Message him.'

'And say what?'

'I don't know. Just ask him. Ask him why he set it up. See what he says.'

I pulled out my phone and went to message him. 'Shit. Mush. He's blocked me.'

'Why has he done that?'

My brain was racing at a thousand miles an hour trying to piece it all together. 'I chucked a drink on his head didn't I?' I chucked my phone onto the table on top of the offending magazine article. 'Fucking hell, Mush. I have never in my entire life been so horrible to a person. And what if you're right? What if he's . . . ?'

'Right. Leave it with me,' Mush said, picking up his phone.

'What're you going to do?'

'I'm sorting this once and for all. I'm messaging him. And you're going to apologise. Jesus, Charlotte. Forget a year of not saying sorry – you need to put this right before you can move on.'

He was absolutely right. First of all, I'd screamed at him on the Metro. Then I hid behind the underwear in the department store. Then I accused him of following me in the supermarket. Then I chucked a drink on his head and stormed out of the pub leaving him sitting there like some kind of drowned bad date. But I was still struggling to get my hopes up. Or perhaps it was easier to still think of him as the bad guy – that way, I hadn't lost anything. 'Don't forget he still might have set this up for all we know.'

'Yeah. And he might not have either. In fact, I've got a better idea . . . '

Mush explained the plan. I was indignant. 'No, absolutely not. No way.'

'You've got a lot to be sorry for. If you really like him, you're gonna have to.'

'But I made a commitment.'

'Yeah and we talked about that. It's not about never saying sorry, it's about only saying sorry when you mean it.'

'But what if . . . '

'What if what? Seriously, just do it.'

31

It was out there. Charlotte Thomas was sorry. Charlotte Thomas was more than sorry.

Charlotte Thomas hadn't unsuccessfully tried to dive out of the way of a drunk woman with an espresso martini. Charlotte Thomas hadn't apologised to her male boss for refusing to go for after work drinks with him. And no, Charlotte Thomas hadn't apologised for being a woman.

Charlotte Thomas had apologised because she absolutely meant it.

It wasn't even just in text. It was a huge graphic with the words in bright red.

I'M SORRY GREG X

Beneath the graphic was simply a hashtag #FindFit Manspreader.

Social media went wild for it once more. It was everywhere. There was no way it couldn't get back to him. He might have blocked me, but he couldn't block the entire internet.

Charlotte Thomas was sorry. And Greg Lancaster needed to know about it.

Out of everyone in the world, if there was one person who deserved my apology it was him. The very man who started all this.

After an initial burst of excitement, however, I was still blocked. There were local radio interview requests coming in, and Twitter polls running to decide whether or not we'd get together. Whether or not the magazine was right and it was all a set-up. And whether or not I deserved to be forgiven.

All in all, positivity shone through. Well, except on Twitter where everyone decided it was a huge set-up and I was the world's worst human being. But generally, people wanted a love story.

Then it happened. A message. On Instagram. From Greg.

```
For what? For the time you accused me
of being a stalker? Or the time you
chucked a drink over my head? Or was it
the time you screamed at me on the Metro?
```

My heart sank. I held the phone out to Mush.

'Look, he's messaged you,' he said, trying to keep my enthusiasm up. 'He's taken the time to unblock you and message you. He's a bloke. He wouldn't be doing that if he didn't want to hear back from you.'

'What shall I say?'

'Say yes – you're sorry for everything.'

I typed in my reply.

```
Yes. I am sorry. For all of it. I've
been a cow. I know you don't have to
forgive me. But . . .
```

'Shall I just do it? Shall I just ask him out? Again?'

'Aye, why not. What's the worst that can happen? He'll block you?'

'Ha.' I carried on typing . . .

```
But if you do forgive me, I'll buy you
a pint to make up for it. And not pour
it on you . . . xx
```

We sat waiting. The 'seen' notification popped up below my message. I saw him start typing. Then stop again. Then start again.

'Mush, if he's taking this long to decide . . . '

'Just . . . wait and see. Remember you thought this about the job too.'

I put the phone down on the table, turned it upside down, and tried to ignore it. Then I picked it back up, my mouth dry in anticipation. Still nothing.

'I've totally fucked it up haven't I?'

'I don't know. But on the bright side, you've got a new job and a paid ambassador role. This time next year you could be on *I'm a Celebrity . . . Get Me Out Of Here.*'

I was barely listening to Mush. I was too preoccupied. Why would someone do that? Why bother blocking you, then unblocking you, having a go, then letting you hang in abject agony after you'd said your apology and asked them out. My heart was in my mouth and I felt sick. Like there was all this emotion charging around inside my ribcage, churning me up and making me feel both really bad and really anxious at the same time. Was there still a chance? Had I really – properly – pissed him off for good this time?

My phone pinged and I nearly fell off my seat grabbing it in such a frantic move. It wasn't him.

```
Charlotte. Are we doing this presentation
together or what? X
```

I knew I was in bad books when my mam opened a text with my name like that. I rolled my eyes and typed out a reply.

```
Sure, whatever.
```

I really couldn't face being on anyone else's naughty list right now.

It pinged again. I picked it up with a sigh. But it wasn't my mam this time.

```
I'm not sure it's a great idea TBH. I'll
ha . . .
```

My heart sank. It was a half-finished message. He'd obviously clicked send before he was supposed to. But it was clear that he wasn't interested. Sometimes sorry doesn't make everything better.

32

I spent ages reading and rereading all the pages on the employee advisory website. *How to raise a formal grievance.*

They all seemed to be suggesting that it's best to raise the problem with the person in question first of all. That made me feel sick to my stomach. I mean, I'd already told him I thought it was inappropriate to ask me out for wine to talk about a job. And his response was to behave like an absolute cock in my appraisal. And then try to jeopardise my interview.

But what I overheard in the corridor. That was another level.

Nah. I'd given him the opportunity. I wasn't going to make excuses. Apologising wasn't just about my obsession with the word sorry. It was about not standing my ground, not standing up for myself.

Not standing up for others.

There was a revelation as far as the 'whistle-blower' was concerned too. Turned out it was Pete. I honest to God wasn't expecting that. I don't know why, really. I guess maybe because he's a bloke. But that wasn't exactly fair.

I ended up just asking the question of David and Pete. I asked them on direct message. I didn't fancy putting them on the spot face to face.

David replied with a simple 'no' and asked nothing more about it. But Pete, he replied instantly.

```
Yes it was me. Sorry if it made you
uncomfortable. It's just that you looked
really uncomfortable in the pub that
night.
```

I explained that I did and thanked him, but I did wonder why that was all it took to raise a grievance – even if it was just an informal heads up. It transpires he's been there too. In a previous job. One of the older senior managers kept asking him to stay behind to work late. Except there were never any urgent deadlines or specific priorities to attend to. Nope, the perverse old cow just wanted her young employee to stay behind with her. And things got a bit . . . inappropriate.

He knew the look, he said. He knew how the dynamic of manager and employee could make things difficult. He left his job. He never even put in a complaint. Said he didn't feel comfortable doing it, but has regretted it ever since.

He also said he didn't want to bother me with it because it was a grievance against Jamie. Not against me. And why should I be made to feel uncomfortable for something someone else has done.

Now it felt as though I was doing it for Pete too.

I started typing my letter. Subject header: Formal grievance – concerning Jamie Potter.

I didn't really know where to begin. I mean, there was so much. And it had escalated so quickly. The relief I felt when I began typing the events, though, was enormous. Seeing it all in black and white just felt . . . justifying. All these little things build up and it's like you become immune to them. As though they don't matter because alone they're not too much. But then they go by and get bigger because there's no consequence. Because we're all acclimatised, I guess.

No more. I was standing my ground.

The website said you should think about what a satisfactory outcome would be but, to be honest, I had no idea. I no longer felt threatened by Jamie, the power dynamic had changed and suddenly he seemed so much smaller. I knew Harriet could see straight through him, and we were both going to be reporting into her now. Peer to peer not manager to subordinate. But what if he does it to someone else he manages?

I wasn't sure what I wanted. Trying to get people the sack really wasn't my bag. If I grew up feeling sorry for lonely broccoli on a plate, there was no way I could simply switch my empathy level to minus ten – even if Jamie had been an absolute arse. But I knew that it needed to be acknowledged. I knew he needed to be told that he couldn't carry on like that. I didn't want his head (or anything else) on a plate. I needed him to not do it again to another woman. It's like every little thing, on its own, isn't that big a deal, but when you put them together . . .

No. Most of these little things *were* big deals on their own. He needed calling out. He needed to apologise.

I needed to hear him say sorry. And then, whatever else happened after that, well, that wasn't down to me. That was out of my hands. And I felt pretty comfortable with that to be honest.

33

'I can't believe I've agreed to do this.'

Mush glanced up from his cereal bowl. 'Aye, but your mam's done loads for you over the years.'

'Yep but I've never asked her to stand up in front of a bunch of people and talk about her fanny. . . '

'No, but you kind of brought the topic to the forefront. Personally, I think Mother Thomas is a pioneer of her generation.'

'Give over. She's only giving a talk about the menopause.'

'Then why are you so worried about doing your bit?'

It was a fair point. Mush drained the milk from his bowl as if he was drinking from some mega-sized mug and grabbed his keys. 'Come on then.' He was giving me a lift to my mam's work. It was based out of town, but he didn't need to go too far past his law firm's offices to reach it. The difference in backdrop, however, was stark. One minute you're on the Quayside, the next in industrial warehousing. Still, her office was on the edge of the Ouseburn Valley which was pretty cool. Packed with microbreweries and up-cycling stores and cool little arts places. Not that me mam will have been too taken by those. She was a house dry white wine girl through and through.

'Good luck with fanny craic,' Mush hollered from the car window as loudly as he possibly could. I flicked him the Vs and watched him zoom off down the road towards his permit-only multi-storey parking by his posh office. It was all paid for by the company, of course. It made sense for Mush to drive to work and back. Me, not so much.

I walked up the hill of the industrial park until I reached the sign for Mam's work. I'd been here a million times before as a kid. She'd worked here for ever. Since I was about seven or something. But in those days the only things I would have been exhibiting were pasta pictures I'd made in playschool or dodgy self-portraits from Year Seven art class. This was a whole other ball game and I felt sick with nerves. All of a sudden I had to be this other person. This pretend person who was all over the internet, when, in reality, they all knew me as the little girl who had unwittingly created some kind of phallic symbolist artwork using pasta and a paper plate as a kid.

There seemed to be a long-running theme blighting my life.

I walked up to reception and told them I was there for the women's wellbeing talk. The lady on the desk had been with the company for seemingly ever too. I recognised her from the pasta plate days. 'Your mam's ever so proud of you lovey.' She beamed at me as she called upstairs to let Mam know I was here. She was pristine. Silk blouse and hair styled to within an inch of its life, settling on her shoulders in a layered style that barely moved as she did. She put the phone back down and smiled. 'She's on her way. Want to grab a seat while you're waiting?'

She gestured to the grey fabric corner sofa and I sat on the edge, by the water cooler and the front doors to the building. I watched the digital screen rotate PowerPoint slides – no doubt some kind of internal comms thing. There was something about *slips, trips and falls* with a big black boot hovering over what looked like a banana skin – only it was in mono so I wasn't totally convinced. I grabbed a little plastic cup of water and waited with just the slides for entertainment.

As one slide disappeared from view, I saw the promo for our little double act.

Women's wellbeing at work event.

A deep dive into menstruation, menopause and bossing your smear test . . .

Oh sweet Jesus. Bossing? Since when did Mam ever use that word? And deep dive? Surely she's had some grief for that?

I knew there was going to be Mam introducing things, then a talk from a menopause expert, then our little bit – consisting of my mam talking about her menopause experience, and me discussing smear tests and my now famous tilted cervix.

I heard the lift clunk to the ground and the doors were barely open before I heard her. 'Hi sweetie!' She practically bounded out of the lift, beaming from ear to ear. 'Isn't this great, a mam and daughter partnership event.'

'Just . . . you know. Don't say anything too embarrassing will you?'

'And I thought your generation was supposed to be the most liberated?'

'Yeah, I mean. Just, you know, no embarrassing mam stuff.'

She tutted at me and shook her head dramatically as we headed into the lift and hit the button for the fourth floor. It pinged way too quickly for my liking but at least this was it – I'd have it done and dusted within an hour then I could get back to . . . ugh. What exactly. Waiting for a response to my complaint and lamenting over the loss of the great Greg Lancaster love affair.

I was ushered into a chair on the 'stage area' – as Mam called it. We were speaking in what looked like a kitchen area for staff. It was buzzing, I'll give her that. Mind you, as office manager she was also in charge of topping up the milk and ordering the chocolate biscuits, so I could see why she was so popular. Plus, if I'm honest, I couldn't've asked for a better mam. Everybody loved her. And she wasn't that embarrassing. Not really.

She introduced Miss Menopause – a menopause educator who gave talks in workplaces. I had never really thought about the menopause before. I guess I just thought there were hot flushes, then you just stopped bleeding. End of. Period.

But no . . . there was intermittent bleeding, spotting, long periods, short periods, periods so heavy they stain your bed clothes. Mood swings, libido changes, anxiety, panic, depression . . .

It all sounded miserable . . . until she mentioned something about a woman's mid-life crisis being a time of new horizons and adventure and excitability. I quite liked that.

At least I did until me mam got up and started banging on about her sex drive! I had to concentrate really, *really* hard on the pattern of the floor tiles to stop myself being overwhelmed with nausea. And what was my mam doing fancying that bloke off the telly when she should have been fancying me dad?

I guess I just always thought of her as a mam. I never really considered she was a woman in her own right. Then she talked about some of the problems she went through during menopause and I literally had no idea. Hysterectomy, fibroids, panic attacks on public transport. I felt a pang of guilt shudder through my chest. Nearly thirty years old and I was still seeing my mam as some kind of 2D cartoon character parent. I made a mental note to ask her how she was more often.

Then it was my turn. After the applause for her menopause talk died down she took a deep breath, smiled over at me and made her announcement. 'And here's the girl who brought the tilted cervix to the fore! My lovely daughter, Charlotte.'

As I went to stand up my mam dashed to the laptop and fiddled with something on the screen, which I thought odd seeing as I wasn't using slides or anything.

I stood in position taking my spot in front of all her work colleagues and then it hit the room like a gigantic bubblegum explosion. The unmistakable pop sound of the Spice Girls.

Oh. My God. I couldn't help but glower at her like a sulky teenager. Everything I'd just told myself I now considered null and void. Mortified didn't cut it.

I stood in my spot ready to speak but she continued playing the song at full volume. 'Who Do You Think You Are' was in full swing and showed no sign of abating. I let out a giggle through gritted teeth, remembering that awful time when I was dragged up onto the stage on a family holiday by the Elvis impersonator and had to literally just stand there as he warbled some song at me. A slow song. It was excruciating.

Dear God, mother, please don't play this song in full.

After what felt like an age, she finally turned the volume down, looking incredibly pleased with herself. I tried to compose myself. 'Well, um, thanks for that Mam.' I tried to make light of it. My voice sounded unbearably mouse-like and hollow after the nineties pop parade.

'Hehe,' I shot her a look as I faked a laugh, reminding her not to interfere any more in this talk. 'Yes, so, my mam reckons I'm like one of the Spice Girls because one in five women have a tilted cervix so . . . '

'And doesn't she look like Sporty Spice with her long hair?'

'Mam!' I snapped, rather too loudly, before shaking it off and reminding myself that I wasn't a teenager. 'Um. Haha. Yes, so basically, one in five women have a tilted cervix and apparently I'm one of them. And apparently, according to my mam, the odds are on one of the Spice Girls being one too.'

It conjured a ripple of giggles from the audience, who had been sitting fairly quietly until that point. Seeing their faces made me relax, and I wondered if perhaps I should thank my mam after all.

I took a breath and began my talk . . .

'It all started when I realised that I had literally apologised for being a woman . . . '

34

Walking into the office knowing that Jamie knew that I'd filed a formal complaint felt strangely liberating. I thought it'd make me feel smaller. But I knew, 100 per cent, that I was in the right. I had nothing to apologise for. I only wish I'd done it sooner.

The weight that lifted after making the decision was unbelievable. I hadn't realised how much strain all this Jamie stuff had put on me for so long. I was constantly on edge, constantly treading on eggshells, trying to say the right thing even though I was continuously responding to the wrong thing.

Everything about the way he had behaved was wrong.

I chucked my bag underneath my desk and threw my keys and phone on top. Jamie was passing by and I saw him look up at the clock, clearly aggrieved that I was in late. He didn't say anything though.

I'd cleared the whole Mam HR presentation thingy with Harriet. I didn't want to risk being accused of being 'lewd' again for talking about real life. Honestly it almost made me laugh now. I didn't look at Jamie and feel threatened. In many ways I felt sorry for him. It was all a bit pathetic, really.

I pressed the on button of my Mac and let it fire up as Pete's head popped up from across the desk divides. 'Cuppa?'

'Ooh go on then,' I said. It was like we had this whole new bond. Not the nicest of circumstances to bond over, but it's strange isn't it, how you can work with someone and, on face value, you're convinced you've got nothing in common, but when you dig a bit deeper, the thing you do have in common is so much more powerful than wearing the same brand of trainers or dancing in the same clubs.

My emails were busy with rate updates from a couple of media outlets, a new brief from a long-term client and, ah, an email from John – Harriet's counterpart.

I hadn't really had much to do with John before, so it was a bit of a surprise that he was taking on the 'investigating officer' role in regards to my complaint. But then again, I did read in the policy that it would be somebody neutral. However, his email went on to say, it would be unlikely that we would need to go through the formal process, as he had been author-ised to inform me that Jamie was leaving the company due to a more senior role with another agency. However, he would be very happy to sit down and discuss any further action I might need to take, or to arrange any additional support I might need.

My chest deflated in a mixture of relief and disappointment. I had got myself all geared up ready to fight my corner. I'd decided to make a stand and to unapologetically hold my slimeball of a boss to account. And now it seemed he was getting away with it.

Or was he? Was he *really* leaving for a better job? Just like that? It didn't seem likely.

At least I knew I had done all I could. I'd taken steps, I'd acknowledged what was wrong. I couldn't take on a whole world of Jamies. I'd done my bit. And, even if he wasn't formally held to account, perhaps he'd think twice and save someone else from having to constantly bat off his unprofessional, inappropriate, disgusting sleaze.

He was on his way out. And I was on the up.

'Here you go.' Pete returned with a cuppa. 'You OK?' he asked, perching on my desk.

'Yeah. Well. I think so. That complaint I put forward isn't being investigated . . . '

'You're kidding me. See this is the problem, this . . . '

'No, no, I mean. It's not being investigated because, well, I don't suppose I'm meant to tell anyone so strictly between us,' I felt I could talk to Pete like this now, 'Jamie's leaving.' I whispered.

'Hallelujah!' he whispered back. Then he clinked mugs with me as we quietly sat in a moment of peace.

'Thank you,' I said. 'You know, for . . . '

'No need. It's what we all need to do. Look out for each other.'

I nodded, then noticed an Instagram message pop up. But not just any Instagram message. I couldn't help but get distracted when I saw a new direct message from Greg Lancaster in my phone.

'I'll leave you to it.' Pete smiled.

I opened the message.

```
Sorry Charlotte. The bairn distracted me.
I left the messages in drafts. Sending
now . . .
```

Oh . . . ? This was . . . interesting. I was meant to be the one saying sorry – now here he was just dropping it in. Clearly not everyone had the same hang ups as me.

I waited, desperate to see what the full message was going to be. My heart in my mouth. Butterflies zooming around my belly as though they were powered by high-speed engines. What was the original message. What did he intend to write. Then it came through . . .

```
I'm not sure it's a great idea TBH. I'll
have to think about it . . .
```

If he needs to think about it . . .

```
I mean, I've got my dry-cleaning bill
to consider . . .
```

Dry-cleaning bill? He's clearly still angry. Is he just toying with me? Can't say I blame him after everything. Including his apparent dry-cleaning bill.

I saw the little grey dots appear, indicating that my romantic fate was about to be revealed. I braced myself for disappointment . . .

```
I've thought about it. Yes. That'd be
lovely X
```

I jumped up out of my seat, my arms thrown up in the air like a champ, completely forgetting myself. The entire office looked over, in anticipation of a new client account win or something.

I immediately felt daft. But after all I learned, I decided to embrace it.

'Fit manspreader said yes to a date. With me!' I squealed, bursting with excitement.

And it seemed the entire office had followed my emotional, angst-ridden, rollercoaster of a quest to find the man of my dreams. One by one they began clapping. Maya stood up and whistled. Pete nodded admiringly. And Harriet popped her head out of her door, whispered to someone, then hollered 'Get in there Charlotte!'

And that was exactly what I was going to do this time. I was going to go all in. No messing. No pretence. Greg Lancaster was about to find out that I wholeheartedly, unapologetically, fancied the pants off him.

35

I knew he wouldn't be seeing it on the first date, or possibly ever, given my track record with Greg so far . . . but there's something about a trim and edge that makes me feel more confident. And so if I wanted to make it to date number two, I decided I needed to do some lady-gardening beforehand. I wanted to feel good – for me, not for him. So I booked in for my usual – a not-quite Brazilian.

My favourite salon was reserved for special occasions. And this was a special occasion. Ripping your stragglers out with wax wasn't exactly a low-cost affair, but it'd be worth it.

My usual beauty therapist was away for some kind of Valentine's break with her fella or something, so they booked me in with Frannie. I'd never met her before, but I thought her name rather apt. I felt reassured. Especially when I saw her and noticed the care she took over her appearance.

She had that young dewy skin that shimmered – but without giving away any preparation secrets. You might truly believe that she was naked from a make-up point of view – if you could ever believe somebody over the age of eight could possibly have skin that nice.

'Can I take your coat and bag?' she said as I followed her into one of the little treatment rooms, her hair swishing like Holly Willoughby's

'Thanks' I said, unwrapping my scarf and removing my coat.

She placed them neatly on the little chair. 'So I think from your notes you've had the Brazilian before?' she asked.

'Yeah. Well, I always call it the not-quite-Brazilian.'

'OK.'

'As in, a fairly generous landing strip.' I clarified, feeling slightly nervous at her dismissal of my obvious desire to provide instruction.

'Sure,' she said. 'Just pop your jeans and things over there and pop these on. I'll be back in two ticks.' She handed me one of those fucking awful paper G-strings and left the room. I never understood the point of them but, what the hell.

As I struggled with my boots and tight jeans, flashbacks of my smear test lodged themselves in my brain.

Never apologise for being a woman.

On reflection I felt a glow of warmth towards that nurse. She might have been matronly in attitude but my God, it was the kick up the arse I needed.

Or should I say the speculum up the fanny.

I knew my lady parts were perfectly wonderful in every way, and today, I was paying homage to them. I was showing them how much I respected them by treating them to a spruce up.

I wiggled my way onto the bed, complete with my strange paper G-string, and pulled the soft fluffy towel over my nether regions. The G-string an exception, everything else in this place was like a five-star experience compared to the blue paper towels and stained ceiling of the nurse's room at my GP surgery.

There was chilled music playing – some kind of new age hippy stuff that you could barely hear but that forced you to slow right down, and the lighting was low and soft.

I lay back, my head on the comfy pillow, and breathed in slowly. Bikini waxes were never exactly enjoyable but they did everything they possibly could to help you relax.

There was a knock at the door. 'All ready?' she shouted through in her perfectly polite voice.

'I am,' I shouted back, wiggling my bum a bit more to make sure I was as comfortable as can be before the stripping commenced.

'I'll give you a complimentary head massage to relax you before we start.' This was my favourite bit. Although I sometimes wished they did it afterwards. But still, I got the point of it was to make the whole hot waxing experience less painful.

She wafted a couple of tiny bottles of essential oils under my nose. 'Just tell me which you prefer' she said, switching it out to another. It was like a fiesta of peppermint and lavender morphing into jasmine before becoming something altogether more deep and musky.

'They all smell delicious,' I said, feeling like a novice at a wine tasting event. 'I'll go with the first.'

I closed my eyes as she gently massaged my temples and I felt myself close to drifting off to sleep as her fingertips carefully moved my skin in slow circles. I hadn't felt this relaxed in as long as I could remember. It was the perfect antidote to Warrior Mud Challenges, job interviews, appraisals and viral posts . . .

Clear. Your. Head.

I tried to clear all the stress from my head but then Greg's smile popped in there. Oh my God I was actually going on a date with him. I had to stop myself from smiling. I didn't want Frannie thinking I was getting off on her massage.

I decided instead to plan my shopping itinerary. The Lunar Cup fee that had just hit my bank account meant that I could really spoil myself today. I was definitely going in jeans for the date, I needed to be understated. And comfortable. But I definitely fancied something new. A pair of nice new boots maybe. And I wanted to check out the new top I saw online.

Before I'd had chance to remember which shop said top was in the massage was over and I was ready for the main event.

'OK, I'll just dab a little on first to check the temperature.'

'OK.'

She placed a small amount of pink goo on the top of my leg with a wooden spatula. 'How's that?'

'Good,' I lied. It was always slightly hotter than I expected it to be, but I thought, if it's hotter upfront, I'll be compensated with less relative pain when it gets ripped off. That was my reasoning anyway. I thought it probably clung better to the hair the higher the temperature.

'OK,' she continued painting the hot pink gloop over my bare skin. 'Special occasion?'

'Date,' I said, immediately feeling slutty. 'Although, well, it's a first date so it's not, you know . . . '

'Lovely,' she said, carefully tapping the edge of a piece of wax to check if it had hardened sufficiently.

My thoughts shifted and I wanted to kick myself for being so lame. Who cared if I wanted to sleep with someone on a first date? It was my prerogative, surely? I mean, we'd been chatting loads. We'd shared a rather, ahem, heated moment on the Metro. We had history. Even if we didn't – I could sleep with who I goddamn liked. Just because I was a woman I wasn't going to feel guilty about that.

My inner feminist only temporarily rose up as I quickly realised that I was lying on my back, legs akimbo, paper G-string barely covering my bits to painfully preen myself for a man. The way we're told we should.

But I preferred myself preened. Didn't I? So wasn't I doing this for me more than him? Or was it only because women's mags told me I should prefer myself hair free and silky smooth?

And who is actually telling the women's mags that's the way it should be?

How do you know, I mean *really* know, if you are being genuine about your own taste when it's all been influenced by magazines and *Love Island*?

Did I even know who I really was?

Besides, I probably wouldn't *actually* sleep with him on our first date. And that was my prerogative too . . .

Frannie suddenly jolted me out of my imaginary identity crisis. 'Off anywhere nice then?'

'Just a drink.'

Jeez Charlotte, your date-night craic had better be more interesting than that.

'Well I'm sure it'll be lovely,' she said, tapping away at the now hardened wax.

I realised that this wasn't meant to be interesting conversation anyway. It was just an exchange of well-used sentences to get through the awkwardness of having to chat to a stranger while you've got your fanny out.

'Can you just pull your skin taut here . . . that's right. OK. Breathe in.' She was physically preparing me for the first moment of pain. The one that's always worse than you remember. 'Now breathe out in three, two, one!'

'Eeeeeehhhhhh,' I said, wincing. 'The things we do, eh?'

'I know. I'll work as quickly as I can. Just tell me if it gets too much.'

'Sure,' I said, wondering exactly what good that would do considering what she'd covered me in had to come off at some point regardless of the pain. Maybe they had sedatives in the cupboard.

'OK, and in three, two, one . . . !' As she repeated the process over and over I looked up at the ceiling wishing there was some kind of stain or dodgy ceiling tile to focus on. Unfortunately, this place was just too damn chic.

'Right then, can we have you lift your leg up now?' Frannie said, moving to the bottom of the bed. This was the most humiliating part of the Brazilian experience, the removal of inner bum cheek fluff. But it was the least painful and signalled the end of your vanity ordeal.

A couple of minimally abrasive wax strips later and it was all over. 'There you go.' Frannie said cheerfully. 'All done. I'll leave you to dress.'

I breathed a sigh of relief and sat up as she waltzed out of the door but then I looked down.

What in the actual . . .

My not-quite Brazilian was certainly a not-quite Brazilian. But not in the way I'd hoped. Not in the neat, ever so slightly wider than normal landing strip. No, this wasn't a softer approach to the most popular fanny wax trend.

Even the most experienced Big Jet TV pilot couldn't land on that landing strip.

A Beatles song immediately popped into my head . . .

'The Long and Winding Road'.

OMG.

I looked like I needed a ruler.

I sat there with my mouth open, gawping at the disaster when I heard her knock. 'OK to come back in?'

I was livid. She was a professional. She had seen the state of it and walked off as though everything was OK.

'Yep, you better had,' I said.

She opened the door. 'Oh, I'm sorry, I thought you were decent . . . '

This was exactly the moment I'd normally grimace, say thanks and vow never to return. Or, if I was feeling particularly bold, I might have apologised and gently suggested I must've moved mid-wax, suggesting I was at fault for a wax job that had left me with a halfway house between a thunderbolt and a boomerang. But that – I reminded myself – was the old me.

Today, I needed to be firm, but kind. I needed to make very clear that this wasn't acceptable, but at the same time, she seemed dead nice, and I didn't want to go to town with my newfound consumer-warrior head on. After all, we all knew what happened last time I tried that approach . . .

'The landing strip is . . .' I started, standing up and removing the towel from my nether regions. 'Well, it's not exactly straight . . . ' I said, pointing at my bits while trying to maintain an air of dignity and compassion for all involved in this disaster.

'Would you like me to straighten it a little with the tweezers.'

'I think it's gonna take more than tweezers . . . ' I said, as firmly and kindly as I could. I was so mortified by the state of my lady garden I didn't notice the reddening of her face . . .

'I'm so, so sorry. I'm new, I . . . ' Her words wouldn't come out and I noticed that tears were welling in her eyes . . . I was now lying part naked on a bed with a crying beauty therapist.

'Are you OK?' I asked, concerned but, in all honesty, wondering why *I* wasn't the one in tears.

'I'm sorry you hate it,' she sobbed.

'Well, it's . . . '

She let out another big sob and sniffed hard. 'I'll get my manager,' she said, and immediately left the room.

What was I supposed to do at this point? I was waiting for a personal inspection by the manager. I lay still where I was, feeling more exposed than ever knowing that I was about to be given a once over to check if my fanny met with trading standards.

Within moments there was a knock at the door and Frannie appeared alongside her manager – who was as bubbly as Frannie was before I gave her some kind of nervous breakdown.

'Hi there. I'm so sorry to hear you're not satisfied with your wax,' the manager said, her dark brown hair tied up in a neat bun and her presence clearly intimidating Frannie who cowered behind her. 'I wonder if I could take a look?'

I lifted the towel back up again in preparation for quality control . . .

'Oh. My. Yes. I'm so sorry.' She continued looking over it. Why did it need such close inspection? Meanwhile, Frannie stood by the door, tissue to nose, clearly ready to run should she start sobbing again.

I started to feel guilty. Perhaps I shouldn't have made a fuss of it all? I'd clearly upset the poor girl. But I was paying for a professional service. It was both physically and financially painful. And I certainly wouldn't feel confident on a date knowing that Frankenstein's monster was lurking under my knickers.

No. I would not apologise. This wasn't my apology to make.

'OK,' said the manager. 'Frannie is new with us and I know she is really upset that this has happened.'

I nodded, slowly grabbing for the towel thinking that perhaps it was time to cover up, move on and grab some hair removal cream from Boots . . .

'It's always tough starting a new job,' I said softly. Frannie managed a smile and her manager seemed placated by my reaction.

'Yep, you should've seen the aesthetic disaster I created the first time I had to do brows,' she said, joining in with the '*don't be too hard on yourself*' but '*let's acknowledge this as a fuck up, make it better and move on*' approach.

She continued. 'I'm not sure I can straighten it without removing it entirely . . . Hollywood do you? And perhaps I can give you a free treatment to make up for your trouble?

'That'd be lovely,' I said.

'Lash lift? Or brow shape and tint?'

'A lash lift would be lovely, thank you,' I said, secretly feeling smug that not only was I getting the most expensive bikini wax for the price of a Brazilian, but I was also getting my face preened too.

As I removed the towel and flashed my bits one last time, I realised that this was the perfect time *not* to apologise. Nobody should disrespect my fairy. Least of all me.

36

The music was blaring out from my iPad, which was balancing on my bed amongst a wide variety of outfits I'd pulled from my wardrobe before discarding them all in a heap on top of my duvet. As I built myself up to the tricky eyeliner stage of applying make-up, I couldn't help but smile. This was really happening. We'd cleared the air. We'd gotten over our awkward (to say the least) moments. He already knew I had a tilted cervix and we hadn't even been on a first date yet.

Our first date was tonight. And I couldn't bloody wait.

I applied make-up every day. But there was always an added level of jeopardy when applying make-up for a very important date. Should I wuss out and use the smudgy pencil, or really go for it with the confidence of a liquid liner?

I picked up the liquid liner and steadied my left elbow with my right hand while my left hand carefully hovered over my eyelid, preparing for the right time to touch down and strike with the black-inked little brush.

One, two, three . . .

I had committed pen to skin. Mind you, it was always easy to get the first one right, matching the flick to the second eye was where the real tension arose.

'Mush! Mush!'

'What?'

'Can you check my eyeliner?'

His head appeared round the door moments later as I tried to study my work in the mirror. It felt like it might be a success.

He crouched in front of me and carefully studied my face. 'Look straight at me.'

I kept as perfectly still as I could until he said 'Perfect. You'll knock him dead.'

I smiled and my breath caught in a whoosh of excitement. 'Eeeeh can you believe it. I've *finally* got a date with him. No newspapers. No hiding. Just a date.'

'Yep, thank God. Your escapades were close to being made into a bloody soap opera. And I really didn't want to be starring in it.'

'You love it,' I beamed as he left me to crack on with the finishing touches. He was out tonight too. Not a date though. He was off to play Ghetto Golf with his workmates.

My phone started vibrating. Mam.

'Mam. I'm just—'

'You're on speaker . . . '

'Why? Who's there?'

'Just your dad, lovey. We want to say good luck.'

Oh. I forgot I'd told her about the date. Big mistake.

'Thanks. I'm actually just . . . '

I heard dad clear his throat. 'Your mam said he's a nice fella this, Graham . . . '

'Greg.'

'Aye. Him.'

'OK. Um . . . '

'Lovey . . . ' Mam had obviously forced my dad back into the background now he'd said his bit. 'Just don't jump to any conclusions. You know. Don't assume negative intent.'

'What?'

'It's a thing they say at work. In conflict training.'

'I'm off on a date I'm not about to start a fight . . . '

'Well you just make sure to remember that this time. The poor fella.'

'Eh?'

'Glass of wine all over him. The poor . . . '

'OK Mam. I've got to go . . . OK, yes, OK, bye then, bye . . . '

Bloody magazine article.

I turned the volume on my iPad up a bit and threw my wardrobe back open and it was as though it was meant to be. I'd never even spotted it before. My fitted plain white T-shirt. It would offset perfectly against my eyeliner and, oops, nearly forgot . . .

I found my favourite red lipstick in my handbag and struck a perfect pout in the mirror to apply it. There. Strong eyes, strong lips, my long brown hair in a high, messy bun, and a plain white tee and trousers. I felt good.

We decided on somewhere local given that we must live literally a few yards from each other. How had I never spotted him before that fateful morning?

I closed the front door behind me and breathed in the winter air. It was cold and dark but every window and shop and car light looked like a starry twinkle tonight.

I walked down the street with a jaunty spring, wholly acknowledging how smug I must've looked to late night commuters just getting home after a long day's work – having seen daylight neither at the start nor the end of their shift.

The pub was just filling up, and I hoped we'd be able to get a quiet table where nobody would be looking on at the viral couple from the internet. Ha, I wondered how we might fare if we ended up in one of those weekend supplement blind date features. How would he score me?

I walked in and craned my neck to see if he was there. The bar was only one row deep, and there seemed to be a mix of students getting ready for their night out and people marking the end of their working day. Then I noticed something out the corner of my eye. There he was. Looking absolutely bloody gorgeous. Better than ever.

He was wearing a khaki long-sleeved top, with just a few buttons down the front. The material clung to his arms just enough, outlining his toned muscles without being too showy. Be still, my heart.

He waved at me from a corner table, the huge screen behind him on the wall playing the Winter Olympics. We wouldn't need to watch that. I was sure we'd have tons to talk about. It wasn't as though we needed an ice breaker or anything!

I signalled to him that I'd just grab a drink but he picked up a glass of wine signalling back that there was no need. I walked over, and suddenly felt shy. I was looking at him differently today. Today, he was my date. And I could feel my smile breaking through and my cheeks flushing as I caught his eyes and quickly broke away in a moment of nervousness.

'I got you one in . . . ' he said, nodding to the glass then looking straight back into my eyes. My breath caught in my chest and I felt fuzzy with infatuation.

'Thanks,' I said, taking a seat and immediately a sip of the chilled wine. It was a large glass. And it was a Pinot. 'How did you guess my favourite?'

'I didn't guess it. I got an unmistakeable taste of it when you chucked a glass over my head last time.'

I felt ashamed. 'I'm so . . . '

He grinned at me. 'No bother. I reckon we're past all that now.'

I couldn't stop smiling, my cheeks were beginning to hurt from it, like I was sucking on a fizzy sweet. We sat kind of grinning inanely at each other for a few seconds before bursting out laughing.

'So I guess we've kind of already broken the ice,' I said, taking another sip of confidence from the glass.

'Aye,' he said, supping his pint and looking up at me, never breaking eye contact. He was confident. And beautiful. And I couldn't quite believe we were here. Together. On a date.

And to think it all started with me screaming at him. 'You know,' he continued. 'I was never going to go ahead with that newspaper thing. I never entertained it. I just needed you to know about it.'

'I figured that out,' I said. 'In the end.'

'I had wondered if we should turn it on its head, do something in response to it. But I guess I wussed out.' He looked down at his pint, his fingers wrapped around the bottom of the glass, twisting slightly. He was as nervous as me. Vulnerability could be so damn attractive.

I was over the moon to see those dimples reappear. He glanced away briefly, clearly feeling a bit shy around me too. He was never arrogant. He was never smirking all those times. He just . . . he just liked me back all along . . .

'So we've already spoken about your anatomy,' he chuckled. 'Maybe we should backtrack . . . tell me about you.'

'Well, I . . . ha, where do you start, you go first . . . '

He tilted his head to one side with the sweetest look on his face. 'Shy all of a sudden?'

'I can be, you know.'

'OK, I'll go. I'm thirty-one. I er . . . I like football but can't play it. Similar state of affairs with music. And, well, I guess the big thing . . . '

'You're a dad,' I said assuredly.

'How do you . . . ah. Instagram. Our entire lives are out there aren't they?'

'And the department store.'

'God yes, of course,' he giggled silently. 'That feels like an age ago. After everything . . . '

'We've had a few false starts haven't we?' I laughed. 'Listen. I really am sorry . . . '

'Honestly, you don't need to . . . '

'No, really I do. I was an absolute cow. I, well, the day I screamed at you. On the Metro. I'd just realised that I had been apologising for literally *everything*. And I was so angry with myself for being so, well, pathetic really. And you were unfortunate enough to walk directly into my line of fire . . . '

'Mind you, if you hadn't screamed at me we wouldn't be sat here, so . . . '

'True,' I said, smiling at him nervously. 'You know, I made a promise to myself that day never to apologise again for a year . . . '

'Ah right.'

'But I needed to break it cos I'd been such a . . . '

'You *were* a bit of a cow.' He picked up his drink and I could see his ribs trying to stifle laughter. I hit his arm playfully and knocked his drink slightly.

'Sorry . . . !' I said, as he put his pint down and I noticed he had froth on his top lip. 'You've um, you've got some . . . ' I leaned in and wiped it from his top lip, feeling like I was in some kind of cheesy romcom. 'That was kind of cheesy,' I said, my cheeks flushing. There was a beat. It was both heated and slightly awkward all at once. Because I really felt like I could kiss him there and then. But I wanted to savour that inevitably wonderful moment. I wanted to feel like this for a while longer. 'Tell me about your daughter,' I said.

'Gracie. She's a little radgie, bless her. Who said girls were less bother? I've never known anyone with so much energy.

A right little tearaway.' He beamed. I smiled back just as he added, 'Gracie's mam . . . she . . . '

'You don't have to tell me.'

'She passed away. Nearly three years ago now. Gracie was only two and a half.'

'I'm so sorry.'

'It was a short illness . . . brutal but it still gave her time to tell me I had to carry on without her.' His mind seemed to wander before he shook himself away from his thoughts. 'But, that's a story for another time. And anyway, you need to tell me about you. We're on a date! No need for maudlin stuff on a first date is there?'

He pushed his sleeves up from his wrists and for a moment I realised I was just staring at his arms, thinking things I definitely should not have been thinking. I had to shake myself back to the moment before he thought I was ignoring him.

I grinned. 'OK. Erm. I'm twenty-nine. I live with my best mate Mush, who I went to uni with. Work for a media agency. And I just got promoted.'

'Get you!'

'I know. Amazing really after all the social media controversy. But yep. It's in the bag so . . . '

'Well congrats' he raised his glass and I clinked my wine glass against it and I felt so relaxed. I was almost glad we'd gone through all the ridiculous things we'd gone through before reaching our proper first date. Because right now everything felt perfect. Right now was *exactly* where I wanted us to be.

But then I glanced up at the screen, no longer seeing the bobsleigh racing that greeted me when I first walked in . . .

my actual face must've dropped to the floor while my digital face lurched forward on the big screen, a little purple cup on the palm of my digital hand.

Charlotte Thomas knows where to find it . . .

Oh. My. God.

'What is it?' he seemed concerned. My face must've spewed horror. He twisted his head to see what was bothering his date. The date that was going so well until now. 'Oh . . . ' He turned back to face me, raising an eyebrow.

All I wanted was to find the remote, turn the TV off and crawl under the table to hide forever. I hadn't considered this. I hadn't considered big screens in pubs with my face about ten times bigger than it should be and that unmistakable little purple cup. I hadn't considered that news of my tilted cervix was going to accompany me on pub crawls whenever there was a big game or event being televised. I hadn't considered Greg Lancaster seeing me on a big screen while I was feeling coy and daydreamy. But there we have it. In order to secure a sustainable investment in broadband and, more specifically, Disney Plus, I had given my tilted cervix to the world, signing over my rights for it to be broadcast on every big screen in the land.

I looked around me. The pub was full of blokes. They couldn't've cared less if I was on the screen talking about fannies. I smiled. Someone really fucked up the media buying spots for this campaign.

I don't know how I was expecting Greg to react. I mean, I guess he wasn't going to be embarrassed – we'd kind of maxed out on that front already. But there was something about the way he laughed that told me he was happy to be in the no shame club with me. For the first time in a long time there was no 'sorry' trying to escape from my mouth. I took a look – a proper long look – at Greg. And the smile on his face told me that I had absolutely nothing to apologise for.

Epilogue

3rd August 2023 | *Confessions of a difficult woman* | *Lifestyle*

Sorry not sorry

I never intended to start a blog. I didn't think I had much to say so it never crossed my mind. But then the whole tilted cervix thing took off online and I realised that I had actually been saying far too much by not saying enough – if that makes any sense? And the moment I started being 'difficult', well, that was the moment I realised that it was the only way to chip away at the barriers that women face. Compliance only makes such barriers stronger and harder to crack.

Difficult women are a necessity. Sure, men can be feminists, but we can't rely on men to effect change. If we want actual equality rather than just bumper-sticker slogans, there are two things that, from my recent experiences anyway, I believe hold us back.

The first is imposter syndrome. We wonder, relentlessly, if we really deserve our place in the office, or in the bedroom, or sipping mineral water and working up a sweat in the gym . . .

Often, we don't believe we do, which is why we sometimes feel almost as though chance got us past that interview or that it was a fluke that time we ran a 10k.

So we feel out of place and awkward. Flapping around like some kind of beached mermaid, unable to walk with confidence – or sometimes at all – into a room. So instead we become stuck, staying closer to the water, knowing we can hide ourselves if we need to. Because we've learned to be encased with imposter syndrome – reminding us how feminine we are but honestly, have you ever tried to walk in a full length fishtail dress and heels?

I've spent my entire life feeling like a trespasser, an imposter, a fish out of water. It's not something that's simply confined to the workplace – regardless of the fact that most books on the topic are to be found in the business section, with words and phrases like 'leadership', 'glass ceiling' and 'executive' screaming out at you.

Thing is these words and phrases are just a bunch of other things we feel we have to aspire to.

News flash – we don't!

We need to be a managing director of a global organisation about as much as we need to be a bloody pink princess in a tutu.

Sure, some people *do* want to be the managing director of a global organisation. And that's fine. And if you really want to be a pink princess in the tutu, that's fine tootoo.

The problem with imposter syndrome isn't that it stops us from being the things the world tells us we *should* be. It's that it stops us from grabbing what we *want* from life. Nobody should hijack the meaning of ambition or of independence and turn it into a rigid rule.

Ambition for me is being happy, feeling respected, challenging myself, standing up for what I believe in, speaking out and making an impact. And when it came to it, I decided it wasn't the step up to senior management that I was chasing. I realised it wasn't a step up that I needed, it was a step in an entirely new direction that I craved.

My accidental minge-meme fiasco kind of paved the way for me to explore my own personal branding. So here I am, writing my first blog post, exploring what I've learned. And it might sound kind of cliché, some kind of business-speak bullshit, but a personal brand isn't about dressing up as someone else. It isn't about spewing bland, corporate speak and donning a fake facade of confidence and a posh voice when all you really want to do is say *howay, man, this public speaking malarkey is pure ladgeful. But I'll give it a try anyway* . . .

My new job lets me be me. And before I can be a leader of anyone else, I'd really like to be an inspiring leader of *me*.

The second thing I've learned that really holds us back is very closely related – we apologise for literally *everything*.

Why do we do that? Why do we apologise for taking up space?

Why is every girl's T-shirt slogan encouraging happiness and gratitude and kindness when boys are encouraged to be bold and strong and iconic?

Why do so many women's magazines teach us more about giving than they do about receiving in the bedroom?

Why are female victims of sexual abuse judged on what they wear or how they act?

We constantly seek reasons to explain ourselves. We apologise for what we wear and what we say and what we ask and sometimes, even for who we are.

We apologise for leaning across someone in the supermarket to reach for a something – even though they've been hogging the space for ten minutes trying to decide if they want halloumi or mozzarella or a trusty old Red Leicester.

We feel bad when a man behaves inappropriately towards us. Wondering what we did to encourage it. Analysing every single thing we ever said to them and every single outfit we ever wore to the office.

Of course, it's no surprise that the person who pointed out my relentless needless ridiculous apologising was a woman – my smear test nurse to be precise. And as most of the internet knows by now (thanks to my Metro outburst targeted at the man who is now my gift-from-the-Gods-boyfriend), I have a rather difficult cervix. But I should never apologise for it. Because I should never apologise for being a woman.

It's easy to blame earlier generations. The women who tell us that being slapped on the arse was commonplace, almost acceptable, back in their day. But when you think about it, the only reason we have things as good as we do today is because of the women who came before us. Greenham Common Women's Peace Camp, the Women's Suffrage, Ruth Bader Ginsburg, Maya Angelou, Madonna and yes, Mam, the Spice Girls, too.

Apologies have a place in society. When you've fucked up, or lied, or hurt someone – intentionally or otherwise. But they should never be used as 'ums' or 'errs' or 'can I just' or 'no worries if not'. Let's ask for what we need – fuck it, what we *want* – loudly and proudly. Let's fill the space we've been given on this earth without wasting a single bit of it. And please, let's stop absorbing the shame that others project onto us.

It's time to do our generation's bit. And I vote (because, thanks to other women, I now can) that we do this by refusing to apologise when we've done nothing wrong. Let's break the cycle.

Are you with me?

Acknowledgements

Heaps of thanks and admiration to everyone who helped bring this book to life.

First of all thanks to the wonderful team of absolute goddesses at HarperNorth: My editor Gen Pegg, whose passion for the book and cheerleading for the North has been invaluable; Alice Murphy-Pyle - a creative force whose encouraging emails and fun ideas always make me smile; and Megan Jones whose care and attention every step of the way has been so appreciated. Of course, thanks also to the wider HarperCollins team - it takes a city to raise a book.

Special thanks to my agent, Jo Bell, for her unwavering support, encouragement and always getting me quickly back on track when I have one of my signature wobbles, frenzies and confidence dips. It's always much appreciated.

Thanks to everyone who helped make the NWIN 'alternative' book trailer: my ever patient husband and writer/ director, Chris Connel; hugely talented filmmaker Topher McGrillis; shining stars Chess Tomlinson and Dean Bone; my brilliant stepson Sam Nichol and sister-in-law and namesake, Lucy Nichol (yes, it does get confusing); Dot, Simon and team at Recovery Connections for letting us run riot around the fabulous Fork in the Road Cafe (Simon – you're a star in the making!); and Joel and Gary at Go North East for the lend of the bus.

Thanks also to Creative UK / North of Tyne Combined Authority for the funding support.

But most of all, thanks to the nurse at my GP's practice who made me giggle so much during my smear test it inspired the pivotal scene of the book.

Harper North

would like to thank the following staff and contributors for their involvement in making this book a reality:

Fionnuala Barrett
Samuel Birkett
Peter Borcsok
Lisa Brewster
Ciara Briggs
Sarah Burke
Alan Cracknell
Jonathan de Peyer
Anna Derkacz
Tom Dunstan
Kate Elton
Sarah Emsley
Simon Gerratt
Laura Gerrard
Monica Green
Natassa Hadjinicolaou

Mayada Ibrahim
Megan Jones
Jean-Marie Kelly
Taslima Khatun
Sammy Luton
Rachel McCarron
Molly McNevin
Alice Murphy-Pyle
Adam Murray
Genevieve Pegg
Agnes Rigou
Florence Shepherd
Eleanor Slater
Emma Sullivan
Katrina Troy
Daisy Watt

For more unmissable reads,
sign up to the HarperNorth newsletter at
www.harpernorth.co.uk

or find us on Twitter at
@HarperNorthUK

**Harper
North**